the summer we let go

THE DESTIN DIARIES 

HOPE HOLLOWAY
AND
CECELIA SCOTT

The Destin Diaries

The Summer We Met – Book 1
The Summer We Danced – Book 2
The Summer We Made Promises – Book 3
The Summer We Kept Secrets – Book 4
The Summer We Let Go – Book 5
The Summer We Celebrated – Book 6
The Summer We Sailed Away – Book 7

July 4, 1993

Dear Diary,

If I don't write this down this minute, I swear my head is going to explode like one of the fireworks Dad insists on lighting even though Uncle Artie says he's going to burn the dunes down and get us banned from Destin forever.

Tonight was the Fourth of July, which means hot dogs, sparklers, sand everywhere (even in places sand should not be), and that feeling like summer is so big and loud and bright it might actually swallow you whole.

The beach was packed and we basically stayed there all day. Blankets everywhere, coolers, boom boxes, Frisbees, and inner tubes. The air smelled like salt and smoke and sunscreen and freedom.

And of course—of _course_—Peter was right in the middle of it, like he has been all summer long. I wasn't sure he'd keep spending summers with us since he's in college now, but here he is... torturing me.

New form of anguish? He smiles at me different. In a new way. A different way. I swear.

Not just a polite smile. Not a "hey kid" smile—because I'm sixteen now and he can't call me "kid" anymore. A real smile. It started slow, like he didn't even realize he's doing it, and then suddenly it's all there—warm and crooked and devastating.

I swear that smile of his could power the entire Fourth of July. We wouldn't even need fireworks.

He and Eli were in charge of the bonfire again, which has been the tradition since we started spending summers in Destin. This is our fifth year! And every bonfire, Uncle Artie stands there with his hands on his hips, shaking his head and offering fire related pointers, trying to get Eli and Peter to pay attention.

I was on the sand with Kate and Tessa, our towels all tangled up like always. Crista had a full-on hissy fit because she thought she lost her flip-flops (she didn't—they were literally under her towel), and weirdly enough, Dustin Mathers was the one who talked her down. Unexpected!

Anyway, after the fireworks started, I kept sneaking glances at Peter, standing there with the firelight hitting his face, and I had this thought that scared me a little.

<u>What if I always feel this way about him???</u> What if no matter how much time passes, or how old I get, or who else comes into my life, I always kind of love Peter McCarthy?

We finally dragged ourselves inside and the house was chaos and everyone was arguing about whose turn it was to shower, so I came in here and put my headphones on. Everyone assumed I was escaping the madness.

But the madness is in my head! Why? Because I'm listening to "I Will Always Love You" over and over, which I know is dramatic, but Whitney Houston gets me. It feels like that song was written for moments exactly like this, to hold tight to the love I just can't deny.

So, I'm lying here thinking about Peter's smile and the way summer feels like it will never end because it's only the Fourth of July.

Happy Birthday, America!

—Viv

Chapter One
Vivien

Present Day

The moment Vivien Lawson's gaze landed on the man striding up the boardwalk toward the Summer House, her heart swooped around in her chest, not sure if it wanted to soar...or thud.

As if she didn't know. Her heart *always* soared at the sight of Peter because some things never changed—a fact Tessa had delighted in reminding her this morning. Vivien had unearthed yet another diary from the '90s and Tessa had insisted on a dramatic read of the July 4th entry from their sixteenth summer.

The words had made her laugh...and fight a familiar punch of regret. Had she made a huge mistake by ending her budding romance with Peter McCarthy nearly two months ago?

Peter had given Vivien the "space" she'd asked for, using the time to move from Pensacola to a rental house ten minutes away in Crystal Beach to start a new job. They'd had plenty of time apart, but now he was in town, and he'd be a regular here at the Summer House.

Vivien wasn't sure how she felt about that... about *him*.

Backlit by the setting sun and surrounded by the white sands of Destin, her old teenage crush looked as handsome, strong, and confident at fifty-three as he had in 1993, on this same beach for this same Fourth of July celebration.

Older, yes. A few silver strands threaded into his dark blond hair, but no less light in his penetrating brown eyes. His shoulders were broader now, defined by years of law enforcement training and no fear of hard work. His smile was easy, just like she'd pictured it a few hours ago when she and Tessa had sat side by side howling in laughter at their girlhood drama.

Barefoot, he wore a loose linen shirt and shorts, holding a beer in one hand, the other on her brother's shoulder. Eli and Peter talked and laughed on their way back from the beach, their bonfire pit mission accomplished.

Later, that bonfire would be surrounded by friends and family enjoying a hot holiday night.

And, just like she had three decades ago, Vivien would steal glances at Peter, and her heart would still feel like the fireworks were inside of her when he smiled.

She'd truly expected these feelings to be gone when Peter returned to Destin last week, but that was not the case. If anything, they were stronger.

Were his? Or had he accepted her decision and moved on?

Two stories above the men, Vivien leaned against the railing of the Summer House's main deck, vaguely aware of chatter in the house and the start of a new song Tessa had queued up for her perfect playlist.

The first few notes punched, and Vivien stepped away from the railing to narrow her eyes at Tessa, who stood at the kitchen island mixing drinks.

"Really, Tess? Whitney Houston?"

Tessa lifted a glass, squeezed a lime, and rounded the island, offering Vivien the official Summer House drink—a gin and tonic—a teasing smirk on her lips.

"I thought you'd like this choice," Tessa joked, flipping back some long blond hair and peering past Vivien at the boardwalk. "For the one that got away."

Vivien took the glass with a nod of thanks. "The one I *sent* away, more like."

"It made sense at the time, Viv."

Tessa returned to the kitchen before Vivien could respond, leaving her to consider how right her friend was.

Fresh out of a twenty-six-year marriage, new to Destin, and steadily building her interior design business, Vivien simply hadn't been ready for the complication of a romantic relationship.

Not that Peter McCarthy was complicated. He was what her mother would call "a straight shooter"—literally, as a police detective, and figuratively, as a decent, stand-up guy. A guy who'd professed his love for her the night they'd broken up, then immediately agreed to give her the space and freedom she requested.

So far, that had been easy. Peter had returned to Pensacola when his local case was closed, but he'd already accepted a new position with the Okaloosa County Sheriff's Office, starting as a senior criminal investigator right here in Destin.

He'd made that decision before she dropped her bomb, leaving her to wonder if he would have done the same thing if he'd known she was going to break up with him that night.

Didn't matter. He was officially a local. And the truth was, her crush on him still burned as bright as that bonfire would later tonight.

She had no idea how Peter felt. He'd been warm when they saw each other for the first time a few days ago. They'd only been alone for a moment in the kitchen, and they'd had a perfectly *nice* conversation. There'd been no long glances, no casual touches, and certainly no sweet kisses like they'd shared in the spring.

They were old friends, nothing more, nothing less, part of a blend of family and friends who had a long history on this beach.

But looking at him now...she couldn't remember the meaning of *space* or why she'd thought she wanted it. Her poor body had the same numb ache that plagued her as a teenager, longing to just be close to him. Was it the beach? Destin? History? Or was Whitney right...and she would always love him?

Peter slowed his step as he and Eli got closer to the house and lifted his gaze, meeting hers. His smile wavered as they locked eyes, but he looked away and reacted to something Eli said.

Oh, Peter. What was I thinking?

"That's the face of a woman in torment."

She turned at the sound of her daughter's voice, hissing in a breath and hoping she hadn't just said her thoughts out loud. "Torment? What do you mean?"

Lacey snorted a soft laugh and narrowed her big baby blues. "I mean you're practically hanging over the deck like Rapunzel or Juliet or some other lovestruck character on a balcony."

"Lovestruck?" Was she *that* obvious? "I'm just looking at that beach, which promises a glorious sunset, don't you think?"

Lacey rolled her eyes. "Come on, Mom. It's me. I've known you my whole life. I've been sharing a bed with you for the last five months, which is something no self-respecting twenty-five-year-old should admit. I know what you're thinking."

With an easy laugh, Vivien didn't deny a thing. "You should have claimed Tessa's old room when she moved into that beach house, Lace. Then you wouldn't have to share the main suite with me."

Lacey shrugged. "I knew Aunt Crista was coming this month. Plus, I like rooming with you. C'mon, now. Back to Peter."

"Peter? I didn't bring him up." Vivien took a sip, the cocktail tasting bitter on her lips. "Where's Roman?"

Lacey looked past her toward the water and sand drenched in the gold of sunset. "If you really were staring at the beach and not your ex in bare feet, you'd see my boyfriend out there doing what he does—throwing a football with Jonah and Peter's son. Connor is very nice, by the way."

Vivien turned and looked beyond Peter and Eli as they disappeared into the downstairs of the three-level beach house. Out on the sand, Roman Matteo was definitely showing off his NFL skills with Vivien's nephew, Jonah, who was holding his own with the second-string wide receiver.

Connor McCarthy, a dental student who'd joined his father for a long weekend in Destin, caught a few impressive passes to show he'd clearly inherited Peter's athletic prowess.

In the mix, Vivien's seven-year-old niece, Nolie, hadn't caught a thing but was prancing between the much bigger men. Mostly she was kicking up sand and giggling wildly with Aunt Pittypat, a tiny Yorkie who rarely left the child's side.

"I was surprised when Crista and Nolie showed up without Anthony," Vivien said, referring to her brother-in-law, who they'd all expected to join them for the holiday.

"Aunt Crista said this new management position has him working long hours," Lacey told her.

"Over the Fourth of July?" Vivien asked, remembering the shadow in her younger sister's eyes when she came inside late last evening after a long drive. "I guess, but poor Crista is four months pregnant and had to haul a seven-year-old all the way from Atlanta alone. Where is she?"

"Napping upstairs now," Lacey said. "And you are truly an expert subject-changer, Mom. Talk to me about Peter."

"What's to say that hasn't been said before?" Lifting a brow, Vivien leaned in to stage-whisper, "And it was said in the diary of sixteen-year-old Vivien Lawson that Tessa just performed like she was auditioning for the part of an infatuated teenager."

Lacey trilled a laugh. "Sorry I missed that dramatic interpretation of teen Vivien's life."

Vivien sighed, wondering if, deep inside, she still *was* teen Vivien. "Reading it really reminded me that he has always been my weakness and has me wondering why, oh, why did I send him packing?"

"Ahh. We finally get an explanation for the torment in your eyes."

She shot her daughter a look. "A little doubt, some second-guessing, but I'm not *tormented*." Was she?

Lacey laughed. "Hey, I work for Tessa. Some of that drama rubs off. But, Mom, don't be so hard on yourself. Remember that the ink was hardly dry on your divorce papers. You just launched your own business, you moved your whole life to Destin, and you hadn't been a fully independent woman in two and a half decades. Diving right into a serious relationship was...risky."

Vivien appreciated the rationale so much, and it made sense...until it didn't.

"Anyway, I wouldn't worry too much," Lacey added.

"You wouldn't?"

"He didn't move here just to change jobs. Have you seen him looking at you?"

"He looks away," Vivien said. "Every time."

"But he stares when you don't know it. Trust me, he'd jump at the chance to try again if you gave him the green light. What's stopping you?"

"For one thing, he just got here a few days ago. Then there's the fact that there are a zillion Lawsons and Wylies and extras around at the moment. Plus, his son is visiting. I haven't been alone with him."

"Well, don't wait too long," Lacey warned in a sing-song voice. "Good men are hard to find."

Vivien smiled at her daughter, then shifted her gaze to the pro-ball player as he caught a spiraling football. He soft-tossed it to Nolie and danced with her like they were in the end zone, which made Lacey quietly whimper.

"Speaking of good men," Vivien murmured.

She sighed. "Yeah. Roman's a keeper."

"What happens when he leaves for training?" Vivien asked.

Lacey shook her head. "I don't know, Mom. We're what? Two months or so into this romance? I'm taking it one day at a time and enjoying every minute."

Vivien slid an arm around her, adding a squeeze. "I'm happy for you. And, by the way, I like rooming with you, too. Oh..."

Lacey's eyes flashed as they heard men's footsteps coming up the spiral stairs from the pool level. "That'll be

Peter and Uncle Eli. Don't waste time, Mamacita. Show him your heart."

Vivien smiled at the cheesy expression. "I'll talk to him," she promised.

"Good." Lacey gave her a kiss on the cheek. "Now I'm going to play some football with the man I love."

With that, she slipped away as Peter and Eli appeared at the top of the steps. Peter looked right at Vivien, his gaze serious, with interest and a question in his eyes. This time, he didn't look away.

And that gave her the courage to promise herself she'd talk to him tonight.

BY THE TIME the last of the guests had said goodbye, the Summer House had settled into its familiar post-party hush. The music was off. The deck lights had been dimmed. The Gulf air blew in from the open sliders, carrying the distant sound of a few more fireworks and laughter from some people on the beach.

Vivien finished the kitchen clean-up with a slow and sure hand, wiping down the counters and putting away the last of the dishes. The Summer House had been home to her for more than four months, and she moved through this kitchen like it was hers and hers alone.

In a sense, it was—hers and Eli's. All the others came and went.

Some stayed—including Lacey, who would surely be looking for her own place soon, and Jonah, who would probably live downstairs with baby Atlas until he finished culinary school.

Others left. Tessa had moved into a two-unit beach house she co-owned with Dusty Mathers. Eli's daughter, Meredith, had stayed to recover from her ectopic pregnancy, but would no doubt head back to Atlanta soon.

Crista was here for at least a few weeks. Mom and Jo Ellen had decided to spend the summer in the apartment over the garage. That left Eli, her older brother, the home's architect. He'd planned to stay here all summer, but then last week, Kate—his main reason for sticking around—had zipped back to Ithaca in something of a hurry.

It remained to be seen if Destin lost its allure for Eli with his new love interest gone. He might return to life in Atlanta, running Acacia Architecture.

With all the comings and goings, the constant change and the multi-generational, two-family vibe, Vivien had somehow become the Summer House anchor. And she couldn't be happier with that role.

She reached for a dishtowel when she heard footsteps on the deck and a familiar figure appeared in the wide-open sliders.

Finally. She hadn't been alone with Peter all night... until now.

"Did you clean up that firepit?" she asked, playfully fluttering the dishtowel. "Uncle Artie's watching from heaven."

"He'd be proud," he said, his low and silky voice

sliding over her in the quiet of the kitchen. "We met every county regulation and hid all the evidence."

She laughed, maybe sounding a little nervous, but she tried to remember that she had a thirty-year history with Peter and this sure wasn't their first July 4th together. Plus, he'd said he *loved* her...right before she said she wanted to break up.

He stepped into the dimly lit kitchen, his gaze locked on her with that same intentional look she'd seen all night. Like he was respecting her space, but ready to invade it with a word.

It was time to give that word.

"Where's Eli?" she asked, rooting around for small talk before...the big talk.

"He said he was going to take a walk." Peter grinned. "Pretty sure that's code for 'call Kate.'"

She made a face at the mention of her close friend, still mulling over Kate's impulsive return to her job at Cornell University's chemistry lab. "I wish she had stayed for the holiday weekend. We were expecting her for the whole summer. Did Eli tell you what happened?"

He nodded. "Something about a Department of Energy grant renewal?"

"Yeah. They moved up an inspection of the whole EV battery thing she works on in her lab, and she insisted that all the equipment had to be recalibrated and the results demonstrated live," Vivien explained, parroting Kate's litany of excuses. "She wanted to do it herself and headed back."

Peter looked skeptical. "Eli thinks it could have been handled remotely."

Her heart squeezed. "She did leave in a hurry. But that lab is as much a child to her as her teenagers. Still..."

"Things are progressing with Eli and Kate," Peter finished. "He thinks she's scared."

Vivien considered the many things that the fairly new couple had working against them—and not just the thousand-mile separation between Ithaca and Atlanta.

Her brother, a widower, lived and breathed a vibrant faith in God that few people—even Vivien—could understand. Kate held a PhD in chemistry and based her entire life on science and provable facts. Despite tangible attraction, Eli and Kate's personal philosophies couldn't be further apart.

Vivien didn't want to think that was why her friend took off, but it could have had something to do with it.

"If Cornell doesn't get this grant, it could jeopardize millions in funding," she said, wanting that to be the real reason.

Peter nodded, watching her for a beat before speaking.

"Need help?"

"I'm almost done but you can start the dishwasher." She handed him the bottle of detergent, and he took it and pulled open the dishwasher door.

"Where's Connor?" she asked, remembering his son.

"He slipped out right before we started cleaning up the firepit," he explained. "We drove separately in case I wanted to stay late." He said it casually, but his gaze was serious. "I was hoping we'd get a minute," he added.

Her pulse ticked up as she watched him tap the buttons on the dishwasher to start it.

Finished with the task, he leaned on the counter and crossed his arms.

She mirrored the pose, looking up at him. "You good?" she asked. "You've been quiet tonight."

He considered that. "I've been trying to follow your lead."

She didn't reply, but she didn't look away, either.

"You asked for space," he said gently. "So I've been giving it."

"Yeah, I know." Her throat tightened as she considered the best way to handle this. Did she just come out and say, "I was wrong, stupid, and please kiss me?"

It was her move, and they both knew it.

"Peter," she began.

He straightened slightly, attentive. "Yeah?"

She took a breath. "I've been thinking about…"

She needed to say "us" but the word stuck in her throat. There was no going back if she did this. If she revived their romance, she couldn't—

The sharp buzz of Peter's phone cut through the quiet.

He frowned and grunted, glancing at the screen. "Sorry. It's work."

Her heart sank—not because of the interruption, but because of the seriousness that instantly settled over him. He answered without hesitation. "McCarthy."

Vivien watched his posture change—shoulders squaring, attention snapping into focus.

"Yes," he said. "That's my son."

His son? The room seemed to tilt.

He listened, his jaw tightening. "Where?" A beat. "Okay. Was he conscious?"

Conscious? Vivien stepped closer and reached for his arm. "Connor?" she mouthed.

"Any idea who was at fault?" he asked the caller.

Vivien's breath grew shallow as she watched him absorb the information.

"Yes," he said. "He was with me all day. He didn't drink." His voice sharpened. "The other driver failed the field test?" He swore softly under his breath. "I'm on my way."

He ended the call and looked at her, his expression controlled but shaken beneath the surface.

"Connor's been in an accident," he said. "On 98. A truck crossed the center line—driver was intoxicated."

She gasped. "Is he—"

"He's banged up but fine," Peter said quickly. "Concussion, maybe some fractures. They're taking him to the hospital now."

She turned without hesitation to find her purse and keys. "I'll come with you."

He shook his head, already moving toward the door. "No. No. It's late, Viv. Let me go assess. I'll call you as soon as I know more."

"Please," she said, touching his arm. "Let me help."

He covered her hand briefly with his, squeezing once. "I will. But I have to go. Now."

She nodded, forcing herself to step back. "Okay."

He kissed her forehead quickly, firmly. Then he was gone, out the front door in what felt like a blur.

Vivien stayed frozen in the quiet kitchen, her thoughts no longer on what she might have lost, but on the man she cared for racing into the night to get to his son.

She stood there for a long moment, hands pressed together, whispering a silent prayer for Connor—and for Peter—before turning off the lights and letting the house go dark around her.

Chapter Two
Tessa

The flashing lights came down the highway out of nowhere, making Tessa Wylie sit up in the passenger seat of the F-150, the post-party euphoria evaporating at the unsettling sight and sound.

Red and blue lights blared against the dark line of palms along 98, bouncing off the glossy hood of the truck and reflecting in the windshield. Dusty pulled over to let an ambulance barrel past them, siren screaming, followed closely by another, his hand instinctively reaching for hers.

"Eesh," he whispered.

Tessa leaned forward, craning her neck as they passed the intersection. Police cruisers clustered, lights cutting through the humid night. A handful of people stood off to the side, silhouettes frozen in confusion and shock.

"Well," she murmured after they passed, so grateful it wasn't them. "Someone's Fourth of July definitely didn't end with sparklers and watermelon."

"Yeah. Those aren't the kind of fireworks you want to remember." He sighed heavily, not for the first time in this car ride, she realized.

They drove on, the road humming beneath the tires, the night air rushing in through the open windows. Tessa rested her elbow on the door and let her fingers trail against the breeze that carried the scent of salt and smoke and celebration.

She glanced at Dusty, who was quiet and definitely deep in thought.

It wasn't...them, was it? She didn't think so.

Yes, they were dancing around the nature of their relationship, which was intensified by their recent decision to co-buy a beach house. They didn't live together, but they shared a two-unit home, so they saw a lot of each other.

By a lot, she meant daily, nightly, and any chance they got. Each day, she was getting to know this man better.

He looked relaxed at first glance, posture easy, one arm resting casually near the window. But she could read him well enough now to sense something was humming beneath that calm exterior. Something heavy.

They turned off the main road and onto their street, a narrow strip running parallel to the beach. The houses here were a mix of Old Florida charm and newer renovations, some pastel bungalows, weathered rentals, and the occasional modern rebuild rising confidently above the rest.

And then there was the little fixer-upper they called home. Two homes, actually. Hers on the top floor, his below.

The beach house sat a little higher than the neighboring homes, pale against the dark, windows glowing softly. They'd had a quick closing and moved in a week ago, which was a minor miracle, considering that a few weeks before that, they'd ended their brief romantic relationship.

Tessa had made it clear that, at fifty and single for her entire life, she wasn't in a relationship for kicks. Not anymore. Tessa Wylie was done with flings and fun—she wanted *forever*.

But the only love Dusty had ever known—his wife, Kelly—had died after years of illness. He'd been drained by caretaking, broken by loss, and ready for those flings and fun.

Rather than accept that, she'd done the unthinkable—at least for Tessa. She'd insisted that it be her way or the highway.

He'd taken the highway...and then made a U-Turn.

She smiled faintly at the memory of their not so coincidental meeting to see this house—thanks to Lorna, their mutual real estate agent. She'd brought them back together in an empty living room, keys heavy in their palms, the sound of the Gulf drifting faintly through open windows.

The beach-facing house they'd both dreamed about individually was available—but only if they pooled their resources and agreed to share the cost. That decision had been kind of a no-brainer. But them? As a couple? Wanting different things?

She could still hear his voice, low and sincere, as he'd taken her hand.

I'm going to say it again, Tessa. I've missed you.

Her throat tightened as the memory unfolded.

I can't stop thinking about you. I wake up wondering what you're doing. I want to kick myself for being a fool— which is how I think we'd both feel if we don't at least... try.

She wasn't sure if he meant them or the house, and when she'd asked, he'd smiled, not dodging the question, but not forcing an answer either.

The moment had shifted everything. They agreed to buy the house, each take an apartment, and see what happened.

Something was definitely happening between them. They shared evenings and meals, spent late nights on the rooftop, sipping pinot grigio, looking at the stars, and listening to the surf. They continued to learn about each other, kissed each other goodnight, and went to sleep in their respective beds.

Every morning, Tessa woke up with him on her mind and knew he did the same. No, she didn't think their relationship was what had Dusty so quiet tonight.

"Before the party, Vivien and I read a diary entry from this very day in 1993," she told him, partly to fill the silence, partly because some of the entry was still echoing in her head. "Wow."

Dusty let out a low groan. "Oh, no. Please tell me my name didn't come up."

She laughed. "It absolutely did."

He shot her a look, bracing. "What kind of idiot did I make of myself this time?"

"Relax. It wasn't a horror story." She smiled. "Actually, it was kind of sweet."

"That's not usually how stories about eighteen-year-old Dustin Mathers start."

"Well, apparently, you surprised everyone." She leaned back against the seat. "Crista had a meltdown and you soothed her."

"The meltdown I can believe. My soothing? Not so much."

"You were a therapist even way back then," she said.

"Really? 'Cause I thought I was a troubled mess who was usually drunk and secretly pining after the blonde in very short shorts."

She snorted. "They weren't *that* short, but I do remember thinking you were a hero."

He stared straight ahead for a moment, then shook his head slowly. "Huh." Then he threw her a look. "I'll take that as a win."

Even as he smiled, she felt that subtle strain again. The way his gaze drifted, his expression tightening. The fact that he dropped the subject of her short shorts.

The car rolled into the driveway, tires crunching over shell-strewn gravel. Dusty cut the engine, and the sudden silence settled over them, thick and intimate.

They sat there for a beat longer than necessary.

Tessa reached for the door handle, then hesitated. "You okay?" she asked gently.

"Yeah." The answer was too quick, and he looked like he realized that. "Just tired. Long week. Saw a lot of patients."

That made sense. Dusty's work as a therapist specializing in grief counseling wasn't easily left in his home office. And she'd seen lots of cars in the driveway spot they reserved for his clients, so it had been a busy week up to the holiday.

"More work tomorrow?" she asked.

"Maybe. I have one patient..." His voice faded as they each got out of the truck, the sound of the surf faint but constant.

As they reached his first-floor front door, he sighed. "I don't know if I'm dreading seeing this patient or really looking forward to telling her something." He adjusted the dark-rimmed glasses that she'd grown to adore because they made him look smart and professorial, like her father had been. "It's weighing on me."

So it *was* work. He really couldn't talk about his patients for confidentiality reasons, but she could practically taste his need to unburden himself.

"How about a glass of wine on the roof?" she suggested.

He threw her a wry smile. "So I can talk about what I can't talk about?"

"Maybe you can speak in hypotheticals," she said, putting a hand on his shoulder. "And I'll pretend I'm asleep so you're not breaking any rules."

He studied her, something vulnerable flickering in his eyes. Then he nodded toward the stairs. "Yes, please. But don't pretend to be asleep."

"I'll go in through your place," she said, following him

inside, "and change into something less party-ish and more like pajamas."

There was an outside entrance up to her second-floor apartment, but because the house had once been a single-family dwelling, there were also stairs inside his unit. They used that convenient connection so frequently, it made her wonder if in some ways they *were* living together.

Inside, his living room was cool and quiet, the scent of fresh paint and ocean air lingering in the open spaces. The whole house was full of potential that he would soon draw out with the handyman skills he'd used to renovate the home where he and his wife had lived before her death.

Here, the living area stretched out before them, flowing into a modest kitchen, everything functional but dated.

Beyond the French doors, the small deck and plunge pool glimmered in the moonlight. She used his pool as often as he used her rooftop, and that worked for both of them.

"Meet you on the roof," she said, heading up to her apartment.

"I'll bring the wine," he said. "You bring the short shorts."

"Shut up." But she was smiling as she went upstairs.

THE UNOBSTRUCTED GULF view from the roof, even at midnight, was a glorious thing to behold. And tonight, there was the occasional flash of a diehard celebrator with one last screaming crackler to make the blue-on-black horizon and moonlit sky even more enchanting.

Tessa hadn't done much in the way of decorating her apartment yet, but she'd put in a lot of effort up here. The day after they moved in, she'd sprung for comfy chaises with a cocktail table, and an umbrella-topped dining set where she and Dusty shared breakfasts, lunches, and dinners together.

They'd hung some vineyard lights, which cast a golden glow over the little slice of paradise. Up here, the world seemed far away, with the view and the stars and the sky to envelop them like a privacy bubble.

She hoped that vibe helped him unload what was on his mind tonight.

He poured wine into two stemless glasses, and they toasted lightly before settling on their chaises. But Dusty didn't lean back. He took a long drink, staring out at the horizon, silent while Tessa sipped and set her glass on the table.

She stretched out her legs, flicking the bottoms of her sleep pants, and crossing her bare feet.

"Okay," she said quietly. "Pretend I'm asleep and you're dictating patient notes."

He gave a soft scoff.

"Tell me as much as you can," she urged. "At least enough to get this burden off your heart."

He turned to her, his eyes narrowing behind his glasses. "How are you so perceptive?"

"One of my million great qualities."

"Seriously."

"I am serious," she teased, sitting up a bit to take another drink. "But honestly, it doesn't take telepathic talent to feel something's working on you, honey."

His expression softened at the term of endearment, which might have been the first time she'd called him that. She hoped it wouldn't be the last.

He exhaled, slow and heavy. "There's a woman I've been counseling for almost a year. Brace yourself, because it's tragic."

So many of his patients had tragic stories. How he faced death, sorrow, and personal loss every day and maintained a great sense of humor was a mystery to her.

"I'm braced," she assured him.

"Her name's Morgan and she's twenty-six. About two years ago, Morgan had a baby girl, named Olive."

Olive. Tessa swallowed at the mention of a baby with a precious name, dreading the rest of the story. *Not the child, please, God, not the child.*

Closing her eyes, she whispered, "Go on."

"It's not what you think," he said quickly. "The little girl is fine, but Morgan's husband and her parents were in a fatal accident on the way to the hospital the morning after Olive was born."

She gasped, putting her hand to her mouth. "No!"

"Yes," he said simply. "Obviously, I can tell you all this because it's public knowledge."

But how poor Morgan handled the loss probably was not. She waited, still, while he gathered his thoughts.

"She doesn't have family," he said. "Her parents are gone, and she had no siblings. Her late husband's family is basically estranged. They don't want anything to do with Morgan or their granddaughter, who they blame for their son's death, for reasons I will never understand. Morgan's very young, not just chronologically but emotionally. She's more like a teenager and..." He huffed a breath. "She's on very shaky ground and needs more than I can give her. That's the problem."

Tessa let out a soft whimper of sympathy. "What will you do?"

"Well, I'm going to tell her the next time I see her—which could be tomorrow, depending on her mood, because I will always make room in my schedule for her—that I have a possible solution."

"Good," Tessa said.

"But it's not perfect," he replied. "I've contacted a psychiatrist colleague of mine who could get her into an inpatient treatment at a facility not far from here, which I believe she really, really needs. And fast. Her insurance will cover most of it, but..."

"Does she need money?" Tessa asked, leaning forward. "Because I'll help. I really would. I—"

He reached over the table, showing the first smile she'd seen since they got up there. "You're so sweet."

She'd been called a lot of things in life, but sweet? She just shrugged. "I'm human, Dusty. I can't imagine the pain she's going through."

"It's bad," he acknowledged. "I worry she might..." He didn't finish, but he didn't have to. "She's not stable and needs serious psychiatric help. But I don't think she's going to take it."

"Why not?"

"Because the program requires at least one full month in the facility. She's afraid—and rightly so—that Olive would become a ward of the state. She's terrified she'd never get her back."

"They'd keep a child from her mother?"

"She has a, um, history." He shook his head. "I can't go into that, Tessa, but she's on shaky ground with that kid. No one is threatening to take her, but I just don't see any path forward for her and that's the problem." His voice roughened. "Morgan doesn't want Olive to end up in the system. She loves her more than anything, but she knows she's not in a place to care for her properly right now."

They sat in silence, the waves whispering below.

"And this is what's weighing on you?" Tessa finally asked.

He nodded. "I don't know how she'll take the news that I found a place and...Olive..."

"Should stay with us." The words were out before she really gave it too much thought.

And Dusty whipped his head around. "*What?*"

She stared at him, trying to gather up a rationale but not sure she had one other than it seemed right.

"We could take care of her for a month," she said. "How hard can it be?"

He didn't answer right away, but searched her face in the gold vineyard lights as if he were trying to see if she was kidding.

"You'd...take on a two-year-old for a month?"

"Of course." Tessa waved a hand like he'd said a weekend. "I love little girls. I told you I saved Nolie from repeating third grade with her dyslexia. And I have a houseful of Wylies and Lawsons to help. My July is not that busy—well, there's one wedding, a birthday event, and an anniversary party on the Tessa Wylie Events planning calendar. But Lacey is itching for more responsibility. How much trouble could a two-year-old girl actually be?"

He choked a laugh. "Well, neither one of us knows because I've never been a father and you..."

Gave up my son, Roman, for adoption.

And that thought just made the need to do this burn a little brighter.

"I'd love to help her—and you," she said. "I mean, would we have to qualify or do some kind of home visit?"

"Not if it's only for a month," he said, his voice rising just enough to tell her he was considering this crazy idea. "We'd just be, well, babysitters. No legal binding or issues."

"Then let's take her."

"Tessa." He breathed her name.

"What?"

He got up and sat on the side of her chaise, reaching for her hand. "You're amazing, that's what."

"And I didn't even wear my short shorts," she joked,

as she always did when the attention was too much to bear.

"I mean it," he said, leaning closer. "You are...wow. What a good, good heart you have."

"Tell anyone and my reputation is ruined." She'd made that joke a few times in her life, too.

Why did she put such a protective wall around herself? She didn't know and right then...she was starting to feel like it should really come down.

She put her hand on Dusty's cheek, grazing her thumb over his close-cropped beard.

"I don't know how *good* my heart is," she said, "but it is tender. And I can't stand for this poor Morgan to have so much pain and grief and a two-year-old to worry about. Let her get help. Little Olive—how I love that name—can stay upstairs in my apartment with me. I'll meet Morgan and if she's one hundred percent comfortable, I'll take her. We can share parenting duties and get our taste of something we never had."

He took a slow, deep breath. "Okay."

"Okay?" She sat up, a smile pulling as she realized just how much she wanted this. "Really?"

"Of course." He reached for her. "You're making it very difficult, you know."

"Making what difficult?"

"Not to...fall."

She smiled, knowing what he meant. "All part of my evil plan."

He just shook his head and pressed a kiss on her hair.

"Nothing—not one cell in your body—is evil," he said. "You are good and beautiful and funny and I..."

She held her breath.

"I can't wait to co-parent with you."

And let it out with a soft laugh. "It'll be our next great adventure."

He pulled her close, and kissed her—slow, grateful, full of promise.

And for the first time in a long while, the future felt wide open.

Chapter Three
Maggie

Maggie Lawson woke at dawn to the sound of someone in the kitchenette clanging a spoon against a mug so loud it could have been a shovel and a metal trash can.

Really, Jo?

Maggie lay still, listening. The two-bedroom apartment above the Summer House's garage had its own rhythms—soft ones and...the sound of Jo Ellen making tea. At first, it was annoying. But now? It was a reminder to Maggie that she wasn't alone, and she liked that.

She liked everything about waking up in this apartment, to be honest.

The gulls outside her window were white against the blue morning sky, squawking a greeting. The distant sound of a car driving down Gulf Shore Boulevard gave her a weird sense of being somewhere that wasn't suburbia. Even the ticking of that living room clock Jo Ellen called "quaint" and Maggie called "deafening" was... home.

The idea still startled her, especially since she'd only been here about a month. How could this small apartment on a beach in Florida be *home*? Maggie, born and raised in Atlanta, had never lived anywhere but Georgia. She enjoyed a spacious suite and all the amenities—including her flawless rose garden—as a permanent resident in her daughter's sprawling brick Colonial.

That was home. Wasn't it?

At the thought, she blinked away sleep and stared up at the ceiling fan, which whirred silently, the soundless spin adding to the overall sense of comfort.

That's what she felt here. And not the "I'm settled into my routine" comfort that any self-respecting seventy-eight-year-old should relish in her sunset years.

This was a bone-deep comfort. The feeling that she... belonged.

Good heavens. It was a brand-new, monstrous beach house that rose up from the sand where an old cottage had once stood. This structure had no real memories. These walls didn't hold sentimental value. This apartment was practically an afterthought to raise the value of an already ridiculously overpriced piece of property.

But somehow, it felt so right to wake up here every morning—on the beach, sharing an apartment with an old friend who always managed to make Maggie laugh. Not a rose in sight, except one in a pretty container on the windowsill, and yet it felt right.

Quick panting and movement at the bottom of her bed made Maggie stir, inching up to smile at Aunt Pittypat.

"Have you missed me, sweetheart?" she whispered, reaching for the teacup Yorkie. Pitty had stayed in Atlanta, cared for by Maggie's granddaughter, for the past month. But Crista and Nolie arrived recently with Pittypat, who didn't seem to feel at all at home in this apartment.

She slept with Maggie, as she always did, but the dog was restless—no doubt looking for the little girl who showered her in love and dressed her up in lace doll frocks.

"All right," she said, sitting all the way up. "Let's find Nolie for you. I have a feeling I've lost you to another woman, you little traitor."

She turned to get out of bed the way a woman her age always did—slowly, carefully, and with an inventory of what might hurt today.

Nothing, if she didn't count the low-key neuropathy that made her toes tingle or the old ache in her back that had become part of life.

She stepped into a golden strip of sunlight that cut across the hardwood floor. Even the shades of the floor, the warmth of the sun, and the distant sound of Jo Ellen humming an old Motown song felt *homey*.

When had this happened and what did it mean? The apartment had two bedrooms and a living area and kitchenette that functioned well for them, but it wasn't a six-bedroom showplace with an expansive deck and an egg chair that looked out at her garden.

Still, it hadn't taken long for Maggie to find herself sitting in the swivel chair by the window every afternoon. She contentedly watched pelicans and listened to Jo Ellen natter on about her word puzzles on the iPad or ask really dumb questions of Oscar, that ridiculous AI thing on her phone.

Grabbing the light robe that matched her steel-gray pajamas, Maggie walked into the kitchenette, where Jo Ellen stood holding a mug and looking out the window. There wasn't an actual water view from here, but there was plenty of sky and green horizon and sand dunes in the distance.

"Morning, Mags." Jo Ellen turned, silver hair up in a youthful-looking ponytail. "And Pittypat!" She beamed down at the dog. "I thought she might choose to sleep with Nolie in the house."

"She will tonight," Maggie said. "I'm afraid her loyalties have shifted." On a sigh, she looked around, the casual beach décor like an invitation to sit and not move all day. "Some of mine have, too," she added on a whisper.

"Oh, no. You want to leave." Jo Ellen put her mug down and tightened her flamingo-covered bathrobe that used to be absurd but now made Maggie just feel good every time she looked at it. "I knew it. You're going back to Atlanta with Crista and Nolie. You hate the beach. You want to go back to your rose garden and your lady friends."

Maggie bit her lip. "My *lady* friends?"

"The gardening club you went to Europe with. The other rose ladies. Not...me."

Maggie wanted to laugh, but the fact that Jo Ellen was so far off base was not funny.

"On the contrary," Maggie said. "I was just musing

over the fact that I don't want to leave this place. And that's just wrong."

"I feel the same!" Jo Ellen gushed. "I feel like if I never see snow again or walk through that dreary house in Ithaca that just feels empty without Artie, then I'll be just fine."

"Well, we're here for the summer," Maggie said, reaching for Pittypat's leash by the door.

"And then what?"

As she bent over to clip the leash to the collar, Maggie looked up at her friend. "Then my kids will either sell this place for a huge profit or keep it. I gave them this house when Eli finished building it, and come November, they can legally sell it."

"I don't think Eli needs the money and I sense that Vivien would never leave unless she had to," Jo Ellen said, sounding like she'd given the situation a lot of thought. "Crista is the wild card."

The statement about her youngest echoed as Maggie made her way to the patch of grass at the side of the house. Speaking of wild cards—where was Anthony? Why wasn't he here? Did it mean he'd taken a stance against selling?

As Crista's husband, he certainly had a say in whether or not the Lawson siblings kept this house, the only asset that Maggie hadn't been forced to turn over to the government after her husband's arrest thirty-plus years ago.

"Pittypat!" Nolie's high-pitched voice echoed from

upstairs, on the side of the massive deck. "Grandma! I'm coming down! I can walk her for you."

Maggie smiled up at her beloved girl, almost as excited as Pitty, who was dancing and wagging at the sound of Nolie's voice.

A moment later, the little girl came flying out, waving an empty plastic bag. "I wasn't sure if you had a poop bag!"

Maggie rolled her eyes at the uncouth phrase, but took the hug sweet Nolie offered.

"I've been hoping you'd get up early," Nolie said, breathlessly dropping to her knees to cover Pitty in kisses. "Everyone in the house is still asleep and Mommy said I had to let you sleep, too."

"She's up?" Maggie asked.

Nolie nodded. "On the deck."

So it was a perfect time to talk.

Maggie secured the leash in Nolie's tiny hand. "Stay with her until she does her business, darling. I'm going to have coffee with your mommy."

"Okay!" She pranced away and Maggie headed right to the stairs that would take her to the deck. There, she found Crista deep in thought, staring at the horizon.

She wasn't holding a coffee. She wasn't scrolling her phone. She was just...looking out. Hands resting on the balustrade railing, shoulders tense, dark hair pulled back, face with an expression of...well, she certainly didn't look like someone enjoying a beach morning.

She looked *troubled*.

Crista didn't turn until Maggie was almost beside her.

"Oh," Crista said quickly, blinking as if she'd been caught doing something wrong. "Hi, Mama."

Maggie eyed her carefully. Yes, Crista was four months pregnant, and no doubt had lost sleep, especially during that first trimester. But the shadows under her eyes were deep—deeper than they were when she'd been pregnant with Nolie.

"Nolie didn't wake you, did she?" Crista asked.

"Please. Jo Ellen is the loudest tea brewer in history," Maggie said. "It's like the symphony percussion section has arrived every morning."

Crista made a small laughing sound. "She's... something."

"She's a delight," Maggie said.

Crista glanced at her, surprised, probably because Maggie had never had anything nice to say about Jo Ellen Wylie in recent decades, but that was a long time—and a lot of revelations—ago.

"I'm glad you two are enjoying each other's company," Crista said.

"Oh, we are. I forgot how much fun she is."

Crista swallowed and her gaze slid back to the horizon, too deep in thought to even react to Maggie's appreciation for fun. It wasn't something she was famous for.

Crista blinked, hard, as if the sun was in her eyes. The silence stretched a beat, long enough for Maggie to dive in.

"Are you happy you came down?" she asked.

Crista hesitated. "Of course."

"And Anthony? Sad to miss it?"

Her eyes flashed. "Work," she said simply.

"Ah, the new promotion really has him putting in the long hours, huh?" Maggie asked.

"Something does," her daughter mumbled, the words almost lost as she turned. "There's coffee brewed. Want a cup?"

"If it will get you to tell me what's wrong with you."

She gave the first smile that was deep enough to show her one dimple, the only one of Maggie's three children to inherit Roger's signature smile. "I'm fourteen weeks pregnant, Mama. I'm exhausted, and...yeah. That's what's wrong."

Maggie followed Crista into the kitchen, both of them fixing coffee. Without a word, they took matching white mugs back to the deck and sat across from each other in two comfortable chairs.

"I've been thinking about this house," Maggie finally said after first sips were taken.

Crista went still. "What about it?"

"The fact that you kids can sell in November. Have you and Vivien and Eli discussed it?"

"I think they're dug in," she said. "To stay."

"And you?" Maggie ventured. "You used to want to sell, but..."

Crista's eyes flashed, but she didn't finish the sentence for Maggie.

"Have you decided?" Maggie pressed.

Crista opened her mouth, closed it, then said, "Thinking about it."

"About selling or..."

Crista looked at the house again, and her expression changed—something like longing crossed with resentment.

"It's worth so much," she finally said. "Do you have any idea what we could do with that money? We could pay off everything. We could—"

"You and Anthony are not struggling," Maggie reminded her.

Crista's eyes snapped to hers. "You don't know everything."

Oh. Maggie's stomach tightened as she whiffed the scent of a secret. "Then tell me, Crista."

Crista laughed once, shaky. "It's not—"

Maggie cut in, calm but unmovable. "Crista."

Crista's eyes filled instantly, as if her body had been waiting for permission to fall apart. "No, Mama," she whispered. "I can't."

Maggie leaned over, putting a hand on her daughter's arm. "You can. You always can tell me anything. Will I judge?"

Crista snorted.

"Of course I will," Maggie conceded. "And then I will move heaven and earth to help you."

"You can't move anything to help me," Crista said, so softly Maggie wasn't sure she'd heard.

"Is it the baby?" Maggie asked, her body tense as she waited for bad news.

Crista blinked, startled by the question. "The baby's fine," she said, and her hand went to her slight baby bump in a protective gesture. "And Nolie's great, too. Letting her watch little Pittypat while you were down here was such a good idea. It's given her...I don't know. A sense of taking care of something, which will be good when the baby comes."

"Well, if it's not the baby or Nolie, then—"

"I think Anthony is cheating on me."

The words were soft and careful, as if Crista was afraid they might hurt someone if spoken too loudly. Well, they did. Maggie felt them like a physical blow.

"No," Maggie breathed. "Absolutely not."

Crista flinched. "Like I said, you don't know everything."

Maggie leaned forward to make the obvious point. "Crista, you're pregnant and that can wreak havoc on a woman's moods. Anthony adores you. That man looks at you like you hung the moon. There is no universe in which he—"

"I thought so, too," Crista sighed, sounding nothing like the drama queen she usually was, not emotional, just...certain. And scared to death.

"What are you basing this on?" Maggie asked.

Crista swallowed. "You know he was promoted. He's running an entire engineering division now. He's in meetings constantly. He's...different."

"He's under pressure," Maggie said quickly. "He wants to impress the higher-ups and earn that big pay raise. That doesn't make him unfaithful."

"He has a new administrative assistant," Crista said. "She's young. She's pretty."

Maggie scoffed. "Women have never been his weakness."

"He takes calls outside now. He never did before. And he doesn't want me to see his phone."

"Work calls."

"I picked his phone up once," Crista said. "I saw texts with his admin. I was too scared of getting caught to read them. But the next time I looked, those texts were gone. The third time, there was a password."

Maggie's breath caught. "Honey, you shouldn't—"

"And the debit card," Crista interjected, ready to pop now that she'd taken off her seal of silence. "I found a brand-new one in his wallet. A separate account. One I know nothing about."

Oof. That one hit hard. Maggie's mind flashed to another man, another marriage, another set of hidden finances that had nearly destroyed everything. The money was the first sign that Roger had been up to... something.

"Well," she said slowly. "That is...odd. But it does not automatically mean—"

"I feel it, Mama," Crista said. "In my gut. Something is wrong. He's not being honest with me."

Maggie knew that intuition, too. "Have you asked him?"

Crista shook her head. "He'd say I'm hormonal. That I'm imagining things. And maybe I am. But what if I'm not?"

Maggie searched the face of her beautiful, fragile, complicated daughter.

"You do have a tendency to...overdramatize," she said gently.

Crista's eyes filled. "This isn't drama. This is my marriage. What should I do?"

Maggie closed her eyes and considered every aspect of the question and how best to answer it.

"Stay here," she said finally. "Stay for a few weeks and be with your family. Let him miss you. Let him remember what life feels like without you and Nolie in it."

Crista stared at her. "You want me to leave him?"

"I want you to breathe," Maggie said. "And I want him to remember what he stands to lose."

Crista fell back against the sofa.

Before she could respond, footsteps sounded behind them. They both turned to see Vivien in the doorway, already dressed, her purse on her shoulder, her face drawn as she nodded to them.

"Is everything okay?" Crista asked, searching her sister's expression.

"Peter's son, Connor, was in a car accident last night," she announced quietly. "He's okay. Concussion. Broken bones. They kept him overnight. I'm going to the hospital."

Maggie rose instantly. "Oh, I liked that young man. How awful."

Crista groaned as if this was just more bad news on her heart. "I talked to him for a while last night. Really nice kid with a disarming sense of humor for a dentist-to-be. I can't believe he..."

"He'll be okay," Vivien assured them, looking from one to the other. "It was serious but could have been much worse. Eli knows," she added. "I told him last night. I'll be back in a bit."

She blew a kiss and headed out the front door. When Maggie heard the door close, she exhaled and leaned forward, knowing their private time together was going to come to a close.

"This family will hold you," she told Crista. "No matter what."

Crista nodded, tears threatening as if Connor's bad news had somehow made hers worse.

"And about the house, Mama? You can see why I started thinking about...selling. If we get..." She swallowed noisily. "If I'm right and we aren't together..." A sob squeezed. "I'll need money," she managed to finish.

Maggie leaned over her, hands on Crista's shoulders. "Lots of 'ifs' in that shaky plan, Crista. *If* you are wrong..."

Crista exhaled. "Then I wouldn't sell this dream house. But I'm not, Mama. A woman knows things."

She couldn't argue that. But Maggie also couldn't believe Anthony would cheat. She simply couldn't and there *had* to be a way to get to the truth.

She'd just have to find it.

Chapter Four
Vivien

Vivien reread Peter's last text after she pulled into the parking lot of the HCA Fort Walton-Destin Hospital.

Connor's awake. In some pain. Going to be fine.

Three short sentences, clinical in their reassurance, yet still taut with something else—relief, possibly, or exhaustion. Maybe just the lingering aftershock of a phone call no parent ever wanted to get.

She turned off the engine and sat for a few seconds, hands resting on the steering wheel, looking at the three-story hospital building. The creamy stucco was bathed in morning sunlight and surrounded by cheery palm trees, with a few people moving in and out under a large portico.

She watched a nurse in scrubs, a patient pushed in a wheelchair, a random visitor with a phone pressed to his ear looking like he'd rather be anywhere else on Earth than at this small-town hospital.

Vivien exhaled slowly.

When she'd tapped on Eli's door last night and told him what had happened, her brother had instantly dropped his head and moved his lips in prayer. And this morning, he looked a little tired and she'd noticed an open Bible on his bed. Hopefully, faithful Eli had a direct line to The Big Guy and Connor was protected and would heal fast.

She wrapped her hand around the two paper cups of coffee she'd just picked up. One black with a "drive-by" of real sugar, as Peter called his coffee preference. Hers had cream and sweetener, though she suspected she wouldn't touch it.

Her stomach was burning, but it would be better when she could see Connor, the kind and serious twenty-eight-year-old young man she'd met yesterday.

He was Peter's son, so she loved him already.

Slow down, Viv. Peter still thinks you want space and you're blowing in with coffee and love.

Holding the cups, she jostled her bag higher on her shoulder and headed toward the main entrance.

Inside, the hospital smelled slightly metallic, with sleek tile floors and a front desk manned by one rather sleepy-looking receptionist. She bypassed the desk for the elevators to the third floor, following the directions Peter had texted.

He hadn't called her, which was a bit of a disappointment. But why would he? She wasn't his girlfriend, just a concerned family friend.

Obviously, this new turn of events had nothing to do with them as a couple. But how long would their talk have to wait? She didn't know, but she'd find out soon. Since she was ready to tell him she didn't want all that space after all, waiting would be interminable. But the timing had to be right and respectful, even if it delayed her confession by a few days.

Based on the way he'd looked at her last night—a little guarded and uncertain—she had to wonder how he'd respond. What if *he* had changed *his* mind in the few months they'd been apart?

She shook her head as the elevator doors slid open.

None of that mattered now.

What mattered was Connor. And Peter. And the fact that she could be here to show him he wasn't alone.

She tried not to rush down the hall, silently observing the hospital surroundings. An IV pole rolled by, directed by an orderly who looked at his phone as he walked. Nurses at the station murmured to each other. A television played softly behind a half-closed door. Somewhere, a call bell chimed.

Vivien adjusted her grip on the coffee cups and slowed as she scanned the room numbers, pausing at Room 318.

She took a breath and knocked lightly.

The door opened almost immediately and the woman standing there was not Peter. Or a nurse, based on the sweatshirt and jeans that looked like they'd been put on in haste.

She was slender, petite, with pale skin and auburn hair that fell from a ponytail in wisps around her face. The style accentuated a delicate bone structure and a peppering of freckles that were showcased on a face that didn't wear a drop of makeup.

Faint lines around her blue-gray eyes and mouth gave

away her years—probably the same as Vivien's. Her expression was surprised during the split second when they stared at each other.

"Oh," Vivien said, briefly wondering if she had the wrong room number. "Hi. I—"

Before she could finish, Peter appeared in the doorway, much taller than this lady who couldn't be five-foot-three, his finger lifting to his lips.

"Hey, Viv," he whispered. "He's sound asleep."

He gestured gently for them to step into the hall. Vivien backed out automatically, the red-haired woman joining them. Peter eased the door shut behind them.

Only then did Vivien really get a look at him.

There were shadows under his eyes that hadn't been there last night. His hair was rumpled, as if he'd run his hands through it one too many times. He smiled when he saw the coffees—but it didn't reach his eyes.

"Thank you," he said softly as she handed him one. "You didn't have to do that."

"I wanted to," she said. "I just...thought you might need it."

He nodded, and exhaled. Then, as if remembering himself, he turned slightly.

"Sorry, Vivien, this is Holly," he said. "Connor's mom."

Oh. She was his *ex-wife.* The realization landed with a jolt. Well, of course Connor's mother would be here. *Duh.*

"Hello, Holly," Vivien said, smoothing her expression

into something warm and polite. "It's nice to meet you, although not under these circumstances."

"And you are?" she asked, shaking the hand Vivien offered.

"Sorry," Peter mumbled again, exhaustion and stress in the word. "Vivien Lawson. From—"

"Oh, of course." Holly's smile was quick, tired, but genuine. "The summers when Pete was a teenager."

Pete? Had anyone besides Eli *ever* called him Pete?

"I've heard so much about you, Vivien," Holly continued. "I've met your brother, Eli, of course. He came to Pensacola once so many years ago. With his wife, Melissa." Her expression fell. "Who, I guess, is gone. Anyway, Pete talks about your family and those summers like they're legend."

Vivien blinked, a little thrown by the present tense. He *talks* about her family? Hadn't they been divorced for nearly a decade now?

"They were legend," she replied. "And, well, I guess they are again." She glanced at Peter without meaning to, seeing something fleeting in his dark eyes.

Instantly, she knew what he was silently communicating. He hadn't told Holly about their relationship. His ex-wife had no idea she was standing in front of a woman "Pete" had said he loved two months ago.

And stupid Vivien had replied with...*I need space.*

She shook off the thought and concentrated on the moment, digging into her memory vault for all the things Peter had told her about Holly. Starting with...her name.

Did she know it was Holly? Had he ever called her anything but "my ex-wife"?

Maybe. She couldn't remember. But she did recall him sharing that their split had not been amicable. Connor had just gone to college when they filed for a divorce he said was inevitable. They'd been waiting until both sons were out of the house to break up the family.

His biggest regret, he'd said once, was that they hadn't been able to stay friends. Or even civil. That he'd hated knowing his sons felt the tension every time they were together. When he shared that, he'd been doling out unsolicited but greatly appreciated divorce advice, telling Vivien to take the high road with her ex-husband, Ryan.

She had, and that had blown up in her face.

"I'm sorry I didn't bring you a coffee," she said to Holly. "I didn't realize—"

"Oh, that's okay," Holly said quickly. "I've had about six already."

Peter huffed a quiet laugh.

"How is Connor?" Vivien asked. "I know you said he's okay, but..."

Peter's expression softened instantly. "He's incredibly lucky," he said. "Really. I saw the accident report, and it could have been so much worse."

"Thank God," she said. "So you have details of how it happened?"

"Oh, please. Pete's a cop," Holly said, as if Vivien didn't know that. "He gets all the inside info."

"It's not a lot more than what I told you, Viv," he said, taking a sip of coffee.

As he did, Vivien couldn't help but notice a flicker in Holly's eyes—surprise that Vivien knew anything already? That she and Peter were in contact? That he called her "Viv"?

"Connor was driving back from the party when a pickup crossed the center line," he added. "Connor swerved to avoid a head-on collision, but the truck clipped the side of his car. Sent him spinning off the road into a shallow ditch. The other driver wasn't hurt, but they brought him here, treated him for scratches, and he was arrested on a DUI."

Vivien winced.

"The airbags deployed," Peter went on. "Paramedics said that probably saved him from something much worse. He was conscious when they got there, but disoriented. Kept asking the same questions over and over."

Holly folded her arms tighter around herself, closing her eyes with a whimper. "I can't stand that my baby went through that."

Vivien gave a sympathetic nod. She'd be a hot holy mess if Lacey were laying in that room after being "clipped" on the highway by a drunk driver.

"What do the doctors say?" she asked.

"Moderate to severe concussion," he said. "Broken clavicle. Fractured wrist. Painful, but nothing life-threatening. Because of the head injury—and the hour—they admitted him overnight and are monitoring for internal bleeding from the airbag or seatbelt, and any neurological changes."

"So he's stable?" Vivien asked quietly.

"Completely," Peter said, relief unmistakable in his voice. "Awake earlier this morning. Pretty wiped out now from a load of heavy-duty painkillers."

"He's in dental school," Holly volunteered—as if Vivien didn't know that, either. "So when they want to give him anything, he asks a million questions and already knows the answers. He's so smart."

"Then we can be sure his wonderful brain is perfectly intact," Vivien said.

Peter smiled at her, a glimpse of light in his eyes.

"I'm so relieved he's going to be okay," Vivien added.

"Okay, but not great," Holly said. "It's his right arm, which has to heal before he goes back to school and needs to work on patients. But I guess right is good, since he broke his left when he was nine." She gazed up at Peter. "Remember that trip to the ER? Ugh. I was a wreck. *You* were a wreck!"

Vivien took a step back, the intimate memory and Holly's rattling on making her suddenly feel out of place. She didn't belong in this family scene, did she?

"Speaking of wrecks," Holly continued, "I was a mess last night. When Pete called, I couldn't leave Pensacola fast enough."

"She got here about two hours after he was admitted," Peter told Vivien. "We've been up all night."

Vivien didn't want to say they looked it, but she could certainly see the long night and stress had left shadows on their faces as they stood side by side, like...a couple. A couple that was united again by something bigger than old resentments.

"I can't imagine the stress you've both been under," Vivien said. "But I'm so relieved he's going to be okay. Truly."

"Thank you for coming," Peter said. "It means a lot."

"Of course." She took another step backwards, sensing it was time to leave. "And if there's anything I can do—anything the family can do—please don't hesitate."

"Oh, we're good," Holly assured her, inching closer to Peter as she looked up at him. "Pete's got everything covered, so I can stay with him while Connor recovers. Yes, I'm going to be a hovercraft mom because that's what I do. Right, Pete?"

He replied with a tight smile, but it wasn't cool or bitter or acrimonious the way he'd described their relationship.

Well, that was a good thing. That had been what he'd always wanted for his sons. He'd told her that.

But...Holly was *staying?*

"I just wanted to check in..." Vivien said awkwardly.

"And we really appreciate it," Holly added.

We. Before Vivien reacted, Peter looked past her. "Oh, here's the doctor finally."

Vivien turned to see a tall man glancing at a tablet as he walked toward them.

"Thank goodness," Holly said, putting her arm on Peter's shoulder. "Let's ask him about that weird mark on the X-ray, Pete. I didn't see it, but your eyes are amazing."

Feeling very much like an extra piece from a different puzzle, Vivien moved away. "Good luck, both of you. And nice to meet you, Holly."

"And you, Vivien," she said warmly. "I'm sure we'll see you again."

Vivien stole a quick look at Peter, but his gaze was locked on the doctor, and he was clearly focused on the next step in this process.

"I'll see you," she said softly to him.

He shifted his gaze. "Thanks for coming, Viv." For one second, she thought he was going to hug her, and she was surprised at how much she wanted that. But he just smiled. "We'll be in touch," he promised.

On that, she pivoted and passed the doctor, hating that her chest burned a little. Nothing was wrong, she reminded herself. They were concerned parents who should be together at a time like this. Holly had been nice, and Peter had been distracted.

And Vivien...was not dating Peter anymore, so she had no right to feel like she belonged here in this situation.

That made her eyes sting as she walked to her car.

VIVIEN PULLED into the Summer House driveway just as Eli stepped out the front door, moving with the kind of single-minded purpose that made it clear he was not headed out for a casual errand. His shoulders were squared. His jaw set. He didn't even glance toward her car as he marched toward Gulf Shore Boulevard.

"Eli!" she called, shoving her door open and hopping out. "Where are you going?"

He stopped, blinking as if he'd been pulled out of a thought mid-sentence. "Vivien." Then, without answering her question, his gaze sharpened. "How's Connor?"

She froze for half a beat, then moved closer to meet him.

"I never actually saw Connor," she said, realizing it only as the words left her mouth.

"Really?" Her brother looked surprised, his sky-blue eyes wide. "He's not allowed visitors?"

"I think he is," she said, "but he was asleep on pain meds and his mother was there." She lifted a brow toward Eli. "Holly? You've met her, I believe."

"Eons ago," he said. "I don't remember her too well. Small? Redhead? Talks a blue streak?"

Vivien pointed at him. "Bingo. Connor is evidently doing as well as expected. A concussion they're watching, broken wrist, fractured collarbone. The other guy was arrested for DUI. That's really all I got, since Peter seemed focused on talking to the doctor. Oh—and I guess Holly's going to stick around and help her son navigate life in a cast."

Eli's face softened, something like relief loosening his shoulders. "Good. That's... good."

The moment stretched, then Vivien tilted her head. "Where are you headed like you're about to stop a crime in progress?"

His mouth curved faintly, but the tension didn't leave his eyes. "I don't think I can stop this crime, but I'm going to Left Coast Bridge."

She blinked. "Left...oh, you mean the *Let Go* Bridge."

He exhaled a dry laugh through his nose. "That's not its real name."

"Not officially," she said. "But tell me one person over forty who's ever spent a summer in Destin who calls it anything else."

His gaze slid past her, toward the road. "They're tearing it down."

She choked. "They're tearing down the Let Go Bridge?"

He nodded once. "It *is* an eyesore, but still. There was a council meeting last week and it got put under 'safety and infrastructure.' Apparently, way too many teenagers jumping into the water is a liability nightmare."

"Well, a lot of us did almost die." At his amused look, she laughed. "It felt that way at sixteen, but seriously, isn't it a historic landmark? Does sentimentality count for nothing these days?"

"In Destin? No, but I wanted to take one more look at it."

"Me, too," she said, motioning for him to keep walking. "If they're going to erase it, I want pictures of it first."

He hesitated, then fell into step beside her as she started down the drive.

They walked in companionable silence for a block before she said, "So. Holly."

He shot her a look. "I take it you've never met her?"

"No, but she's nice. I do remember that Peter once told me he wished their divorce hadn't been acrimonious, so I guess this is a good place for them to...heal. Along with Connor."

Eli shot one more look, this one skeptical and humorous. "I'm sure you two will be great friends."

"Shut it," she muttered. "Peter and I broke things off, remember?"

"Mmm. I do. But..." But here she was, walking to the very bridge where once, many years ago, she'd tried to let him go. Obviously, the bridge had failed and so had she.

He didn't say anything—Eli was too cool to press a point like that. But she had no such compunction with her brother.

"Have you heard from Kate?" she asked as they reached the marina, the scent of salt and fuel mixing in the air.

"Yeah, we text. Talked last night. She's..."

"Busy with that grant stuff?" Vivien suggested when he didn't finish.

"She's working things out," he said, as clear as mud.

"Eli." She jabbed him with her elbow as they reached a roundabout and slipped into what had become a construction zone over the past year. They followed a chain-link fence that enclosed this section of a massive jetty.

"Working what things out?" she urged, not ready to let the subject die. "The grant issues or...the love issues?"

"Will you calm down?"

She laughed. "I'm serious. What is she working out?"

"We care about each other," he said after a moment.

"We do. But...some things don't line up. And you can't fix that with affection."

Some things don't line up. "You mean...your faith?"

"Yeah, obviously, we have different beliefs."

"That's one way of putting it."

Eli slid her a look. "Another way would be this," he said. "I read the Bible every day and live my life grounded in a love of the Lord that I hope permeates my every action. She is a card-carrying, chemistry-loving Senior Research Scientist and Director of the Energy Storage Materials Lab who does not, cannot, and will not give credence to...*religion.*"

He said the last word as if he were echoing someone's distaste for the subject.

"Both are valid positions," he continued. "But there's not a lot of room for compromise."

"Anything else?" she asked. "Besides...God?"

He almost laughed. "*Is* there anything else besides God? Yes, we have issues. We live a thousand miles apart. I have a business in Atlanta and practically have an office here in Destin. She has a big job, teenage kids, and a house in Upstate New York. So there are many road-blocks, but I'd be lying if I didn't say that faith is at the center of anything keeping us apart."

"I hope you work it out," she said glumly as they started walking up a deserted beach, the bridge far enough away to look perfectly fine from here.

"I hope so, too, because I haven't met a woman I care for this much since Melissa died."

Wow. She wasn't sure she knew it was *that* serious.

They cut around the edge of the jetty, stepping carefully over rocks and sand to get to the orange mesh safety fence surrounding the base of the Destin side of the bridge. As they got closer, it was easy to see the dilapidated wooden bridge was held together with rusted metal, some sun-bleached boards, and railings that leaned at precarious angles.

The bridge was over a channel that led to the harbor, connecting two "east" and "west" jetties, which was probably how it got the "Left Coast" name. Of course, the tradition of sixteen-year-olds in Destin jumping off to "let go" of something had transformed that name into something far more lyrical—the bridge where you literally "let go" of things.

Vivien had forgotten about the bridge, with no reason to come out this way, but not her own rite of passage at sixteen.

A yellow sign had been bolted to one post: *Danger. No Trespassing. Demolition scheduled.*

The structure wasn't that high and the water under it was calm, so the jump wasn't particularly dangerous. But oh, so fun.

"Dang," Eli whispered as he read the words. "I didn't want to believe this rumor."

"This place," she said, voice thick, "was everything."

They stood there, letting the breeze push against them, the water slapping rhythmically against stone and metal.

"Do you remember your jump?" Eli asked.

She swallowed. "Perfectly."

Her legs had shaken so hard she thought they'd give out. She'd stood in the middle, heart pounding, clutching a folded scrap of paper with a name on it she wasn't ready to say goodbye to. She'd jumped anyway because everyone was watching and because sixteen felt like a cliff's edge.

"You?" she asked.

"I chickened out," Eli admitted. "Climbed halfway up and decided I didn't have anything to let go of."

She smiled at him. "That tracks."

They edged closer, careful where they stepped, peering at something that had seemed so much bigger when they were kids.

"The summer we jumped," she said softly, "Kate let go of her fear of being a nerd and still she jumped in with her glasses on."

Eli cracked up. "Yep. The woman with lost glasses."

"And Tessa jumped three times, one for every bad decision she'd made...the week before."

They both laughed at that.

"And you?" he asked. "What did you let go of?"

"Not what, *who*." She looked up at him, squinting in the sun. "Three guesses and the first two don't count."

He frowned. "Why? Why would anyone give up on a guy like Peter McCarthy?"

"I've been asking myself that for a month or so," she said wryly. "But at sixteen? He was utterly unattainable, already in college. I was a child and he was...your best friend."

"Yeah, I wouldn't have approved of that when you were sixteen."

"It hurt to like him so much," she said, her voice giving away her emotions. "Have you ever wanted anything so much you could taste it, but knew you couldn't have it?"

He smiled. "Sometimes I feel that way with Kate."

"Well, imagine you're sixteen and stupid."

"You weren't stupid, Viv."

"I was sixteen, though. So I jumped with a vow to let go of my crush."

"Did it work?" he asked.

She snorted. "Hardly. The fact is, this bridge is... precious and not just because of our summers. Everyone's summers. Who's calling the shots? Where's the historical commission when you need them? Who tears down a landmark without a fight?"

Eli just smiled and turned around to go home. "I don't feel like fighting City Hall, Viv," he said. "I'm busy praying for things that really matter."

She walked back with him, taking a few glances over her shoulder at the bridge that somehow still seemed important. It could be cleaned up. It could be preserved. It could be a tourist attraction instead of a blemish on the beach.

Who else would understand? Peter, of course.

Why did all roads—and bridges—lead back to him?

Chapter Five
Maggie

Maggie loved the beach most in the late afternoon, when the sun softened and the wind carried just enough salt to make everything feel clean. The heat of the day eased. The sand cooled beneath her feet. The sky stretched wide and pale, and she could get perspective on her problems.

Which, since her conversation with Crista this morning, had been mounting.

Jo Ellen, on the other hand, appeared to be fueled entirely by the events of the last twenty-four hours.

"...and I'm just saying, if Connor hadn't whipped that wheel at exactly the right moment, that truck would have T-boned him! He could be dead, Mags. Thank God for young reflexes. Also thank God he hadn't had a sip of alcohol. I watch those things, you know. That boy was clean and sober."

Maggie nodded absently, her gaze fixed on the thin line where sea met sky.

Jo Ellen continued, undeterred. "And Kate being back in Ithaca—honestly, I don't know how she does it. I mean, now that I've been here, washed by this sunshine, the thought of a winter there? I know, I know, it's July, but the cold comes fast. I'd just lie down on the sidewalk and let nature take me. Now, I'm close with Kate, but not enough for her to tell me if there was another reason for her leaving so quickly. Like...you know."

"Mmm," Maggie murmured.

"Or *do* you know?"

Maggie shot her a look. "What are you talking about, Jo?"

"Well, everything but what's really on your mind, I suppose."

"Nothing's on my mind," Maggie lied.

Jo Ellen not-so-secretly rolled her eyes, but didn't press.

Instead, they walked in rhythm along the wet sand, their bare feet sinking and lifting with each step. Gulls cried overhead. A pelican skimmed the water's surface, wingtips brushing the waves.

I think Anthony is cheating on me.

Crista's announcement replayed in Maggie's head like a cracked record.

It was impossible. Entirely fiction. A hallucination born of hormones and fear and too much time alone with her thoughts. Crista always overreacted, in any situation.

Anthony adored Crista, anyone with eyes could see that. He doted on Nolie. In the three years Maggie had lived with the family, she'd never seen anything that indicated Anthony had a cheating bone in his body.

He'd worked closely with Nolie when she was diagnosed with dyslexia, and he cared for his home like a natural protector. He was not the kind of man who betrayed his family.

Maggie knew people, and she'd bet her last dollar on Anthony Merritt.

There *had* to be another explanation. A logical one. A boring one. A financial one. A professional one. An unexpected one. Anything but the thing Crista feared.

Deleted texts. A password. A separate account.

Anthony was busy. He was ambitious and stepping into a new role. Okay, he had a pretty assistant and took his calls outside. None of that equaled *infidelity.*

"Magnolia Fredericks Lawson."

Maggie blinked at her full name. "What?"

"You have not heard a single word I've said in the last five minutes."

Maggie turned to her friend. "It hasn't been a *single* word, Jo. It's been a continuous broadcast with no commercial breaks for applause or breath."

Jo Ellen stopped walking, flipping back a few silver locks that Maggie used to think were too long for a seventy-eight-year-old but she kind of loved now.

"Excuse me for breathing," Jo Ellen murmured.

"Am I right?"

"You're...brutal." Jo Ellen laughed. "But that's why I love you. The truth is I have been delivering a perfectly curated monologue about the emotional state of every human in the Summer House—including dear Atlas, who smiled at me and it was *not* gas—and you have been nodding like a dashboard ornament." She leaned in. "We should get a few of those for Scarlett," she added, referring to their playful name for the red T-bird their friend had unexpectedly gifted them. "Maybe a Georgia Bulldog bobblehead for old time's sake?"

Maggie wasn't thinking about the car. "Whatever," she muttered. "I'm just...worried about other things."

"Then share them," Jo Ellen said, putting a hand on Maggie's shoulder. "Or I'll start guessing, and I'm going with a brain tumor."

"Jo Ellen!"

"A long and sexy conversation with Brick the Biker?"

"Would you stop?"

"Oh, I know!" Jo Ellen practically danced on the sand. "You're planning your toast for Eli and Kate's wedding! How's that for wishful thinking?"

Wedding? "It's...crazy. Like you." Maggie wanted to share all her fears, but somehow, repeating Crista's allegations made them feel true.

"What's going on, Mags?" Jo Ellen asked gently. "I'm here for you, no matter what."

Maggie looked out at the water again, feeling herself succumbing to the temptation to tell.

"It's not fun, it's not pleasant, and, most of all, it's not true," Maggie started. "And you have to promise not to breathe a word to anyone and I do mean anyone—not Kate, not Tessa, not Meredith, and please not Crista. Not a soul."

Jo Ellen raised her right hand. "I swear I will not breathe a word of whatever you are about to tell me. I swear on the sisterhood of Delta Delta Delta, in the spirit of the Tri-Delt honor code, the secret handshake, and the eternal bond of our sorority. I swear upon every pastel cardigan and pearl necklace I have ever owned that this dies with me."

Despite herself, Maggie laughed. "All right."

Jo Ellen leaned in, vibrating with anticipation. "I'm a *vault*."

Maggie took a breath. "Crista thinks Anthony is cheating on her."

The smile vanished. "What?"

"She told me this morning."

"No." Jo Ellen shook her head. "No, no, no. That's not—"

"She's convinced."

"But they have Nolie. And a baby on the way. He couldn't possibly...could he?" Her voice broke on the last two words.

"No," Maggie said simply. "I don't believe it."

"So why would she think that?"

Maggie carefully explained what she knew—which was little—and why Crista seemed concerned.

"Okay, that's all...fishy," Jo Ellen agreed after taking it all in. "But this is Crista. Need I say more?"

"I know," Maggie said on a sigh. "She tends to...blow things out of proportion."

"Drama is her default," Jo Ellen said. "It always has been. Even as a little girl, she was given to meltdowns and tantrums."

Maggie frowned, never a fan of anyone saying anything negative about her kids, even if it was true.

"She was the youngest, and all the others were

teenagers," Maggie said. "Crista always felt like the odd man out with our kids and the only way to get attention was by crying."

"Well, she's not the odd man out now," Jo Ellen said as though she didn't buy the rationale.

"She lost her father at ten, Jo," Maggie added, the words coming out more clipped than she wanted, but how could she not defend Crista? "In the span of a month, her two siblings went to college, her father went to jail, and a few months later, she and I moved out of a beautiful custom-built home that was confiscated by the U.S. government and into a one-bedroom apartment. And I started working, leaving her to fend for herself for a few hours when she got home from school. The next thing she knew, her father died. Of course she's dramatic."

"We weren't speaking in those days," Jo Ellen said, her voice rich with sympathy. "And I hate that our rift meant I couldn't be there for you in that dark time."

Maggie shrugged. "We survived, but Crista is... volatile. Maybe a little afraid of how easily a storybook life can blow up. I don't fault her for the theatrics, but I don't for one minute believe she's right about Anthony."

"Then there has to be a different explanation," Jo Ellen said. "None of those things automatically mean there's another woman. She didn't catch him in the act."

Maggie grimaced at the thought.

"She hasn't confronted him?" Jo Ellen asked.

"He'll say it's hormones. That she's imagining it. She doesn't want to be dismissed."

"I hate to say this, Mags, but a woman knows. At least, I think. Artie certainly never cheated."

"Neither did Roger," Maggie said. "Unless you count the loan shark who cheated him out of...everything."

Jo nodded slowly, thinking. "Someone has to prove to Crista that she's wrong."

"Of course," Maggie agreed. "But she's not listening to common sense."

"We need someone on the ground. A private investigator?"

"No, I can't hire—"

"We could do it, Mags!"

Maggie slowed her step. "We?"

Jo's mouth curved. "Who better?"

"Um...anyone?"

"I'm serious!" Jo Ellen insisted. "We just need to get up there and follow him around and verify that he's not having an affair."

"You're out of your mind." Even as Maggie said the words, a whisper of déjà vu rolled over her...along with quite recent memories of a road trip to Miami. "We couldn't possibly..."

"Why not?" Jo Ellen shot back. "We fire up Scarlett, pack our bags, and start Senior Sleuthing."

Maggie choked. "Excuse me?"

"I just made that up," she beamed. "So alliterative, don't you think? Must be all that Wordle I've been doing."

"Are you on drugs?"

"Wordle isn't a drug! Although it can be addictive."

Maggie narrowed her eyes. "Be serious, Jo. What are you suggesting?"

"That we drive up to Atlanta and keep an eye on Anthony. We give Crista the proof she needs—not that he is guilty, but that he isn't."

Maggie actually considered the idea, which was mad.

"Well, if we make up some reason for me to go home —like my roses need tending—then Anthony will just... behave. Then we'll *think* we're right, but we won't *know*."

"True," Jo Ellen agreed. "So he can't know we're there, but we can very surreptitiously follow him and watch what he does, where he goes, who he goes with..."

Maggie fought a shiver despite the summer sun. The suggestion was so wrong...and so right.

"I can't agree to that," she said, giving voice to her thoughts. "If Crista found out, she'd be devastated. If Anthony found out, he'd be furious. If anyone else found out, they'd think I'd gone off the deep end and am an overbearing control freak trying to rule this family like the Queen Mother."

"You're not?" Jo Ellen teased.

"I'm attempting to change," Maggie admitted on a sigh. "Being here—and being with you—has made me remember a time in my life when I was young, carefree, and didn't control everything."

"What are you trying to control?" Jo Ellen countered. "Nothing," she finished before Maggie could speak. "You're trying to help your daughter and grandchildren. You're trying to save a marriage. You're trying to make the world a better place, one secret drive-by at a time."

Maggie snorted. "Where did you come from, Jo Ellen Wylie?"

"Ithaca, New York, and we could say that's where we're going on a road trip but Kate's there and I don't really want to drive from Destin to Ithaca. Unless you do. I'd do anything for you, Mags."

The admission touched Maggie, making her stop on the sand and look hard at her closest friend. For a long time, she didn't speak but simply held Jo Ellen's gaze.

"I have keys to a house," Maggie finally whispered, half hating herself for saying it, but also seeing that it was the answer and the only way.

"Keys? To what house?"

"To a neighbor's house two doors away from Crista and Anthony's. Barbara Johansen goes to see her daughter in Wisconsin every summer and leaves me the key to take care of her plants."

"Does she have a camera?" Jo Ellen asked. "Cleaning people? Any witnesses of any kind?"

Witnesses. The word made Maggie's heart clutch. "No."

"Good. We'll stay there and...monitor the situation."

Maggie felt a smile pull. "You mean spy on Anthony?"

"I mean...we'll casually observe his comings and goings."

Maggie launched a brow. "I can't believe..."

"That you're about to say yes," Jo Ellen finished for her.

"Honestly? I can't believe I didn't think of it myself."

Jo Ellen let out a giddy laugh. "I can! You're so by-the-book, Mags. You know I'm going to come at every problem with a more creative solution."

"And by creative, you mean you'll lie your way out of whatever predicament we're in, including jail."

"Well, it wouldn't be the first time." Jo Ellen elbowed her. "Oh! We could call Brick and have a motorcade protection service."

In spite of herself, Maggie felt her cheeks warm at the second mention of the tattooed biker with a beard like a wizard. The man had taken to texting her, "Good morning, Mags the Magnificent!" every single day, even after she'd told him to please ride off into the sunset and don't bother with a helmet.

"Don't bring Brick into this," she said. "But we have to come up with a plausible reason for why we're going to leave for a while. We did the spa lie last time."

"Okay..." Jo Ellen pursed her lips and tapped her cheek, the gesture deepening the tiny creases around her lips, but Maggie was thinking too hard to remind her to stop.

"We could tell them we're meeting girlfriends from college?" Jo Ellen tried. "Tri-Delt reunion?"

"They're all dead."

Jo Ellen's shoulders dropped, then she brightened. "You and Brick need a chaperone for a long weekend away."

Maggie's eyes shuttered.

"Okay, okay," Jo Ellen said. "Brick is a touchy subject. How about something close to the truth? That's always smart. We're running up to Atlanta to see...a lawyer about the house or something like that."

"Why wouldn't I stay at Crista's house where I live? And they'd have questions. Eli will want to know everything."

"Maggie!" She frowned again, causing more lines. "We have to just—"

"I've got it," Maggie exclaimed, resisting the urge to reach over and *make* her stop frowning.

Jo Ellen lit up. "Tell me!"

"We tell them we're getting...work done."

"Work?"

Maggie lifted a hand and made a small, circular motion in the air near her cheek. "Strategic. Subtle. A nip and tuck, if you will."

Jo's mouth fell open. Then she gasped. "We're telling them we're getting *plastic surgery?*"

"Not surgery," Maggie said quickly. "Consultations. Procedures. Very modern things that don't involve knives. Lasers. Needles. Whatever vampire plasma they're selling these days."

Jo stared. "But we'll come back looking exactly the same."

"We'll get facials up there. And no one will notice. They'll try to be nice and say it really worked, and it will explain why we'd go to Atlanta, where I know a doctor. We'll say we're staying in a special recovery hotel that's part of the surgery center."

"They have those?" Jo Ellen asked.

"For the really rich," Maggie said. "And we can just

come back wearing hats and oversized sunglasses and pretending we can't smile. We'll grab some products and slather up with Retin-A."

Jo clasped her hands. "Yes, Mags! We'll commit. We'll need serums. Ice rollers. Overnight masks. We'll return glowing like we've been reborn in a Korean skincare lab."

Maggie shook her head. "I cannot believe this is my life."

"You're welcome," Jo trilled.

"Thank you, Jo," she conceded. "You're a good friend."

"Come on." Jo Ellen looped their arms together. "Let's pack to save a marriage and have some fun."

For the first time all day, Maggie believed they could do both.

Chapter Six
Tessa

Tessa's phone buzzed on the counter just as she was smoothing the play area rug for the third time.

Dusty: *be there in 2 min*

Her stomach churned as she stared at the brief text he'd probably sent from a stoplight.

"Okay," she told no one, and lifted her chin like the apartment could hear her and talk back. If it could, it would tell her she'd used too much organic lemon cleaner and the amount of toys she'd purchased bordered on ridiculous.

Too bad. Olive Leighton was going to have fun or Tessa would die trying.

With two minutes left, she did one last lap around her small but cheery home, inspecting it for baby readiness. The outlets were covered. Candy Land, Chutes 'n' Ladders, and no less than five wooden puzzles were stacked for easy access. The tiny table and chairs were ready for their first tea party. A basket of rubber blocks and thick board books sat on a coffee table that had padding on sharp corners.

She wandered down the hallway to look at the guest

room—now Olive's room, the doorway protected by a small gate. The toddler bed that Dusty had built with impressive Allen wrench skills and an endless supply of patience was nestled in the corner under a window. Tessa had covered it with a pink gingham comforter and a few too many stuffed animals.

Was there such a thing as too many stuffed animals? "I think not," Tessa murmured, moving her last-minute inspection to the hall bathroom.

There, a nightlight glowed faintly in the corner and a little stepstool waited at the bathroom sink.

She'd even set out a brand-new Little Mermaid toothbrush on the counter. On the tub, a bottle of bubble bath stood next to four rubber duckies lined up like a squadron of cheery yellow soldiers.

Tessa paused in the doorway and tried to picture Olive splish-splashing and giggling while she blew bubbles. She could hear a small voice asking for another story, *pwease, Miss Tessa!* She could already sense the love in a hug goodnight before lights-out time.

It wasn't hard to imagine any of that, because she'd been thinking about having Olive stay here every minute since she'd made the suggestion. At Dusty's request, she hadn't told anyone about their plans. She knew anything could happen—Morgan could change her mind or run off or find another solution—but none of those things had.

More importantly, she had to respect client confidentiality and Morgan's deeply personal situation.

In about one minute, she'd have this little girl in her home for a month. When the time was right, she'd tell friends and family they were doing a favor for one of Dusty's patients. For now, for today, all that mattered was that she bond with Olive.

And bond she would. Through toys, games, special treats...whatever it took to give this child joy and fill this home with girlish giggles.

Confident she could do that, Tessa walked back into the kitchen just as she heard a car pull into the driveway.

Okay, then. *Showtime.*

The sound of footsteps on the stairs would come next —Dusty's steady stride, his voice calling up, the door cracking open, a high-pitched, "*Hewwo.*"

She waited, but heard nothing. The quiet stretched long enough for her to go to the front window and see Dusty's truck parked in the driveway, no people, no child, no bag, nothing.

Finally, the driver's door opened, and Dusty stepped out and looked right up at her, as if he fully expected Tessa to be looking out her window. Instantly, she saw a look of frustration and a plea for help in his eyes.

Tessa didn't hesitate. She darted to the door and down the outside stairs to the driveway.

When she got there, Dusty had moved to the passenger side of the truck. As Tessa walked closer, that door opened and Dusty reached a hand to help Morgan out of the truck.

"C'mon," he said gently. "At least stand out here to say goodbye and I'll get her things. Look, Tessa's here."

Tessa quickened her stride, watching Morgan step out slowly, moving with zombie-like energy.

She looked more fragile than when Tessa had met her the first time. Or maybe she carried herself differently today, with her shoulders rounded forward, her face pale under the bright July sun.

When she'd come in to see Dusty and he'd presented their idea and introduced Tessa, Morgan had seemed brighter and slightly more hopeful. Not today.

Her hair was pulled into a sloppy knot, and she wore sweatpants and an oversized hoodie that looked downright painful in this heat. Her expression teetered between terrified and despondent, her vitality so low it was a wonder she managed to dress and pack for herself, let alone a child.

She looked in Tessa's direction and lifted a sad hand in a partial wave.

"Hey, Morgan," Tessa said.

Wordlessly, Dusty opened the cab door, leaning into the truck's back seat. He spoke in soft tones, too quiet for Tessa to hear, as he unlatched a car seat belt and reached in for Olive.

A second later, he turned, holding a tiny child wearing a mismatched pajama top and bottoms, sneakers with no socks, and a wild mess of yellow curls that hadn't seen a hairbrush in...a while. Easing her to the ground, Dusty slowly straightened as if he expected his little visitor to run.

But she stood rooted to that spot, gaze down, thumb in mouth, tiny shoulders rising and falling with each breath.

"Well, you must be Olive," Tessa said, stepping around Morgan to greet the child. "Hello. I'm Tessa."

When Tessa bent closer, the little girl took a step back, refusing to look up.

"I can't wait to show you all the toys I have for your stay," Tessa continued, undaunted. "I sure hope you like stuffies. I pretty much cleaned out Target."

No response. No eye contact. But no tears, either.

Morgan stood a few feet away with her arms folded tight over her chest, staring at the driveway, either disinterested or distracted. Whichever, she wasn't stepping in and encouraging her little girl to *say hello to the nice lady*.

Dusty pulled a very small pink roller bag with faded images of Hello Kitty on the side from the back and glanced at Tessa. "That's everything. The car seat can stay in the truck."

"Do you want to come inside with Olive?" Tessa asked Morgan. "You might feel better if you see her room." She leaned a little closer to Olive to stage-whisper, "It's the one with the brand new big-girl bed."

Olive looked up, the first spark of interest in her blue, blue eyes.

"No," Morgan said, her voice gruff. "I can't...no. You...take her."

"Well, you probably want to say goodbye." Tessa put a light hand on Olive's shoulder. "Kiss Mommy, honey. She wants to hug you before she leaves."

The interest in her eyes turned to raw fear as she looked from Tessa to Morgan to Dusty and back to

Morgan, her little brain visibly putting two and two together and coming up with...desertion.

Instantly, her mouth opened, her eyes filled, and the air rocked with the high-pitched wail.

"No, no, don't cry—"

Tessa's plea was drowned out by a scream of "Mommy! Mommy!" as Olive shot straight to her mother, arms out, feet jumping to get up.

Morgan didn't reach for her child. She just looked down at Olive, silent. Like she didn't hear the cries or see the desperation in her child's outstretched arms.

For some reason, that stunned Tessa—more than if she'd reprimanded the little girl.

"It's okay, it's okay," Tessa murmured, resisting the urge to scoop her up and comfort the poor thing. "Mommy will be back soon. Until then, we'll have fun. So much fun. More fun than you've ever had, starting with...dolls. We have baby dolls. And a stuffed, um, turtle or six. And a farmhouse. And games. So many games. Candy Land! Do you play?"

Olive wiped a runny nose, put her head back, and howled, "*Mommmy!*"

Morgan took a step back and gave Tessa a silent plea for help.

"You can pick her up," Dusty said. "In fact, you should probably take her inside."

She didn't have to be asked twice. Tessa lifted the tiny body—she couldn't weigh twenty-five pounds—and pressed Olive to her chest, ignoring the kicks and attempts to get free.

"*Mommmy!*" She screeched the word at an unimaginable pitch in Tessa's ear, who held tight and turned to Morgan.

Tessa still couldn't fathom that the young woman didn't want to at least give her daughter one last kiss before a month apart.

But Morgan had two hands over her face, her own shoulders shaking with a sob.

Instantly, Dusty slid his arm around Morgan. "You got this, Morgan. I promise you, it's going to be fine." He ushered her into the truck, helped her with the seatbelt, then closed the door. Rushing around the front of the truck, he slowed when he neared the walkway where Tessa stood with a squirmy, teary two-year-old.

"Is she okay?" Tessa mouthed, her heart breaking for Morgan.

He lifted a shoulder. "I'm checking her into the center right now. Can you handle..."

"Yes," she said with far more confidence than she felt. "We got this. Right, Olive Oyl? Just like Popeye's girlfriend, huh? We are girls on a mission to have fun. Ready?"

The squirming slowed and the wailing quieted. Her body was still tense, but it was a start.

Dusty leaned forward and gave Olive's curls a pat. "You're in good hands," he whispered, then leaned in to brush Tessa's cheek with his knuckles. "And you're a goddess."

She smiled. "Hand me that suitcase," she said.

She took the bag from him, surprised at how light it

was. Didn't matter. She'd cleaned out the toddler clothes at Target, too.

"Let's go, princess. I believe there's a peanut butter and jelly sandwich with your name on it. I say we have lunch on the rooftop, huh?" She prattled on as she walked up the stairs, turning back once, expecting to see Dusty already behind the wheel, whipping out to get Morgan help.

But he hadn't moved from the spot, staring up at her with raw affection and admiration in his eyes. Her heart tumbled a little at the sight.

"And that, my little friend, was worth the price of admission," Tessa whispered. "Which is free for you. Here we go."

As she opened the door to her apartment, she lowered Olive to the floor. For the very first time, they held each other's gaze.

Olive's eyes were red from crying, and shadowed with uncertainty and a distant pain that Tessa wanted to wipe away with every ounce of strength she had.

"Well, welcome home, Olive Oyl."

The little girl took a step back, shuddered on a breath, and then stood stone still. She was dead silent for ten, fifteen, twenty seconds and...*oh*.

A wet spot formed in the front of her pajama pants and dribbled to the floor.

Apparently, Morgan had forgotten to put a diaper on her daughter.

Tessa set the suitcase down and let out a sigh. "Why

don't we start with a warm bath, fresh clothes, and then we'll get that sandwich."

Olive looked down at the puddle around her untied shoes.

"And you'll be thrilled to see I bought a pair of light-up sneakers, because every girl should have those." She took her hand and led her toward the bathroom as the reality of what she'd agreed to settled in.

This wasn't a month of babysitting.

This was a lifeline for a drowning child.

Chapter Seven
Lacey

Even a regular Tuesday night at Boshamps felt like having dinner on a vacation postcard—salt in the air, string lights everywhere, the harbor water catching the last streaks of sunset like it was showing off.

Boats idled and eased past in the distance, kids ran around on the outdoor deck, and somewhere nearby a band was warming up for a set that would drift over the hum of conversation.

Lacey took it all in from the outside table on the second level where she sat kitty-corner from her boyfriend. She sipped a strawberry daiquiri, waiting for the cloud of contentment that always settled over her when she was with Roman Matteo.

Because contentment went hand in hand with love, which was all she could feel when she looked into his lion-gold eyes. He'd changed her life so dramatically, she could hardly believe that three months ago, she'd never heard of the man.

Then she'd done some digging, found out his name, and curiosity led her to contact the son that Tessa had secretly given up for adoption. Before she knew what was happening, Lacey had agreed to a scheme to "pretend" to be dating Roman so that he could meet his birth mother without betraying her past.

Only it was *pretend* for about ten minutes before Lacey had fallen flat out, head over heels, and desperately in love.

Roman, it seemed, came along for that same fall, the two of them embarking on a summer romance that had yet to have a downside.

Well, until the summer ended with his inevitable departure. That side would be…down.

Roman's life as a second-string wide receiver for the Jacksonville Jaguars had been on hold during the off-season. But that life was about to start again very, very soon.

How could she stand not seeing this amazing man every day?

Tonight, he looked unfairly spectacular. He wore a light cotton shirt with the sleeves rolled up, forearms tanned and strong. Dark blond hair that looked sun-lightened at the tips grazed the collar. And when those eyes—amber, warm, unmistakably like Tessa's—tracked her closely and constantly? It was a heady high she loved.

The server brought a spinach and artichoke dip with the warm tortilla chips that Lacey also loved. Then, when they were alone again, Roman smiled over the dip at her.

"You wore that dress to torture me, didn't you?"

She scooped up some dip on a chip, holding her hand under it as she brought it to her mouth. "And to test my skills to not spill on pale pink."

"Well, I love it. I'll think about you wearing pink every minute of training."

She managed to swallow. Barely. "I'll send pictures if you forget," she said sweetly.

He sighed as the proverbial elephant in the room lumbered across the table, sat right next to the dip, and dared them to go on yet another lovely date without facing the fact that this delightful relationship had an inevitable end.

"I won't forget," he murmured, any hint of a smile fading. "I swear, Lace, I won't."

Her stomach dipped. She set a chip on the small appetizer plate, definitely not sure she could swallow another when his eyes were that direct and warm.

"I know," she said. "But you'll have a lot on your mind."

"I already do." He finally ate a spinach and artichoke-covered chip, chewing, then dabbed at his lips with a napkin. "I talked to my trainer today. We did a video physical, which was pretty much hell."

Lacey's heart did a small flip. "I hope he told you you're perfect and should never change."

Roman huffed a laugh. "He told me I'm tight in my hips. Actually, his words were, 'Matteo, you have the hips of a ninety-year-old.'"

"Rude," she said. "Plus, I'd like to see *that* ninety-year-old."

"Right? Could Grandpa carry you out of here?"

She laughed, knowing Roman could do just that with one hand and tight hips.

"Anyway, after that, the training camp schedule came through."

His quiet sentence thudded like a door closing.

"Yeah?" Lacey's smile stayed on her face for half a second too long, then wobbled. "And..."

Roman took a sip of beer, the only sound some chatter and laughter, and distant music. His thumb traced the rim of the glass as he held her gaze, then looked down.

"Report date is in seventeen days."

Her throat tightened. "Seventeen days," she echoed, like she hoped he'd correct her and say...seventeen days and one year. Because that's what they needed to strengthen and secure this still very young relationship.

Roman nodded once. "Yeah."

Lacey tried to make her tone light. "Well. Jacksonville is only, what, four hours from here?"

"It's closer to five."

"Five?" Wasn't Florida narrow? How could it be five hours between Destin and Jacksonville?

"Five," he repeated. "It's literally in another time zone."

Her eyes shuttered. "I know."

"And what do you think?"

The truth was she'd been trying *not* to think about it at all, because the future looked murky and dark and like it could dissolve with the first preseason game. That's when he'd go back to being Roman Matteo, a pro-ball player who probably had legions of gorgeous girls waiting outside the stadium for an autograph, phone numbers at the ready.

But this summer, he'd just been her boyfriend, sweet and fun and honest and perfect.

He leaned forward, forearms on the table. "Lacey?" he pressed. "Surely you've thought about this. About us, and the future."

Her breath caught and she pushed the straw around in her drink. "Sure I have. And...people do long-distance all the time."

One strong shoulder lifted. "People also break up all the time."

"Roman—"

"I'm not trying to be negative," he said quickly. "I'm being honest."

Lacey stared at him, at the seriousness in his face, at the way he didn't look away. She loved that about him— as much as his easy laugh, his genuine, caring personality, and world-class shoulders. He was so steady, like a rock. And, boy, she needed a rock.

"I don't want to do the long-distance thing," he said. "I'm afraid I'll lose you."

Her pulse thundered and she fought the desire to laugh out loud. As if he could lose her.

Roman's eyes held hers, unflinching. "I don't want to come home after practice and stare at a wall and pretend I'm fine."

Lacey's mouth opened, but nothing came out. She wouldn't be fine, either.

"I want to come home and have you there. I want to

share life with you, ups and downs and...everything." His expression softened. "I want to be with you."

The harbor noise faded around her, replaced by the thrum of her heartbeat.

Be with her. What, exactly, did that mean? What did that look like? What did that do to her world, her job, her...*heart?*

"Oh." It came out like a croak.

"You know I have a place in Jacksonville, but it's not great. I think we could get something bigger. On the water, even. Jax Beach and Atlantic Beach are nice. Downtown, on the river, close to the stadium. There are suburbs, too, and..."

His voice trailed off as she stared at him, vaguely aware that her jaw might be wide open in shock.

"You want to...live together?"

"Yes." The word came out so fast and with so little hesitation or doubt, she inched back.

"Really?"

"Yes, really." He laughed and reached for her. "This isn't our first date, Lace."

"No, but it's like our...I don't know. Roman, we've only known each other a few months."

"Fifty-six days," he corrected, then laughed again. "I don't know what it is about you that has me counting days like that. I guess because there haven't been enough of them, and I wanted to be sure we knew each other long enough to...discuss this."

Discuss moving in together? After fifty-six days?

"I'm not asking you to marry me tomorrow," he said,

like he had to clarify that. "I'm asking you to come with me. For camp. For the season. Come see what my life is like. Let's experience being together over there. And how it goes for us to be a couple, and public."

Public. Because Jacksonville wasn't Destin. Jacksonville was where cameras appeared and fans swarmed and people would absolutely notice if Roman Matteo had a girlfriend living with him. Heck, he'd been stopped for autographs *here*—imagine what it would be like at the home of his team.

And she'd tried. She'd imagined life as an NFL girlfriend. Game days. Tailgates. Stadium lights. Roman coming off the field sweaty and grinning, searching for her in the crowd. Her learning his routines, his rituals, the way he took his game-day coffee, the way he liked silence after practice.

"I..." she started and then stopped because her voice did something weird.

Roman's hand finally closed over hers, warm and steady. "You don't have to answer this second."

Lacey smiled. "Just sometime in the next seventeen days."

"Well, yeah. But I can tell you that I'm sure," he said simply. "I have no doubts about us."

No doubts about us. The words made her heart soar so high it was almost dizzying.

"Neither do I," she whispered, and it sounded like surrender.

Roman's shoulders loosened, just slightly, like he'd

been holding tension in the center of his body. Relief flickered across his face—subtle and quick, but real.

He squeezed her hand once. "So," he said, and the hint of a grin returned, "do you think we could make living together work? I mean, with your job and your family and my travel and...everything?"

Lacey exhaled a shaky breath. "I guess."

Roman's grin widened. "Is that a yes?"

Lacey's mind spun—Tessa, the business, her life in Destin, the fact that she'd finally found a career that fit. It was a lot.

"I think," she said carefully, because she needed a thread of caution to hold on to, "I think we could make that work."

He dropped back with a look of relief and happiness. "I'm so happy to hear that, Lace. Really. I just don't want to imagine the season without you by my side. I don't want you here in Destin and us so far apart."

Lacey laughed, a little breathless. Air just wasn't going into her lungs.

"You okay?"

"Yes, I'm...yes. I'm great. I'm also"—she made a vague gesture at her chest—"having an internal situation."

Roman's mouth lifted in a curve. "An internal situation."

"That is the official medical term."

He leaned closer. "Should I call an ambulance?"

"Do not."

Roman's laughter was low and warm, and she could hear the genuine happiness in the sound.

"I'll have to talk to Tessa," she said softly.

"Well, let me know if she won't let you take a sabbatical or work remote. I have some pull with my birth mother."

But what if *Lacey* didn't want to take a sabbatical or work remote? Did she? She honestly had no idea what she wanted beyond the man in front of her.

"I'll talk to Tessa," she said, hoping that promise wasn't another betrayal of Tessa. She'd found Roman—after Tessa said she didn't want to seek out her son. And now...she'd leave with Roman?

Would Tessa understand? "We're working tomorrow at the Summer House in the morning," she told him. "I'll talk to her."

He looked surprised. "Oh. I thought she moved Tessa Wylie Events permanently to her new place."

"So did I, but last week she started coming back to the Summer House for work," she said. "I mean, when she works, which is not much this past week. She's been super distracted and busy. She said she'll explain what's going on, but in the meantime, we've been working at ye olde dining room table on the beach." She shrugged. "Either way is fine with me. Plus, with her so busy, I've been getting some plum assignments."

He nodded. "Well, you talk to her and if you need help—"

She held up a hand. "I got this."

But did she?

Their event management business wasn't just a job. It was the first time in Lacey's adult life that she woke up excited to work. The first time she'd felt competent and creative, like she'd found the world where she belonged.

But Roman was Tessa's biological son! Surely she'd want them—Lacey *and* him—to be happy. And couldn't she work remotely? It would be challenging, but possible if she—

"Are you sure, Lace?" He searched her face, looking for the truth. "You look like you're second-guessing the decision."

Wait. She hadn't made a *decision* yet. She'd just said she'd talk to Tessa. "All I know is that I love you, Roman."

He beamed and leaned close to her lips again. "I love you, too."

"I want to be with you," she murmured into a kiss.

He drew back, his expression softened, his golden eyes warm with affection. He reached his hand to her cheekbone, brushing his thumb along her skin like he was memorizing her face. "Then we want the same thing," he said. "It's just a matter of working out the playbook."

Smiling at his football analogies, she leaned in and kissed him, certain that she and Tessa would figure something out. Tessa loved them both and she was the biggest cheerleader of this relationship, even if it meant Lacey had to give up her job.

At the thought, she slid her hand around Roman's neck and pulled him closer to deepen the kiss, telling herself that he was the only thing that mattered. The only thing.

~

LACEY WAS STILL HOLDING that thought the next day when she made her easy commute to work. In comfy clothes, she merely had to go downstairs, stop in the kitchen for coffee, and head either to the back office—they shared it with Eli and Meredith—or the dining room table.

Today, the architects had some client calls up at Pippin Lake, so Lacey walked to the small but totally functional shared office with two coffees in hand.

Tessa sat at the desk, hair pulled back, a pen tucked behind her ear, looking slightly...different. Not frazzled—nothing really threw Tessa. But distracted. And tired.

"You sleep okay last night?" Lacey asked.

"One word about the bags under my eyes and you're fired."

Lacey snorted and dropped into the chair across from her, setting the coffees on the table. "They're barely noticeable."

"And she lies."

"No, she doesn't," Lacey countered, taking a sip. "What's first on the agenda, boss?"

Tessa tapped the laptop keyboard. "We have some very daunting scheduling problems," she announced.

Did they ever. But not with clients and events—with love and football.

Lacey swallowed coffee and the conversation she knew she had to have, letting Tessa take the lead.

But her boss just threaded her fingers through messy hair, turned her phone over to check it, and sighed.

"Seriously, Tess. Are you okay?" Lacey asked, trying a different version of the same question.

"Mmm." She checked the phone again. "Long story, but let's get through this agenda and if we have time, I'll fill you in as much as I can."

Intrigued, Lacey opened her tablet. She had a long story of her own, which she was happy to delay while they worked.

"Let's talk about the wedding," Tessa started.

"The wedding?" All the blood drained from Lacey's face, leaving her lightheaded. "We didn't...there isn't..."

"The Shakespearean-themed extravaganza for the lovebirds who met at a Renaissance Faire? Billy and Daria?"

"Oh, yes." Lacey shook off her issues and climbed into work, tapping her tablet screen. "The beach meets the Bard. I talked to the bride yesterday."

"Perfect. Where do we stand?" Tessa asked. "I know it's not until September, but there's a ton of work to do."

"Yes, yes." She pulled it together. "What we have are a whopping twelve bridesmaids in corseted gowns and flowing skirts, each one a different jewel tone. Flower crowns. Bare feet in the sand. Oh, Daria said she now wants a hand-lettered program quoting *A Midsummer Night's Dream*."

Tessa blinked. "Of course she does. What else?"

"The officiant needs to wear a velvet doublet," Lacey said, reading her notes. "And the groom is insisting on carrying a sword."

Tessa grunted. "If a single groomsman loses an eye, we double our fee."

"They also want a falcon release."

"No!"

"Fear not, I researched."

"Of course you did," Tessa said with a sigh of relief. "And?"

"It is against Florida falconry law, which says..." She tapped the screen and read her notes. "That a captive-bred raptor may only be released with permission from the wildlife commission's executive director, whose office says it is not happening. We're looking into doves and a handler, and I've scheduled that call for this afternoon."

"Perfect." Tessa's shoulders dropped. "Does she still want gardenias?"

"I told her they bruise just looking at them." Lacey smiled. "White roses it is."

"Excellent." Sipping her coffee, Tessa leaned back, stress clearly lifting. "Now, the anniversary party?"

"Under control," Lacey assured her. "I talked to the caterer and approved the menu—God bless that new chef at Blue Heron Banquets."

"They got a new chef?" Tessa asked.

"A woman named Amalie, from France. Amazing. Anyway, we also have a meeting with the florist, and I found two quartets for the Gilsons to hear locally and choose for music. Invitations are printed—thank goodness for Elsie at Printers Plus, who did a rush for me and..."

Lacey looked up when Tessa let out a half-sigh, half-groan.

"Oh, you're worried about those two things being the same weekend." Lacey snapped her fingers, in the zone now. "I've got that figured out, especially since the party is at the Crystal Castle. The staff there is superb."

"Perfect," Tessa cooed. "Oh, and add this to the list. Seamus Donahue called me last night."

"From the marina? The guy who loved to fish with your dad?"

"The very same," she said. "You know he runs that ministry for underprivileged kids, helping them get refurbished fishing gear and a chance to go out on the water? The Abundant Catch?"

Lacey nodded. "I remember. I also remember he's the one who saw Roman and knew he was Artie's grandson." She winced at the memory of how Tessa had found out she and Roman had gone behind her back.

"All is forgiven a hundred times over," Tessa said, no doubt remembering the same thing. "But he's having a little fundraiser at the marina."

"And we're going to organize it?" Lacey guessed, dreading yet another event to add to her seventeen-day—now sixteen-day—deadline.

"No, no, it's a very casual thing. But he needs donations for a silent auction, and I was thinking...a signed football."

Lacey grinned and pointed at her. "As a matter of fact, I know a guy..."

Tessa laughed but suddenly, her face crumpled and she looked upset.

"What's wrong, Tess?"

"Nothing is wrong," she answered with conviction. "Absolutely nothing is wrong because you, Lacey Knight, are a superstar event planner who deserves a raise, better hours, and my undying love for the way you pick up my slack."

But did she deserve to...quit and go to Jacksonville? Lacey just smiled. "You've been..." She wanted to say distracted, but that didn't sound respectful. "Busy."

"While you became...indispensable."

Oh, dear. That wasn't good. She wanted to... dispense. "I don't know about that, Tess—"

"I do. You know the vendors by first name. You've been to the venues. You anticipate the problems. You calm the clients, you call in favors, and you make everyone—including me—happy. I would roll up and cry without you."

Lacey took a shuddering breath, not sure how to react to the praise. Grateful, of course. But she didn't want to be someone Tessa couldn't live without because she was someone Roman couldn't live without.

"You're doing an amazing job," Tessa continued, making everything worse.

"Tessa—"

"I'm serious," she said. "This?" She gestured at the calendar, the files, the tablet with five tabs open. "This is running because of you."

"That's not true," she said automatically. "This is— this is you. You're the one who—"

Tessa cut her off with a shake of her head. "No. I started it. You made it smooth. You keep the trains from crashing into each other." Tessa looked hard at Lacey. "And, girl, I need you to do that on steroids for one more month."

"One more..." She swallowed. "Why?"

Tessa didn't answer right away. She folded her hands on the desk, staring at them for a long beat and Lacey knew that whatever was working on Tessa was about to be revealed. After that, Lacey could tell her about Roman and Jacksonville.

Finally, Tessa said, "I am going to need to dial back for a month. A lot. Like, I won't be around to do anything but put out a fire. Five-alarm or more."

Lacey blinked at her. "Are you sick?"

"No," she said on a laugh. "Crazy, maybe. Dusty and I agreed to help out one of his patients by watching a small child. I can't say anything more than that, but I am now the proud caretaker of a two-year-old little girl. And she's...needy. Wonderful and dear, but needy. And that means I'm needy. Like, I need you to run this business."

Tessa hesitated, then reached into a folder and slid a paper across the desk. Not a contract, not a vendor quote, this was a simple spreadsheet with numbers highlighted.

"I've given this a lot of thought and want to make it fair."

Lacey glanced down and felt her eyes widen. "Is this...a pay increase?" 'Cause it was sizeable. "Tessa, what—"

"I know you've been wanting to move out of the Summer House—not that I can imagine why, since what could be more fun than sharing a room and a bed with Vivien." Tessa smiled. "I did it for seven summers in the old place and all we did was stay awake and laugh."

But Lacey didn't laugh. She couldn't think straight.

Last night had rearranged her plans so completely she hadn't even caught up yet. The idea that Tessa was offering her a path forward—more money, more stability—felt like the universe doubling down.

"Listen, I know I'm asking a lot," Tessa said softly. "I wouldn't if it weren't really important. I can't give you details, but trust me when I say a life literally depends on it. Two lives—a hurting mother and a small child, still in diapers."

Lacey searched her face, seeing the raw need and the depth of the request. This woman had never asked anything of Lacey, but had brought her into her business with bold confidence and true friendship. Even when Lacey risked that friendship and looked up a person Tessa had specifically said she didn't want to meet, they'd stuck together.

And now, Tessa needed her. Really needed her. She could tell. Was Lacey going to flippantly deny her friend and mentor, with disregard for a little kid, just because Roman wanted to move fast and furious into living together?

And it wasn't just going to be short term, she knew. Maybe Tessa's commitment was, but this kind of money meant her job was serious, secure, and had a long-term future—here, in Destin.

"Okay," Lacey said slowly, because the word felt like

mud in her mouth. "I'm honored. Truly. And yes, I'll take on more responsibility, absolutely, but..."

But she'd promised her boyfriend she'd move!

"But what?" Tessa pressed.

"But...I do expect I'll be in Jacksonville—"

"For home games," Tessa said. "Which don't start until early September, right? Pray the weekend of the Renaissance wedding is an away game."

By then, Roman thought they'd be living together. He wanted her there for preseason games and training and...

"Right?" Tessa urged when she didn't answer.

"Right," Lacey confirmed.

She had no idea what was right and what wasn't. All she knew was she had two lives colliding. Two futures, two loved ones, two directions.

Which road should she take?

"I'll figure it out," she said, as much to herself as to Tessa.

Roman was leaving soon. Tessa was counting on her. And Lacey—trying to love everyone—was going to break someone's heart. Maybe her own.

July 17, 1993

Saturday night. Hot as Hades (as Uncle Artie likes to say). No breeze at all.

And the Let Go Bridge was hopping.

We knew we had to do it this summer, because we're all sixteen. I mean, if you spend your sixteenth summer in Destin with your best friends and you DON'T jump off Left Coast Bridge and let go of something that's drowning you...are you really even alive?

We sure felt alive tonight.

Tessa led the charge, to the surprise of absolutely no one. She announced this morning that we were doing our jump this very night, and of course she told Dustin Mathers when we saw him at the beach today so he made sure we had an audience of noisy boys just like him.

I think Kate confessed to her mom that we were going (I did not dare tell Maggie, who would have blown a gasket). But when we left, Aunt Jo Ellen whispered "Be careful" to Tessa and reminded Kate not to lose her glasses—like telling the sun not to rise—so I think she knew.

Anyway, the three of us flipflopped our way down Gulf Shore and tore out to the jetty, up the beach, and made it to "Let Go" bridge in good time. Like always, kids were pretty much everywhere—but not Peter and Eli. They were watching YET ANOTHER "Lethal Weapon" (two wasn't enough?) they rented from Blockbuster and didn't even know we were going.

That was good. I didn't need Peter to witness my formal "letting go"...of him.

Because, yes, secret diary, the little piece of paper I stashed in my pocket said "Crush on Peter." It's time to let that weight of misery off my shoulders. I'm never going to be anything but Eli's little sister to him.

It was a pretty spectacular night, even if it was blistering hot. The sand was still warm, even at night. Cicadas were screaming and the sky was that deep plum color that only happens in Florida right before night fully settles.

The bridge looked different in the dark. Bigger and higher and, dang, was it worth it to climb up there and jump?

Tessa practically danced through a crowd of boys, announced our intention, flirted with a few lucky souls, and grabbed our hands. She ordered Dustin to "play something good for us to die to!" as we headed toward the stairs to climb up.

Kate looked downright horrified. So much, that she climbed up the bridge still wearing her glasses, of course.

Once we got to the middle, we stood there with our toes over the edge while a car rumbled by, making the whole thing shake a little. Down on the jetty, Dustin's boom box blasted "Smells Like Teen Spirit" which made us laugh even harder.

"Okay, girls," Tessa yelled. "Let go of whatever is too heavy in your life! Ready?"

"Goodbye, fear of being a nerd!" Kate yelled.

I told her she wasn't a nerd and she just side-eyed me and touched her glasses. "These are going in the drink and I'm getting contacts."

I knew her mom kept several pairs of glasses in hiding. I also knew Kate couldn't bear the idea of putting something in her eyes, even for vanity. So I just smiled.

When we asked Tessa what she was letting go of, she howled with laughter and said she'd made so many bad choices she'd be jumping all night long. And that was just for what she did last week.

And me? Well, when they asked, I almost lied.

I tried to think of something small and safe. Like my fear of a breakout, or my inability to stand up to my mother. (Okay, that's not small and I should let go of that sometime in this life, right?)

But the truth was a knot in my chest and it had a name—Peter.

Not Peter-the-person, exactly. Peter-the-

feeling. I used to love the way my crush felt—the way my stomach flips when he smiles. The way my heart thuds when he walks into a room. The way I feel invisible and incandescent at the same time around him.

But come on. He is nineteen and I am sixteen. He is summer and confidence and bare feet and tan skin and that crooked grin. I am… a kid.

Now my crush just hurts and distracts me, and I just don't want to cart it around anymore.

I couldn't lie, though. These were my best girls, and they deserved the truth. "I'm letting go of him."

They didn't laugh. Tessa squeezed my hand and pronounced it "About time!" Kate said, "Good."

"I'll go first," Tessa said. "If I die, it was nice knowin' ya!"

With that, she flung herself off, screaming like she was being abducted by aliens.

"If I don't go now, I never will!" Kate took the next leap, arms wide, fearless, glasses lost forever.

I stood there alone, heart banging against my ribs, thinking about every smile that melted me, every time he ruffled my hair and said, "You're gonna be trouble one day, kid."

One day? When would that be? Never.

"Let go," I told myself, pulling that tiny piece of paper out of my pocket. "No more crush on Peter McCarthy!"

I jumped and opened my hand, so the paper fluttered down much slower than I did.

The fall felt endless, even though it was probably less than fifteen feet to the water. My stomach floated up into my throat. The air tore past me. Then the water hit like a slap, cold and shocking and hard. I went under, deeper than I meant to, the world turning dark and green and silent.

For one perfect second, there was nothing in my chest—no longing. No ache. No hope.

No Peter.

When I burst back to the surface, coughing and laughing, hair slicked to my face, I actually believed it worked. I floated on my back, staring up at the stars, thinking: It's gone. I let it go.

Later, we came back to the house wrapped in towels, still soaked. Our parents were out on the back deck playing a raucous round of Hearts that sounded more like a drinking game than cards.

So we ran up and over the dunes and...there was Peter.

He and Eli and some other guy were down on

the sand, laughing too loud, pretending they weren't sneaking beer.

"We did it!" Tessa called, running toward them and letting her towel fall, which of course got Eli's attention. "We jumped off Let Go Bridge!"

Peter turned and looked right at me. Not Tessa in her wet T-tank top, not Kate (who couldn't have seen him anyway), but me. Me.

All at once, they demanded to know our "let go" promise.

"It's a secret," Kate said softly, trying not to steal a glance at Eli. She probably should have hung on to her nerdiness and let go of HER summer crush.

Peter lifted a beer bottle to his lips, suddenly looking older and unattainable and absolutely drop-dead BEAUTIFUL.

"Your secret's safe with me, kid," he whispered. "What did you let go of?"

I looked up at him and realized that maybe letting go isn't something you do once. Maybe it's something you have to choose, over and over, like stepping off a bridge every day.

I don't know how to do that yet.

I just know that when he looks at me, I still feel like I'm falling.

"Nothing," I told him.

And it was the God's truth. I hadn't let go of a thing. I still love Peter McCarthy and might for the rest of my life.

Love,
Viv

Chapter Eight
Vivien

Vivien closed the pages of the decades-old notebook with a weary sigh. Usually, she let these journals open where they might and randomly cruised memory lane. But with the Let Go Bridge on her brain, she'd searched for this entry, remembering she'd memorialized her jump in her Destin diary.

Her crush on Peter had reached pinnacle intensity when she was sixteen. That summer, Peter became a "man" in her eyes. He'd been in college for a year, he drank, and he had more swagger. She should have known back then he'd be a cop—already so alpha and cool and protective it hurt.

Literally hurt. Still hurt, if she was being honest with herself.

Enough days had passed since the hospital that she decided she had to check on Connor. And Peter. And, she supposed, Holly the Talkative Ex-Wife.

She had a few client meetings in the morning first, so she dressed in a pale blue tank sheath with a linen jacket —to impress the clients, not Peter.

Okay, maybe a little Peter.

They'd exchanged a couple of texts over the past few

days, which were little more than a note that Connor was home and resting, and one that said, "Thanks again for the coffee."

Nothing like, *Gee, come over and keep me company and we can finish the conversation we almost started on the Fourth of July.*

Did he even remember that moment in the kitchen?

Jonah had made trays of cookies for an assignment the night before, so she stacked a dozen on a paper plate and covered it with plastic for Connor.

After her last meeting, which felt interminable, Vivien drove to Peter's rental in Crystal Beach. She'd been there once with Eli before Peter had moved here, to wait for a refrigerator delivery.

She'd managed to check out the house then, which was right off Highway 98 in a tree-lined neighborhood with sweet beach bungalows wrapped in white picket fences.

Pulling up to the address, a thrill shot through her right down to her toes when she saw a new muscular SUV in the driveway with sheriff's plates...right next to a little white sedan she assumed was Holly's, since Connor's vehicle was a total loss.

Pushing any and all thrills to the side, she climbed out, snagged the cookies, and walked to the front door, surprisingly nervous about the drop-in.

After knocking, footsteps came fast from the other side.

Please let it be him.

The door swung open and Holly stood, small and

mighty, smiling up at Vivien. "Well, hello, there," she said. "Nice to see you again, Vivien."

"Hi," Vivien said, matching her smile, lifting the covered plate of cookies. "I wanted to check on Connor and bring him a little get-well treat. How's he doing?"

"He's doing good," Holly said with relief in her voice. "He's sleeping right now. The doctor said rest is the big thing. He's sore, but he's...he's good."

"That's wonderful." Vivien let out a breath. "I'm so glad."

Holly opened the door wider. "Come in. You want coffee or iced tea? I have snacks and, whoa." She looked at the cookies. "Did you make these?"

"No, we have a budding chef in the house."

"Oh, these look delicious. And dangerous. You know, my boy is in the house, so of course I'm overstuffing the pantry. You'd think I have toddlers again but I'm the one eating Skittles. Please."

Vivien stepped inside, noticing the living room furniture felt like it had come from another house, just a little off for this space. The bookshelves, too, looked like they'd been hijacked from their home, but a giant TV had found a wall it loved.

There were pillows on the couch like someone had slept sitting up, with a baseball cap on the armrest and a pair of very large sneakers kicked under the coffee table.

"Excuse the mess," Holly said—again, as if she lived here.

"I imagine Connor's made that sofa home since he got here," Vivien replied.

"Barely moves. Watches hundred year old movies in black and white until I want to scream. But I told him he had to sleep in bed. It's not good for his arm to roll around on that sofa, so he did just go in the back an hour ago. Like I said, you think they're all grown up and turns out they're really babies in big men's clothing."

Oh, yeah, talkative. Unless she was just nervous around Vivien. Had Peter told her—

"Is that Vivien?" Peter's voice came from where they headed, into an open concept family room and kitchen combination. A wall of sliding glass doors led out to a pool and patio.

Peter, seated at the eat-in table with a laptop open and glasses perched on his nose, stood to greet her. His expression shifted to an easy smile with a glimmer in his dark eyes that warmed her.

"Hey," he said, moving as if he was about to reach for a hug, then thought better of it.

"Hey." Vivien stepped closer, setting her bag down on the table and glancing at the computer. "I hope I'm not interrupting."

"Not at all. I'm just going over some open case files and doing some work from home. How are you, Viv?" He took off the readers as if he wanted to get an unobstructed look at her.

"I'm good," she said, aware that Holly was moving around the kitchen with a surprising amount of familiarity.

"Coffee, Vivien?" the other woman asked. "Or something cold?"

"Water would be great, Holly, thank you."

"Please have a seat," Holly said cheerfully. "Pete, do you want a refill?"

"No, thanks." Peter pulled out a chair at the kitchen table for Vivien, coming around to sit across from her. "It's good to see you," he said softly under his breath.

And, just like sixteen-year-old Vivien, her poor heart skipped a proverbial beat. She half-expected him to call her "kid."

"Tell me about Connor," she said. "Healing well?"

Holly and Peter shared a look that spoke volumes. Not only did that make Vivien worry about Connor, but the silent connection between this former married couple was...palpable.

Holly set a glass of iced water in front of Vivien and slid the plate of cookies onto the table like she was hosting a book club. Then, to Vivien's mild horror, she pulled out a chair and joined them.

"Is everything okay with him?" Vivien asked, looking from one to the other.

"He's absolutely fine," Holly assured her, a note of exasperation in her voice. "He wants to be healed and whole in no time, and he just doesn't understand that this requires rest and recovery."

"He thinks he's invincible," Peter added. "And thinks we're acting like the parents of a five-year-old."

Vivien kept a sympathetic smile in place, taking in all the subtext. They agreed on the problems with their recuperating son. And they were a "we" again, parents together. Small shift, but seismic to her.

"It's just one of those things," Holly said, picking up one of the cookies. "When your kid is hurt, it's like he's a child again, right, Pete?"

Pete just gave a tight smile, and Vivien suspected he suddenly heard what the exchange must sound like and wanted it to end.

"So what's new at the Summer House?" he asked, obviously looking for a change of subject.

She rooted around for a neutral response, landing on the obvious. "Did you hear they're tearing down Let Go Bridge?"

His eyes widened in surprise.

"What kind of name is that for a bridge?" Holly asked.

"It's actually named the Left Coast Bridge," Peter explained. "Between the two jetties just south of Destin Bridge on the, well, left side of town if you're looking at a map."

"Oh, I know that bridge," Holly exclaimed. "We used it years ago to come over from Pensacola. That thing is hideous! Good riddance to bad rubbish."

It was Peter and Vivien's turn to exchange a knowing look, proving they both shared at least some level of reverence for the landmark.

"It wasn't...rubbish," Vivien said carefully. "It actually meant a lot to us when we were kids. All the teenagers in Destin from the eighties and nineties used to, um, congregate there."

"It was special," Peter agreed. "Walking that bridge was...a vibe." He grinned. "As Connor would say."

Vivien laughed at the expression, but Holly blinked. "Wait. You...walked on it?"

"Jumped off it," Vivien admitted.

Holly's mouth fell open.

"It was a ritual," Peter explained. "And for some reason, you did it when you were sixteen."

It pleased Vivien to no end that he remembered that detail.

"Did *you?*" Holly asked him.

"Oh, yeah. Everybody did."

Holly looked miffed that there was something in Peter's past she didn't know about. "That's...wildly unsafe. So unlike you, Pete."

"It's not high and the water is calm and perfectly safe there. It was illegal but overlooked by my predecessors with a badge."

Vivien smiled faintly. "It felt brave at sixteen. We called it the 'let go' bridge and everyone jumped at least once. To, you know, let go of...things."

"Things like your life!" Holly retorted with a choked laugh. "I've seen that bridge. It's not even open to traffic anymore. Half of it is fenced off. It's rusted." She shrugged. "In my opinion, some progress is good."

Peter shifted, clearly uncomfortable. "It's not about traffic. It's...history."

Vivien loved that he understood that and fought the urge to reach over the table and squeeze his hand in gratitude.

Holly rolled her eyes. "Hey, I get nostalgia, I do. But sometimes holding on is just... holding on. And dangerous. Maybe the thing you should 'let go' of is stupid kid memories."

Vivien swallowed. She could feel a response rising—too big and personal. How did she explain to a perfect stranger that some things mattered because of who you were when you experienced them?

She couldn't.

Connor's door creaked open and the young man emerged in nothing but sleep pants and a cast, hair sticking up, eyes half-lidded. "Oh, hi, Vivien." He brightened at the sight of her, dark eyes exactly like Peter's squinted with a smile. "I didn't know you were here."

"Oh, honey, she made you cookies."

"Actually, Jonah did," Vivien corrected. "And he sends his best. How are you feeling?"

"Two steps from death." Connor grinned and ran his good hand through slightly shaggy hair, taking her back in time. In fact, he really was a carbon copy of young Peter, Vivien realized. "Jonah's a beast."

"Can I get you milk with those?" Holly asked, already up.

To his credit, Connor tried not to smirk or share a look with his dad, but he kind of failed. "Don't need cookies and milk, Mom. Thanks." He sat down at the table next to Peter, their equally broad shoulders almost touching. "What are you guys talking about?"

"Some bridge that needs to be torn down for safety's sake," Holly answered for him, rising. "If not milk, then water? Lunch? Pain meds? You look pale."

"A few knocks on death's door will do that to a guy."

He winked at Vivien, so much like his father that it nearly took her breath away. "It's a wonder she doesn't tuck me in."

"But she thinks about it," Peter cracked.

"I stopped by the hospital, but you were asleep," Vivien said. "It's good to see you up and about."

"More or less." He gave a wistful sigh, then added, "Thanks for a fun Fourth of July. I wish I'd have hung out later with my dad to have avoided this nightmare. I had a blast catching a football with an actual NFL player."

"You're welcome to hang out anytime you like, Connor," Vivien said.

"Oh, nobody told me there was an NFL player at this party," Holly cooed, coming back to the table with milk Connor had not asked for.

"Mom." He shook his head.

"Enjoy it while you can," Peter said lightly. "No one's bringing you cookies and milk when you go back to dental school."

The mention of it made Connor wince. "I can't miss one minute of the next semester. Everything depends on it."

"Wait—who was this NFL player?" Holly demanded. "Is he famous?"

"Not terribly," Vivien said. "My daughter is dating him." She almost added that Tessa was Roman's birth mother, who'd given him up for adoption, but something stopped her. Holly wasn't part of their inner circle and that was Tessa's story to tell.

Vivien changed the subject to Connor's classes and

plans, asking questions while Holly fussed. After a few minutes, Vivien stood, taking her glass to the sink and wishing Connor well.

He stood when she did, the same six-feet-plus as his dad, giving her an easy smile. "I'll probably take you up on the Summer House offer," he said. "I need sun, water, and..." His voice trailed off.

"No helicopter parents," Peter supplied, getting to his feet.

Connor looked like he was going to say something else, but let it go. "Thank Jonah for the cookies," he finished.

"I'll walk you out," Peter said.

Holly smiled up at her, reaching for another cookie.

"Thanks for the visit, Vivien," she said. "And I mean it—if you let go of anything, it should be that battered old bridge."

Vivien managed to smile and respond politely. But her throat was thick as she walked down the hall, aware of Peter behind her.

At the door, he hesitated, looking down at her like he had a lot to say, but couldn't.

"I'm glad he's healing," she said, knowing it sounded lame but what else could she say?

He nodded. "It's...crowded here."

She exhaled, knowing that was all she needed to hear. "Family is good for him," she said—lame again—fighting the urge to put her arms around Peter and hold tight.

"Yeah. And, look, about the bridge..."

She waved it off. "Silly, I know."

"No, it isn't, Viv. I get it. You know, I can look into some files on that demolition. The Sheriff's Office has to know all about it. Maybe I can find out who's behind it. There may be a way to slow it down. Probably not but we could try."

Her heart caught on the use of "we" in the sentence. "Really?"

"Yeah," he said. "I know it's important to you. It was important to all of us, really."

She looked hard at him, suddenly realizing there was something she didn't know and wanted to.

"What did you let go of?" she asked, taking a small step toward him. "From the bridge, I mean, when you jumped."

The tiniest flicker of something serious, even dark, flashed in his eyes, gone before she could truly analyze it.

"Honey, I can't remember what I had for breakfast let alone some dumb wish I made a hundred years ago."

She didn't know what to grab onto in that sentence— a dumb wish? A hundred years ago? Or...*honey*?

"And yet you'll fight to save it."

He smiled and moved imperceptibly closer. "I never said I'd fight to save it." He put one finger under her chin and lifted her face toward his. "I will fight for you to smile, though."

Her heart—her entire being—melted. Never in her whole life had she wanted to kiss Peter McCarthy more than that very moment.

Affection welled up in her, taking control of her arms,

lifting them like they had a will of their own, and wrapping him in a hug.

"Thank you, Peter," she whispered, anticipating the first kiss, the familiar taste of him, the pressure of—

"Oh, good, you're still here."

They separated instantly at the sound of Holly's voice as she came around the corner.

"Yes, I'm—"

"Connor said I was too harsh about the bridge."

Vivien blinked, drawing back. "Oh, that's—"

"I'm sorry." She kept coming forward until she was standing next to them. "Pete, maybe you can take me to see it, and I can have different eyes. You can tell me about the past, okay?"

Why did she need to ask that in front of Vivien? What else had Connor told her? That Peter and Vivien used to date? That her ex-husband once said he loved Vivien?

Vivien just smiled. "No need for apologies. It's just a silly childhood memory."

With that, she lifted her hand to say goodbye and headed out to her car, more confused than ever about Peter.

Behind the wheel, she sat staring at the house.

Did she love Peter? Or did she honor a lifelong crush? There was a difference and she wasn't sure she knew it.

She only knew it *still* felt like falling.

Chapter Nine
Maggie

Maggie had once considered the Atlanta interstates a form of modern warfare, something to be avoided at all costs. Today, she'd powered her T-bird up from Destin without incident, a much more confident driver after her life-changing road trip to Miami last month.

Still, she was relieved to get off the highway for Jo Ellen's peanut-sized bladder.

"We can take surface streets to Crista's neighborhood," Maggie said when Jo Ellen came out of the mini-mart.

"Good, then let's take the roof off Scarlett and go full Thelma and Louise," she suggested as she settled into the passenger seat.

"It's like you refuse to acknowledge those two die at the end of that movie, Jo."

She shrugged. "I have a scarf," she said, whipping out a piece of bright red silk. "I really want to put it on and ride in the convertible like Grace Kelly and Cary Grant in *To Catch a Thief*." She waved her red flag, then playfully put it over her hair and tied it under her chin. "Do *they* die?"

"I don't remember, but you might die...." Maggie cocked a brow. "Of *embarrassment* if anyone sees you wearing a scarf like that in this century."

Jo flicked her fingers, not caring. "No one *should* see us, Mags," she reminded her. "Remember, we're incognito. Does Anthony know you own this car now?"

"I don't know, but we won't take a chance. He's probably still at work. We can sneak in and park in Barbara's garage. I called her last night and told her I was showing a friend around the neighborhood and asked if she minded if I put you up in her house."

"'What a cool *liah* you are, Melly,'" Jo drawled the line from *Gone With the Wind* with an arguably perfect Scarlett O'Hara accent, making Maggie chuckle. How far her Yankee college roommate had come.

"We'll see how cool I am when I accidentally find myself face to face with Anthony."

"We won't come face to face with him," Jo Ellen said with far more assurance than Maggie felt. "And if we do, I'll make something up. You know it's my secret weapon."

One she hoped they didn't need to wield.

The old Thunderbird purred beneath them, the warm evening sun making Atlanta's wealthy suburbs glimmer like a magazine spread. Maggie took the last curve off a wide boulevard lined with homes that had columns, arched windows, and drama.

What happened behind all those closed doors? Cheating? Betrayal? Or...that happily ever after that every woman wants?

Maggie inhaled, then let it out slowly. "I so hope she's

wrong about Anthony," she murmured, as much to herself as Jo Ellen. "Because if she isn't, I'll never trust my character judgment again."

"I'm sure you're right, Mags," Jo Ellen said. "And we're going to prove it. By the time we turn around and head back to Destin, we will have completely cleared Anthony of any wrongdoing, and we can tell Crista to rest easy and grow that baby."

Maggie threw her a grateful look. "From your lips to God's ears, Jo. I don't want to think about being wrong on this."

They turned into Crista's neighborhood and the street widened, smooth as silk, with lush lawns that looked professionally manicured. Tall oaks arched overhead, their branches meeting like a cathedral ceiling. Everything was green, polished, and orderly, including Crista's dream home that sat in the middle of one of the prettiest streets.

"We do have to pass Crista's to get to Barbara's house," Maggie said. "I hope he's not home early from work looking out the window."

"Or home early looking...at his mistress."

"Jo Ellen!"

"Just kidding," she said quickly. "I know he's not. You know he's not. We're here to make sure Crista knows he's not."

Maggie just bit her lip as they approached the brick Colonial she called home. Funny, she thought as she glanced at the place that really had been a sanctuary for her these last three years. It didn't look like home anymore.

Still beautiful, still a monument to good taste and elegance, but was it home? For Crista, Anthony, Nolie, and a baby-to-be? Of course. But, oddly enough, Maggie didn't have even the slightest twinge of homesickness or longing.

"That's my room, in the front on the first floor," she said, not slowing down too much as they passed.

"Such a pretty house," Jo Ellen cooed.

"Eli designed it. Vivien decorated it. But Crista created perfection." Which was something Maggie always valued. But she'd forgotten about perfection since she'd been sharing a small apartment with Jo Ellen, who never met a surface she couldn't clutter.

She slowed the car two doors away, at a white farm-house-style home with clapboard trim and deep green shutters.

"Our home away from home, Jo," Maggie announced, pulling into the driveway. "There's a garage thingy inside, but I have a key. Come on."

"This is nice, too," Jo Ellen said, looking up at it. "Our houses in Ithaca are so much smaller and older."

"Well, this one is nice architecturally," Maggie replied. "But Barbara, bless her heart, has made some questionable décor decisions."

"Ooh. Fun." Jo Ellen flipped off her seatbelt. "Let's go judge."

Biting back a laugh, Maggie led the way to the side entrance by the garage, using the key that she was so happy she'd kept on her key ring and not in Crista's house.

"This feels like breaking and entering," Jo Ellen whispered as Maggie slipped the key in.

"There's no breaking, Jo. Just entering. Nice and legal."

"Where's the fun in that?" she whined, making Maggie laugh as she pushed the door open, entering the mudroom.

"Oh, yeah. Wallpaper." Jo Ellen looked around at the black and white walls, which were just one giant flower too many.

"Right? Borderline ghastly. One wall, maybe. But four? In a mudroom? Too much." Maggie waved Jo into the kitchen, which would be beautiful except—

"Oh, she likes her copper pots," Jo Ellen noted, looking up at the massive rack above the island where enough pots to cater a wedding hung, blocking the sightline and creating chaos up to the ceiling.

"A little too much, if you ask me," Maggie said. "Brace for the dining room."

"Oh, dear. More wallpaper explosion?"

"Worse. Accent walls run amok."

"I can't wait." Jo Ellen blew through the door into the formal dining room, letting out a groan.

"What is this woman's motto? If one is good, four is... goodest?"

"She doesn't understand the concept of editing," Maggie said, leaning against the door jamb, simply enjoying the heck out of a good judgefest with her best friend. "The living room isn't so bad, but—"

"But the den?" Jo Ellen had already stuck her head into a small room off to the side. "That lamp is...a choice."

Maggie knew the lamp—shaped like a pineapple.

"A choice," Maggie agreed. "And not a good one."

Jo Ellen wandered into the living room, hands clasped behind her back like she was touring a museum.

"And then Barbara reached her *neutral* era," Jo Ellen said in a narrator's voice. "As if once she'd done all the wallpaper, bad lamps, and floor-to-ceiling wainscoting, she stepped into the safety and surrender of blending the two most meaningless colors into one...*graige*."

Maggie cracked up. "You have no idea how right you are."

"I love this!" Jo Ellen exclaimed. "Shall we march upstairs and critique some more?"

As much as she wanted to, Maggie shook her head. "We have to remember the mission, Jo Ellen. Let me pull that car into the garage and then let's change and walk to Crista's house."

Jo Ellen gasped. "And see Anthony?"

"There's a trail that connects all these backyards, leads right to Crista's gate—and my magnificent rose garden—and we can easily see in the back windows of the family room and kitchen. We'll know if Anthony came home on time, if he's alone—"

"He will be," Jo Ellen interjected, making Maggie smile.

"And if he's making himself dinner and settling in for

a night by himself. That's a man who's faithful, loyal, and working so hard he doesn't even think about anything except how much he misses his wife."

"Amen!" Jo Ellen clasped her hands. "Let's get on with the mission then. We'll come back and cast aspersions on the bedrooms later."

"Oh, yes we will! Aspersions with a cocktail."

"Nothing better," Jo agreed.

Having changed into sneakers and capri pants—old lady shorts, Jo Ellen called them—they walked quickly, staying close to the tree line, the sounds of sprinklers and a distant lawnmower fading as dusk descended over the suburbs.

When they reached Crista's backyard fence, Maggie slowed and peered through the slats.

The yard was perfect, of course. A massive wooden deck spilled from French doors, with a firepit and a summer kitchen, and lounge area.

"Oh, an egg chair." Jo Ellen pointed to the oval seat hanging from a hook by the pergola. "I've always wanted to sit in one of those. They look so cozy."

"Anthony and Crista got me that for my birthday last year," Maggie told her. "I can sit in it and look over to the other side, where my rose garden is. It's the prettiest view from up there. Want to see it?"

Jo Ellen squinted at the house, which was dark and looked empty. "Do we dare?"

Maggie didn't answer but stood on her tiptoes, searching the windows upstairs and down for any sign of movement. "He's not here."

"Working late, no doubt."

Oh, how Maggie wanted to believe that.

"Come on, let me sit in that chair." Jo Ellen reached for the gate latch. "And see your garden. Or can we walk there from here?"

"No, you have to go down the stairs on that side of the deck. Okay." Maggie gave a nod. "Let's go very quickly and I'll peek in the windows."

Jo Ellen flipped the latch and they both cringed when the gate squeaked. Not that there was anyone around to hear, but still.

They walked into the grassy area, taking the steps to the deck.

"What a beautiful home," Jo Ellen said. "How lucky that you live here with your daughter and her family. It's perfect."

"It is," Maggie conceded. "But I'm pretty happy down in Destin with you."

"Aww! Maggie!" Jo slowed so she could hug her. "That's downright sentimental for you."

"Stop." She unpeeled Jo's arms. "Sit in the chair and look at my garden. Quick, before Anthony comes home."

"Don't they have cameras?" Jo Ellen asked.

"Nope. But hurry." Maggie ushered her over to her beloved egg chair, but her gaze went beyond it to—

"*What?*" Maggie froze mid-step.

"No! He's here? Oh, my—"

"Look at my garden!" She could barely utter the words as she stared at an overgrown, scraggly mess of roses. Blooms drooping like they'd given up hope. Dead stems still clinging, unpruned and sad.

Maggie stared, horrified on a level that felt deeply personal.

"This," she said, voice trembling with outrage, "is a disgrace."

Jo Ellen grabbed her elbow. "Maggie—focus."

But they were her babies! In a daze, she walked to the side stairs that led to the garden, taking them slowly, trying to breathe.

At the bottom, she crouched and touched a brittle stem like she was checking a pulse.

"No one has deadheaded, fertilized, watered, or loved these roses," she muttered. "He said he would! Look at this. Look at *this*."

Jo Ellen swung like a five-year-old in the egg chair. "Whee! This is fun! We can come back and prune while he's at work."

"You *cannot* neglect roses," Maggie snapped under her breath. "Roses are living things. These leaves are yellowing. That means—"

"That means you're about to get caught," Jo Ellen said.

Maggie ignored her, reaching deeper into the bush. "Where is the fertilizer schedule? Crista would never allow—"

Jo Ellen leaped out of the egg chair and shot toward the stairs. "Maggie!"

Maggie lifted her head, annoyed—and then froze.

The lights inside the house flicked on and the entire backyard flooded with warm, bright illumination.

"Get down here!" Maggie reached a hand up and practically yanked Jo Ellen down the two stairs, pushing them both to the ground so Anthony wouldn't see their heads in the garden.

Not that he ever looked out here because if he had—and he had a *heart*—her roses would be thriving in the summer warmth.

They inched up like a couple of cat burglars, watching the light and movement. He was in the kitchen, then the eat-in area, to the den, then back to the kitchen.

"How do we get out of here?" Jo Ellen asked.

"We can't without crossing the deck," Maggie told her. "Maybe he'll go upstairs and take a shower. Then—"

One of the French doors opened, and Anthony stepped out, his tie loosened, his sleeves rolled up, a phone in his hand.

"Or not," Jo Ellen whispered as both of them ducked into a bush of crispy, nearly dead roses.

"Shh!" Maggie jabbed her. "Listen! He's on speaker!"

They heard the tones of another voice on the phone... a woman's voice.

"Crista?" Jo Ellen mouthed, brows raised in hope.

"I don't think so," Maggie murmured. "Listen."

They heard Anthony's footsteps, coming closer as whoever was on the phone finished talking, still unintelligible from here.

"That's fantastic, Pamela."

"What's his assistant's name?" Jo Ellen mouthed the question.

Maggie could have kicked herself for not asking Crista when she'd talked about the woman. She shrugged and the move caught her top on a thorny branch, making a rustling noise.

They ducked deeper, stayed very still, and listened to…was that the egg chair?

Maggie inched up and stole a glance. Sure enough, Anthony was swinging in the chair, holding the phone out, talking to a woman named Pamela.

Oh, this was not good. Not at all.

"We'll definitely look at it tomorrow," he said, and she replied, but even on speaker, he was too far away to make out anything but the tones of a woman's voice.

"You better come with me." He added a soft chuckle that sounded…oh, not good. "I can't make that decision without you. I need a woman…"

The rest faded as he stood and Maggie bit her lip as he disappeared into the house, leaving the French door open—meaning they couldn't escape this hiding place.

Now what?

"Are you sure we can't get out of this garden without crossing the deck?" Jo Ellen asked on a whisper.

"Unless you want to burrow under the deck. It has been done…by creatures, not old ladies spying on their sons-in-law."

"Mags, look." She pointed to a light upstairs.

"That's their bedroom."

"He's up there. And what's that?"

"The bathroom," Maggie said, straightening and wincing at her back pain. She was too old for this.

"Could we make a run for it?"

She narrowed her eyes. "I don't run."

"Then walk really fast." Jo Ellen tugged on her sleeve. "Ready? Up and across and out, silent and fast like a ninja! Do not stop, sit in the egg chair, or make a noise."

"But I—"

"Now!" With a jerk, Jo Ellen pulled her up the steps, the two of them prancing over the wood like aging ballerinas, neither turning to look at the house. They made it down the other stairs, slipped out the gate, and reached the path breathless.

"We didn't get shot!" Jo Ellen announced on a laugh.

"He doesn't have a gun."

"Oh, Maggie, you had me—"

"But he does have evening conversations with someone named Pamela," Maggie said, still hurting. "We have to find out who that is."

"Oh, we will," Jo Ellen agreed. "How?"

"I'm counting on you to figure that out, Jo. And I'm sure it will involve an elaborate lie."

"At least one," Jo muttered. "Come on. Let's go have a drink and judge the furniture at our free Airbnb."

Maggie tried to smile but it felt forced. Because a tiny, nagging, unwelcome doubt had just slipped into her heart. And after the horrible disregard Anthony showed for her roses?

Clearly, the man was capable of *anything*.

Chapter Ten
Tessa

Tessa was almost used to the silence, which was a sound she certainly didn't expect when she'd suggested a two-year-old stay in her home. Like every other day since Olive had arrived, the mornings at Tessa's house dawned quiet and strangely ordinary.

As always, Tessa had awakened multiple times during the night to tiptoe down the hall and peer into the guest room where Olive slept in a small mound of blankets and stuffed animals. Each time, she stood there listening to the soft whisper of Olive's breath, waiting until her own pulse slowed.

Now, mid-morning, Olive was awake, sitting cross-legged on the rug in her pajamas, lining up wooden blocks in careful rows. She didn't look up when Tessa padded in to watch. She didn't speak. She *never* spoke.

"Good morning, sunshine," Tessa said softly.

Olive slid one block into place.

Tessa had learned that Olive answered with motion, not words. With nods. With glances. With tiny choices.

Hearing only the quiet, Tessa buttered toast and cut it into triangles. She filled a small bowl with blueberries, poured a little orange juice into a sippy cup, and took the whole thing to the table.

The child's silence hadn't bothered Dusty at first, but yesterday he did seem concerned when she just wouldn't answer even a simple question.

"Breakfast," she said. "Come over here, honey."

Wordless, Olive moved to the table and let Tessa lift her into the booster seat. Just as she started to pick at a blueberry, a knock at the door from the inside staircase startled her.

"No worries," Tessa assured her. "It's Mister Dusty. Come on in!" she called.

Dusty stepped into the kitchen a little tentatively but smiled as he took in the sight of Olive eating at the table.

"How are the girls?" he asked lightly.

Tessa stifled a sigh. "Quiet."

He approached Olive slowly. "Morning, kiddo."

She gave no response but looked down at her blueberries, eating with intent. Not wanting to stare at her, Tessa gestured Dusty into the kitchen.

"Coffee?" she asked.

"Yes, please."

They stepped away from the table to the far end of the kitchen counter, where he put a hand on her shoulder. "You look tired."

"Exactly what every woman wants to hear," she said with a fake dirty look. "Are the bags getting bigger?"

"Just a shadow of disappointment and frustration."

She gave him an "are you serious" look. "She has not said a single word since her mother left! Not one. But she's bright, alert, able to build a tower out of blocks and I saw her flipping through a book. Is it me? Her? Trauma?"

"Has she cried?" she asked.

"Not once. Sleeps through the night and has a dry diaper. She just doesn't respond to me."

She waited, searching his face.

"I'm not diagnosing her," he began. "I want to be very clear about that. I'm a grief counselor, not a child psychologist. But I've done a little digging and talked to a few friends who are experts in childhood developmental issues."

"Is it autism?"

"Not at all. The consensus is she's trying to control her environment. But of course, we have no way of knowing that without a professional assessment and I don't want to put her through that."

"Control...by not talking?" Tessa asked.

"My colleagues—again, purely conjecture based on experience, not this child—think the silence isn't delayed speech or defiance but could be something called selective mutism."

She winced.

"It sounds scarier than it is," he said quickly. "It's anxiety based. Olive *can* speak. But a child practicing selective mutism simply won't in certain situations, especially when they feel unsafe."

"Un*safe*?" Her voice cracked. "How could she feel that way? Did I—"

"No! Trauma, instability, loss, upheaval. Tessa, that

girl doesn't know where her mother is and she's never been here before. She's two."

"Of course." Tessa bit her lip, her heart aching with sympathy as she looked at Olive, dutifully finishing her blueberries. "How long does it last?"

He shrugged. "I'm sure every case is wildly different. Hopefully, only until they feel safe, or are just so involved in something they forget everything."

She nodded, instantly considering all her options.

"You just need patience, Tess. You're doing everything right. She needs to be able to make small decisions, even say no to you without major consequences."

"She doesn't say anything, yes or no. I'd love to hear her say no."

"Honestly, the best thing for her is to play," he said.

Tessa sighed. "She likes the beach, so yesterday I picked up some sand toys."

"Good. Get her completely involved in something so she isn't thinking about her surroundings, just focused on play."

"Do you have patients today?" Tessa asked.

"Not for a few hours."

"Great." She snapped her fingers and pointed to him. "Let's go make sandcastles!"

"Brilliant!" He snagged her arm as she started to walk away. "Wait a second."

"You are not backing out of sandcastle construction, Dustin Mathers."

He smiled at the old name they called him when they were young, giving her a flash of that wild child on the beach from her youth. He'd changed so much and she was crazy about the man he'd become.

"What a natural you are, Tess," he whispered. "It's beautiful on you."

Her heart, already feeling mushy, just melted into a pool. "The glow of sleep deprivation?" she cracked.

"Love," he said softly. "Caring. Kindness. Maternal tenderness. All beautiful."

She opened her mouth to make a joke, to flick off the sweet words, to...protect herself. But as she looked into his eyes, she felt a few bricks fall.

She didn't know what to say, so she just lifted up and brushed his lips with an unexpected kiss.

He deepened it for one quick second, sliding an arm around her, but parted quickly with a glance in the general direction of Olive.

"Beautiful." He repeated the word in a low whisper, then eased back. "Come on. Let's make sandcastles...and words."

Oh, heavens. Could she adore this man any *more*?

THE BEACH WAS MOSTLY empty when they arrived, the sun not yet high enough to scorch, the breeze soft and forgiving. The Gulf stretched out in gentle turquoise bands, calm and pretty.

Olive walked between them, one small hand in Tessa's—not from affection, but duty as they crossed the street—the other gripping a yellow shovel Dusty had handed her at the base of the stairs. She moved fast for such a tiny person, eyes fixed forward, expression impossible to read.

To fill the silence and always hoping to elicit a response, Tessa chattered endlessly. She talked about the art of building a sandcastle and picking the perfect place where it could sit. She talked about the birds, the surf, the reason Destin's sand was so white.

"Quartz from the Appalachian mountains?" Dusty asked after she told them. "How do you know that?"

"My sister, the scientist," she said, giving Olive's hand a squeeze. "She's the smartest person I know. You'll love Kate, Olive."

Olive stared straight ahead.

They hit the sand and hustled toward the waterline as Dusty encouraged her to pick the perfect placement for their castle. Eventually, she stopped and plopped down on the sand.

"Okay, here it is, then," he said, laughing at her decision-making process.

"An excellent plot of land," Tessa said solemnly. "High value. Ocean views. Room for expansion."

Olive just stared at the sand as if imagining a castle rising up from it.

Dusty dropped the cooler and the bag of sand toys. Tessa spread a blanket, anchoring the corners with shoes and towels. Then she sat back, deliberately giving Olive space.

Dusty crouched and began scooping slightly wet sand into a bucket, packing it gently.

"You can dump it," he said.

Olive watched. He turned the bucket over and lifted it, revealing a squat, imperfect tower.

Her eyes flickered with interest.

She grabbed her own bucket and knelt, copying him with intense concentration. Sand spilled everywhere. She tried again and again, refusing assistance with just a shake of her head. When her tower finally held—after many failed attempts—she stared at it as though she'd summoned it by magic.

"You're an architect," Tessa murmured.

Olive didn't say a word or smile.

As the sun crossed over the sand, Dusty and Olive stayed hard at work—proving they both had shockingly long attention spans. They scooped and dumped like a two-person construction crew.

Tessa tugged on her brimmed hat and watched from behind her sunglasses, her attention equally divided between the unexpectedly enthusiastic man and the incredibly focused little girl.

Before too long, three small towers appeared, each surviving Olive's constant poking. She dug while Dusty shaped the tops to look more castle-like.

He formed a small mound beside one tower. "This can be the door."

Olive flattened the hill with the shovel.

"Okay," Dusty said. "No door."

She dug faster, working on the next tower.

Tessa watched Dusty closely, taking in his strong, sandy hands, the way he kneeled comfortably under a blistering sun, his ability to meet this frightened child exactly where she was.

For reasons she didn't really understand, it was probably the single most attractive side of him she'd ever seen. And he had many.

Tessa scooted closer, careful not to crowd. She picked up a shell and set it near the evolving castle.

Olive took it and pressed it onto a tower. Then she looked up at Tessa with bright eyes, the first real reaction she'd shown all day.

"It's like jewelry!" Tessa said. "Can't have too much of that. I'll find more jewels for your tower, milady!"

While Olive worked on the next bucket, Tessa found shells and laid them in little piles to let Olive select which she wanted and where they should go. Giving her control, Tessa thought proudly.

Wordlessly—of course—Olive started placing them on the towers—well, sticking them randomly all over the place. She abandoned all construction in lieu of decorating, which Tessa praised to the skies.

Oh, this is perfect, Olive Oyl!

Look at that placement, sweetheart!

Fit for a princess!

Each lavish compliment got a glance in response, but that was all. While they worked, Dusty looked mildly amused, and Tessa intentionally let Olive make every decision.

Just as she finished the shells, a tiny sand crab skittered from a hole near the moat Dusty had created.

Olive froze, then leaned closer, eyes wide. Her

mouth...almost moved. A word rose up, but then she clamped her tiny lips together and watched the crab in wonder until he vanished back into the sand.

"Bye-bye, Mr. Crab," Tessa sang playfully.

Olive pressed her lips together as if she was about to say "Bye" but then she reached for a pretty pink shell. Carefully, she placed it over the hole and looked up at Tessa with an expectant gaze.

"How sweet, Olive. We love Mr. Crab," Tessa said, forming heart hands over her chest.

Olive stared at her, at her hands, and then made a circle with hers in an attempt to make the same heart.

"Olive!" Tessa cooed as if she'd proved the theory of relativity. "You're so smart!"

Stifling a laugh, Dusty stood and stretched. "That's a lot of construction. I need a snack. Anybody else?"

They ate on the blanket—grapes, crackers, juice. Olive sat between them, eating her grapes the way she did the blueberries—one at a time, slow and deliberate.

Afterward, she turned back to the castle, looking around the sand.

"More shells?" Tessa asked. "More jewelry?"

Olive nodded.

"Let's look together," Tessa said, standing and picking up Dusty's empty bucket. "Let's go find every single shell and cover those towers until they are glorious."

It was pretty obvious most of that was lost on a two-year-old, but the little girl took Tessa's hand—not dutifully this time!—and they walked toward the section of sand piled with shells from the last tide.

Side by side, they filled about an inch or two of the bucket, then took it back. And the same way she ate blueberries and grapes, little Olive placed each shell one by one all over the tallest tower, nearly covering it until she lost interest.

While she did, Tessa leaned close to Dusty as they watched her together, praising her work and whispering to each other that she was cute and bright and perfect and dear.

The sun blazed on them, relentless, but Tessa didn't care. She loved this moment, this day, this tiny community of three people life had thrust together—yet they looked, acted, and talked like any other family on the beach.

The very idea made her feel...something. She couldn't quite name it, but knew in her bones it was *good*.

"This castle is perfection, Olive Oyl," Tessa announced. "What do you call it?"

She could feel Dusty hold his breath just as Tessa did the same, waiting for an answer—any answer—to break the silence.

Olive took a slow breath and touched the top shell with one baby finger, staring at the sandcastle. Her lips formed again and they waited, silent and expectant.

Then she turned around and looked toward the house.

Tessa swallowed a soft grunt of frustration, then they quietly packed and went upstairs, where Tessa helped Olive clean up from the sand, eat a few crackers and banana slices before getting her down for a nap.

When she came out, she found Dusty in her living room, his head back, eyes closed.

She slipped onto the sofa next to him. He put his arm around her and pulled her closer, planting a kiss on her head.

"She's asleep," Tessa announced.

"Mmm. We all should be after all that sun and sand-castle building."

Smiling at that, Tessa closed her eyes and nestled her head into the crook of his neck.

"You're a good mom," he whispered.

If she was, wouldn't Olive speak?

She didn't know and right then, she couldn't worry about it. She just snuggled closer to Dusty, and they fell sound asleep on the sofa together.

Chapter Eleven
Lacey

By the time Lacey, Meredith, and Jonah—with Atlas in a harness against his chest— reached the top of the Back Porch's steps, the sky had softened into that familiar Destin palette of peach and coral melting into lavender. The breeze off the water brushed her bare arms, warm but gentle, carrying salt and grilled shrimp and music from a small quartet on the sand.

Lacey walked between her cousins, who were teasing each other like only a brother and sister could. Sometimes, when she was with them, she wished she'd had siblings. But then she remembered that she'd grown up with these two, spent every holiday and many weekends with them, so they truly were the closest thing to siblings she'd ever had.

Which was why she had pushed for a dinner alone with them, so they could really talk. Because Lacey needed advice and she respected her cousins' opinions as much as anyone's. They were older, wiser, and certainly more experienced, and they knew Lacey well.

Atlas snoozed in what Jonah called his "baby pouch," his tiny cheek pressed into the soft gray fabric of his father's T-shirt. Jonah moved with the quiet confidence of someone who had learned how to navigate the world without waking a baby—one arm instinctively curved around the bundle, his steps measured, his body angled slightly forward as if shielding Atlas from wind and noise.

Meredith walked on Lacey's other side, her dark hair pulled back in a low ponytail, a chic linen dress swaying against her knees. She looked calm in that effortless way Meredith always did, but only a close cousin like Lacey knew that nothing was effortless for Meredith Lawson.

Effort was her middle name, her worldview, and her belief system. And in these past few weeks, she'd put a lot of effort into getting over the loss of an unexpected pregnancy.

Jonah, for all his confidence as a father, was recovering from his own shocking grief—the tragic death of his girlfriend, newborn Atlas's mother.

But somehow, they both managed to laugh and prove that they weren't just fine, they were thriving.

And that made them inspirational, amazing, and the perfect people to give Lacey advice on her complicated situation. God willing, by the end of this dinner she'd have clarity.

An attractive hostess greeted them with a smile, adding a surprised coo when she spotted Atlas's little head. "Where would you like to take that darling baby? Inside or out?"

"Outside," they answered in unison, getting a laugh.

Then the hostess put a finger to her lips, quieting them. "We'll wake the baby."

"Nothing wakes this guy," Jonah said. "Unless it's the A/C coming on at two a.m., then he's up and ready to party."

Chatting about babies, they followed her past the open bar and the hum of conversation, along the original "porch" that gave the famous eatery its name.

Outside, they stepped onto the wide deck over the sand, with an unobstructed view of the mirror-calm Gulf.

For a moment, Lacey wished she didn't have such a hard subject on her heart. The evening was tailor-made for relaxing, and she so wanted to chill with two of her favorite people. Well, two and a half.

Lanterns glowed softly above wooden tables. The air was full of laughter and clinking glasses, of couples leaning close, of locals and tourists, all watching as gulls skimmed the surface of the water and flew toward the horizon.

They ordered drinks—Meredith a crisp white wine, Jonah a light beer, Lacey a cocktail with something citrusy and pink. They let Jonah pick appetizers as he shared stories of his adventures in culinary school.

Lacey watched him, marveling—not for the first time —at the man he had become.

The Jonah who'd arrived in a dusty van months ago had been hollow-eyed, guarded, moving through life like a ghost in borrowed skin. The Jonah who'd returned with Atlas after Carly's death had been shattered, raw, barely holding himself together.

This Jonah? He was still grieving, still human, still imperfect—but he was *here*, present, engaged, and managing an infant. It was so far from where he'd been months ago and continents away from the mess he'd been after his mother died when he was fifteen.

When Atlas stirred, Jonah's hand moved without thought, a gentle pat, a quiet sway. The baby settled again.

"It's discipline," he said, in answer to Lacey's question about the mood at culinary school. "Not like we're trapped or scared, but everything in the classroom and kitchens is so purposeful and structured. I'm learning every day and I don't hate it. I do sometimes hate my *béchamel* sauce, but some days, it's my best friend."

Meredith smiled. "That instructor I met the day when I stopped by with Atlas? He thinks you are a superstar."

"Chef Broussard." Jonah looked skyward. "Don't be fooled by his niceness. He's ruthless in the kitchen."

When the server returned with hush puppies and peel-and-eat shrimp, Lacey realized she'd been smiling for ten straight minutes.

The conversation shifted to Meredith, who never liked talking about herself. But she was halfway through what Lacey knew would be her one and only glass of wine, mellowed enough to brush back a stray hair and be honest when Lacey asked her how she was really doing.

"I'm okay," she said softly. "I've enjoyed the break and taking care of this little guy. But if we close on a big local project, then I might stay for a few months and manage a Destin office of Acacia Architecture."

Jonah groaned. "And I'm going to be scrambling for child care, since Grandma and Jo Ellen are always off somewhere, and Kate's gone."

Meredith held up her hand. "I still have time for him and we'll work it out, Jonah. The house is full of help."

"You might stay?" Lacey leaned closer to Meredith. "How did I not hear about this?"

"Uh, I think his name is Roman," Jonah said with a wry smile. "You've been checked out in the end zone, Spacey."

She laughed at the old nickname and didn't bother to deny the allegation. "So much that I missed the possibility of Meredith not going back to Atlanta?"

"I'll go back," Meredith said. "I just love this Lakeside job and if Acacia gets the project and I run it? Major professional coup."

"The only coup that matters to Miss Perfect," Jonah teased. Kind of teased.

She shot her brother a look, but the atmosphere was too lovely for an argument.

The two of them had always had different work ethics—especially after Aunt Melissa died. Meredith was an obsessed workaholic, and Jonah was always more laid-back. But now, he seemed to do a great job of balancing his culinary school schedule and being a single dad.

"So," Meredith said, tilting her head. "Speaking of Roman—why isn't he here with us tonight?"

Because she purposely hadn't asked him. "This is

cousin time," she said, picking up her cocktail. "No outsiders allowed, remember? Club rules."

Meredith snorted. "I forgot about the Cousin Club and that treehouse my dad built."

They sank into the old memory for a moment, sharing a few blasts from the past—like the time Jonah decided to build a swing and the only thing that swung was the treehouse's roof.

"Clearly, we knew then which of us would be an architect," Meredith joked.

"Back to Roman," Jonah said after a few more Cousin Club memories. "I feel like he's not here for a reason."

"Stop being so perceptive," Lacey teased.

Meredith lifted a brow and eyed the appetizer platters. "Oh? Is everything okay with him?"

Lacey laughed nervously. "Wonderful. Exciting. Terrifying."

"Ahh." Jonah grinned. "The romance trifecta."

"He leaves in about two weeks for training camp in Jacksonville," she added.

"You knew that was coming, right?" Meredith asked, plucking a hush puppy.

"Yes, but I didn't know he'd want me to join him. To move to Jacksonville and...live together."

Meredith coughed on the first bite, then covered by waving her hand. "That's hot," she said, even though Lacey suspected the heat wasn't why she'd nearly choked.

"Are you going to?" Jonah asked.

Lacey sighed. "Maybe. Yes. I don't know." She

laughed with them at the vague reply. "Well, I told him I would, but then Tessa announced she needed to pull back from work for personal reasons, offered me a raise, and gave me more responsibility. In fact, she is basically handing me a direct path to a fantastic career as an event planner. Here. In Destin."

Jonah and Meredith stared at her, processing her dilemma.

"I can't say yes to both," Lacey finally said. "Even though, in a way, I already have. And I haven't told my mom yet. I don't know what to choose or do or think or what."

The table went quiet.

Lacey smiled. "And that, dear cousins, is why you are here tonight. Advice and counsel, humor and hope, and very clear direction are all welcome. Hit me."

Meredith cleared her throat and spoke first, hush puppies abandoned. "You've built something real with Tessa, Lace. You have momentum and stability, and a future no matter what happens to you."

Lacey nodded, not at all surprised her career-focused cousin went this way.

"Roman's world is...unpredictable," she continued. "He could get traded to...wherever they have football teams. Far. He could get injured. Anything can happen."

"Anything can happen in *any* relationship," Jonah countered. "If this little guy"—he rubbed Atlas's back—"and what happened to his mother isn't proof of that, I don't know what is."

Lacey turned to him, curious about where he was going.

"I mean, you can't plan a relationship over what *might* happen." He punctuated that by sliding a peeled shrimp into cocktail sauce and popping it into his mouth, followed by a cringe. "*Oof.* There *is* such a thing as too much Worcestershire, you know? Chef B would say, 'Edit, please, edit.'"

Meredith waved a hand as if she didn't want the conversation derailed. "I'm not saying you can't take a risk on love, Lace. I'm just saying, you are what? You had a birthday, so twenty-five? You need a foundation, not a live-in boyfriend."

Jonah shook his head, hard and fast. "You're saying she should choose safety and security over possibility and passion. I firmly disagree, Mer."

Meredith turned to Lacey to make her point. "The fact is you two haven't been together that long. You don't even know him, not completely. What if he surprises you and turns out to be..." She caught herself and took a breath. "Not who you think he is," she finished.

"What better way to find out than to live together?" Jonah asked. "I still say you cannot stay small because life might change. Life is supposed to be about...making more life. A husband, a family. That's what you need."

The two women stared at him.

"I know, I know." He flicked a hand. "I sound all Dad-like."

"You *have* been reading his Bible," Meredith said softly.

"I have," Jonah agreed, unashamed of the fact. "I actually read a little to Atlas and, no surprise, it put him right to sleep." They laughed but his face grew serious. "I like what it has to say about families, love, marriage, and generations. I don't like being a single father, but that was the hand I was dealt. I do like being a father, and I think that's..." He breathed out. "I'm not saying you're not whole without a man, Lacey. I'm saying Roman's a great guy and having a solid relationship and a family life is not a bad thing."

"Roman's great," Meredith agreed. "But he's still a guy and you can't put all your eggs in the basket of hope, only for it to be...stomped on so hard all the eggs are..." She swallowed, unable to finish. "Sorry."

"Hey." Lacey reached across the table and put a hand on Meredith's. "Don't apologize. I should be sorry for making you two address difficult issues just because I have a personal problem."

They took a breather, all of them sipping, tasting, and regrouping.

Meredith broke first. "I'm not saying love doesn't matter. Obviously, it does. I just think you're young, Lacey, and Tessa has guided you toward something you're very good at.

You're not just answering phones in your father's office anymore. You're managing clients. Planning events. You've become indispensable."

"That's exactly the word Tessa used," she replied.

"It's a good word," Meredith said. "I strive for it."

Jonah's eyes flashed with disagreement. "So she

should stay because she's good at something? That's the reason? She could manage clients and plan events in Jacksonville while she's growing a solid relationship into something that could last forever."

Lacey sipped her cocktail slowly, looking from one to the other like she was witnessing two weather systems collide.

Meredith exhaled. "You're romanticizing uncertainty."

Jonah smiled faintly. "You're overvaluing control."

And Lacey laughed under her breath. "It's the club all over again," she joked. "You two taking opposite sides on a theoretical problem. Only the problem is *me* this time."

"Because we care, littlest member of the Cousin Club," Meredith said sweetly.

Jonah gave a playful frown. "Only 'cause Dad said we *had* to let you in."

Lacey chuckled. "I'm glad you did," she said. "And I feel your love. I really do."

"You don't have to decide your whole future, Lace," Meredith reminded her. "Just the next few months."

"And remember," Jonah added. "Sometimes the bravest thing is choosing the thing that scares you."

Meredith threw him a look. "Do you *have* to sound like a fortune cookie?"

Lacey laughed, suddenly hit with how much she loved these two...and also how much she wished Roman were here to enjoy them.

But then she thought about how fun it would be to

have Tessa here, joking with them and being like the hilarious aunt-with-way-too-much-life.

The fact was, she loved Roman *and* Tessa and she didn't want to hurt either of them.

And she knew—deep down—that she would.

"The worst part," she admitted quietly. "Someone I love is going to be disappointed in me. Maybe both of them."

Meredith's expression softened. "I know that's hard for you, Lace."

The server came to clear plates, breaking the intensity. The conversation drifted to lighter things—inside jokes from childhood summers, Meredith's terrible middle-school bangs, Jonah's first disastrous attempt at sourdough.

When dinner ended, they stood near the railing, warm air wrapping around them. Jonah rocked Atlas gently. Meredith leaned against the wood, watching the water.

"You'll figure it out," she said to Lacey.

"Or you'll just choose," Jonah added. "And then figure it out after."

Lacey smiled at both of them.

They walked back toward the parking lot together, teasing Jonah about his "dad walk," taking turns brushing Atlas's tiny hand.

She didn't have clarity but she had love. And right now, in the twilight, with her family, that was enough.

But she'd have to make a decision, and soon.

Chapter Twelve
Vivien

Vivien stared at Peter's text, trying to corral all the mixed emotions his words elicited, unable to just grab one and feel it.

Peter: *Found your bridge guy. Quinn Hargrove, scrap metal multimillionaire. He commissioned the safety assessment and pushed the demo through all channels. Turns out a deputy knows him because he frequents a bar called Breakwater near HarborWalk. Goes there every Friday for happy hour. Wanna ambush? Could meet you there after Connor's doc appt. LMK*

First there was satisfaction—Peter got a name. A living person after days of dead ends, voicemail, and closed doors on the subject of the Left Coast Bridge. But there was also disappointment...a scrap metal multimillionaire? He wouldn't be easily swayed.

She also had a tinge of...hope. Was this a "date" with Peter? Was this a chance to finally have that conversation, or would he come directly from the doctor and bring Connor? And, yikes, Holly. Hope disintegrated at the thought.

What would she say to this Quinn guy if she did

meet him? Whatever it was, she had to say it fast, since the demo date was approaching.

At the light, she typed in "Breakwater Bar" and got the address on her GPS—twenty minutes.

If she went home, changed, waited for Peter, and met him there—it might be well after Quinn Hargrove's "happy hour" window. She replied with a quick "meet you there" and followed the GPS, tapping the steering wheel impatiently as she sat in bumper-to-bumper traffic in the blistering late afternoon heat.

Yes, she'd rather go home to the Summer House, snag a G&T, and fall in the pool until Jonah magically made them all a dream dinner. Actually, she'd like to do all that with Peter by her side and finish the night with a moonlight stroll on the beach, having their heart-to-heart talk and deciding they were better together.

Instead, she was headed to the Breakwater Bar & Grill, a casual restaurant that was frequented more by locals than tourists.

After she found a parking spot—another ten minutes in the car she'd never get back—she walked into the packed bar, trying to decide if Quinn Hargrove would be inside or out. The outside tables were slammed, and she realized she had no idea how to find a man she'd never met.

Inside, she found two empty stools at the end of the bar and ordered that gin and tonic she'd been thinking about. While she waited, she took out her phone and typed "Quinn Hargrove images," and instantly quite a few pictures popped up.

She got a quick snapshot of someone around sixty, salt-and-pepper thinning hair, and what looked like a broad chest—or maybe a big paunch. Hard to tell. The links looked like he had lots of community involvement in the 30A area and was the president and owner of a local company called Hargrove Salvage & Materials.

She skimmed a short home page on their website, highlighting a specialty in the secure and environmentally friendly removal of "aging coastal structures for public safety, traffic efficiency, modern amenities, and increased tourism."

Basically, he eliminated history for the sake of progress and the almighty dollar. Probably made a killing doing that in Destin.

Looking up from her phone, she scanned the bar and...*found him*.

Dang, that was easy. As she stared at him, he sipped a drink and held her eye contact for a good three seconds, then he lifted an eyebrow in her general direction.

She gave a tight smile as the bartender returned with her drink and a check.

Now what? Talk to him alone? Ask innocent questions? Make sure he—

Her phone buzzed and a text box flashed.

Peter: *Complication. Might not make it. Sorry.*

On a sigh, she let the disappointment give a hard and swift kick. What was the complication? Dinner with...*his family?* Hating that she was jealous and sad, she reached for her glass just as the bartender scooped up the paper check.

"This one's been covered by the gentleman down by the taps," he said.

"Oh." She blinked in surprise, then shifted her gaze right back to ol' Quinn Hargrove, who beamed at her.

Well, if this wasn't kismet, she didn't know what was.

She picked up the glass, nodded her thanks to him, and took a sip.

Quinn was up in a flash, headed right toward her. She watched as he walked, studying him. Definitely sixty, maybe more, but he'd been to the gym and possibly the plastic surgeon since that last picture she saw.

At first glance, he wasn't unattractive. Not her type, though.

Her second glance came as he stood next to her and looked her right in the eyes.

"I have never seen you in here before," he said, his voice low and unmistakably flirtatious. "Welcome."

She turned on the barstool to face him, her brain whirring with how to handle this unexpected encounter. She took a breath, conjured up her brightest smile, and extended her hand to keep it professional.

No matter what, she wouldn't lie. She'd just...learn.

"Vivien Lawson," she said. "It's my first time."

He shook a little too hard, his gray-blue eyes taking a not-so-quick trip over her. "Beautiful name, Vivien. Like...the *Gone With the Wind* actress."

"That's who I'm named after."

"Really?"

"Really," she assured him. "My mother has a dog named Aunt Pittypat."

He laughed, hard and from his barrel chest. "I love it."

"And who are you?" she asked, as if she hadn't just Googled the man five minutes ago.

"Quinn Hargrove."

No one would call him handsome, but she sensed an underlying energy that probably made him magnetic. And successful, even if his ill-gotten gains came from demolishing memories and landmarks.

"I take it you're a regular, Mr. Hargrove?"

The corner of his mouth lifted. "Mr. Hargrove makes me feel old. So does being a regular at a bar. Call me Quinn and I'll pretend it's my first time, too."

"Too late for that and you can't lie. About anything." She added a smile. "That's my bar rule."

He chuckled and took a of sip of what smelled like whiskey. "You have rules, huh? Okay." He waited a beat, as if sizing her up or maybe trying to think of something to say. "You a boat person? Or just here for the ambience?"

"Just the ambience tonight."

"Smart woman. Boats are money pits. Ask me how I know."

She lifted a brow. "You own a boat."

"Three of them. Small, medium, and stupid but impressive."

She wasn't impressed, but smiled. "Is boating your profession?"

"Nah. I'm the clean-up guy," he said easily. "I get rid of things people don't want to look at anymore.

And, honey, I've made millions off people's dead dreams."

She tried not to cringe at the term of endearment or the social faux pas of talking income. Her mother would "bless his heart" and walk away.

But he'd opened the door to the very reason she was sitting in this overcrowded bar on a Friday happy hour.

"How does one...clean up dreams?" she asked.

He chuckled. "You make it sound depressing, but it's not. I own a salvage company. What do you do, Vivien?"

"I also clean up people's dreams, and kind of make them come true."

He drew back. "Ooh, I'm intrigued."

"I'm an interior designer."

"Oh, that's—"

"Not as interesting as a salvage company," she assured him. "I'm sorry I'm not familiar with that business. Please tell me more."

"Well, I'd love to." He gestured to the empty seat next to her. "May I?"

"Of course."

He settled on the stool and put his drink on the bar. "I'd love to make it sound glamorous and impress you, Vivien, but what I do is take the trash from a building demo and dispose of it. I'm a glorified garbage man."

She smiled and pointed to a Patek Philippe watch she knew cost upwards of fifty thousand. Her ex-husband used to lust for one. "I've never seen one of those on my trash collector."

He gave a slow grin. "I didn't say it wasn't profitable."

So he was tearing down the bridge for money. Somehow, she managed a smile. "I see. Are your projects all local?"

"Oh, I do work all over Florida. You smell coastal air..." He inhaled noisily and fluttered his fingers in front of his nose as if testing the aroma of wine. "I smell oxidation, sodium chloride, and mold spores. And to me? That smells like *money*."

She took a drink and let him continue.

"Florida is a gold mine of garbage, Vivien. Just look around—anything metal is pitted and green, stainless steel is corroded, and don't get me started on wood. That's not after a hurricane—that's after a summer. This place is one step away from uninhabitable, but that, my dear, is what keeps me in business."

He gave an arrogant tip of his head, waiting a beat for her to be amazed by his prowess and ingenuity.

She dug up a "Wow" and took another sip, trying to figure out how to get him to talk about the bridge.

"Do you have any current projects around here?" she asked.

"Several," he said. "I'm taking down an old shrimping dock behind a bait shop off Harbor Road and a few signs along the beach. Of course, my star event is the Left Coast Bridge."

Her heart stopped. "The...old bridge that joins the jetties?" She tried hard not to sound excited.

"Have you seen that mess?" He chuckled. "That'll buy me a new watch." He leaned an inch closer. "Or you, if you play your cards right."

Ew. She wasn't playing cards, just trying not to show them. "Why are you taking the bridge down?" she asked, keeping her tone neutral. "Is it...hurting anyone?"

"My eyes," he said on a snort. "Tourists don't want to look at that."

"I don't think it's that ugly," she said. "It could be... cleaned up and stay standing."

"Where's the profit in that?" he asked, a little stunned by the suggestion, then he nodded. "Okay. I got you. Li'l bit of a tree hugger, are we?"

"No, I—"

"I'll tell you what I told the city council, some fishing authority, the county commission, and a dimwit at the local newspaper—that bridge is an environmental flashpoint. You can't see under the waterline."

"But you can—"

He swiped his hand, cutting her off. "Those pylons disrupt tidal flow. They trap debris. They choke off seagrass beds. You get algae blooms, erosion, stagnation. It's not just ugly—it's unhealthy. The Gulf doesn't need another artificial barrier from the 1970s rotting into it."

She sipped her drink and let him continue, her dislike for the man increasing with every fake word.

"And then there's the safety issue. Do you know kids *jump* off that bridge? Someone's gonna die."

If that were true, someone would be dead by now. "Kids have jumped off that bridge for decades," she said. "No one has ever died."

"No one has ever died *yet.*" He knocked back the rest of his drink. "I'm doing someone a favor. And..." He called the bartender with a finger flick, then pointed to the bar. "Two more, please."

"No, no, I—"

"Vivien." He put a light hand on her arm. "Relax."

She eased her arm from his touch, deciding to try another tactic. "I've read a few of the older editorials in the paper when the city announced it was coming down. Not everyone is happy."

"Not everyone is ever happy," he countered, then drew back, eyeing her. "Change always upsets people."

"Sometimes it's worth upsetting them," she said. "Sometimes it isn't."

He leaned his elbow on the bar, closer now. "That bridge is a lawsuit waiting to happen. Can we talk about the color of your eyes? Not quite brown, not quite gold. They are the color of..."

"Rust," she joked, inching back from the scrutiny.

"My favorite color, but no, they're more..." He closed a little space between them. "Fiery. Are you fiery, Vivien? I like fiery women."

Sliding her stool back, she managed a humorless smile. "Well, I like beautiful memories and historical landmarks and celebrating legacies, so..."

"Viv!" A man's voice broke through the bar noise, almost immediately accompanied by a hand on her shoulder. A familiar, strong, and unbelievably welcome hand that she only had to touch to feel comfortable again.

"Peter." She smiled up at him with a rush of relief and gratitude. "You made it."

He answered with a light kiss on her hair. Sliding a

protective arm around her, he glanced at the man. "'Scuze me, sir. I believe that's my seat."

Suddenly, all the bravado disappeared from old Quinn Hargrove. His pudgy jowls sagged, his barrel chest deflated, and his smile vanished.

"'Course. Nice chatting with you, Vivien." He stood up and took a step back, giving her one more look. "There's nothing wrong with making a little money off cleaning up the place."

Vivien opened her mouth, but Peter stepped between her and the man, taking his seat.

"Have a nice evening, sir," he said, spinning Vivien's stool to face him.

She drank in the sight of him, a little breathless and so, so happy to see him.

VIVIEN KNEW ALMOST INSTANTLY that something was wrong with Peter. He turned down a drink, looked around like a trapped animal, and let out a shuddering sigh.

"You okay?"

"Now that I don't have to kill that guy breathing down your...front? Yeah." He grinned, but it didn't quite reach his brown eyes. "Sounds like you found your guy and he struck out."

"I struck out, too," she admitted. "But you have the best timing of any man alive."

He gave her a half-smile. "Looked like you needed a

rescue."

She didn't think of herself as a woman who needed saving, but if anyone was going to do that, she wanted it to be Peter.

"He walked away from me, but"—she lifted a shoulder—"I don't think he's walking away from the bridge demo that is going to make him even..."

"Fatter."

She snorted. "I was going to say richer."

His gaze flicked toward the far end of the bar, where Quinn had reclaimed his stool and his bravado. "I looked up some stuff about him while I was in the waiting room with Connor."

"I did, too. Owns a salvage company."

"And has three mortgages on a beachfront house, two ex-wives, and was pulled over two years ago for a DUI but he beat it and had it expunged from the public record. But not the private one."

She let out a soft laugh. "I forgot you have access to something a little more powerful than Google. So he needs money and has friends in high places."

Peter shrugged. "One enemy, though. Natalie Cartwright."

"Who is?"

"A young pistol who is on the board of the Destin History and Fishing Museum."

She shook her head, conjuring up a mental image of the place. "That little brick building on Stahlman? I always thought it was like a fishing-themed shell shop."

"No, it's the closest thing Destin has to a historical

society," he said. "They preserve and honor the history of the area, specifically waterways and fishing-related areas."

"How do you know this Natalie woman is his enemy?"

Peter hesitated, then said, "Also not on the record."

"My lips are sealed."

"She filed a formal objection when the bridge was flagged for review," he said. "She complained that the bridge qualified as a cultural landmark under county guidelines. She requested a pause, but it got dismissed, ignored, and swept under the rug by...individuals with more power."

"Who are probably all sporting their own Patek watches right now," she muttered.

He lifted a shoulder. "Welcome to small-town politics—graft, corruption, and buried files. I found a deputy's summary from a zoning meeting. Quinn called her 'a nuisance' and said she was 'holding the town hostage with history no one cared about.'"

Vivien felt something settle into place. "I like her already."

"I like anyone who can't be bought," Peter said. "She probably knows more about how this got pushed through."

The bartender asked again if they wanted a drink, but Peter shook his head. Then he glanced toward the door. "You okay to head out? It's loud in here."

"Sure," she said lightly. "Lead the way, Detective. Pretty sure Moneybags picked up this tab."

Outside, the evening had softened into gold and navy. The harbor lights blinked on one by one, reflected in ribbons across the water. The sound of steel drums drifted from somewhere behind them, mingling with the slap of waves against docked boats.

They walked along the boardwalk, passing families licking ice cream cones, a street guitarist plucking something nostalgic, couples on dates.

Peter shoved his hands into his pockets, and Vivien silently put her hopes of "the" conversation to bed.

They stopped at a railing where a narrow pier jutted out over the harbor, taking a moment to inhale the scent of fried shrimp and brackish water.

"You okay?" she asked gently.

He huffed a quiet laugh. "I was about to ask you the same thing."

"I'm fine, but you're not."

He hesitated, then sighed. "Connor's broken wrist is...an issue."

Her heart dipped. "What? Why?"

"We saw an orthopedic specialist this afternoon, which is why I was late."

"And..."

"He confirmed what we knew—a fractured distal radius, a hairline clavicle fracture. But he added something—a brachial plexus stretch injury from the impact."

"And the issue?"

"It's basically a grenade in his plans, life, and upcoming residency," he said humorlessly. "The brachial plexus is a network of nerves that runs from the neck, across the shoulders, and down into the hand. It controls fine motor precision, grip strength, and finger isolation. Even sensation in the fingertips. All of which..."

Her heart dropped. "Matter very much to a dentist."

"Bingo." He winced as it seemed to hit him all over again. "Connor calls it 'millimeter work' and knows that he cannot afford even an occasional misfire in a patient's mouth." He shook his head. "And he admitted to me that his grip fades in fifteen minutes and his fingers 'buzz' at night. And if ignores it, the nerve injury could be permanent."

"*Oof.*" She dropped her head back, knowing that would ruin all his years of education and training before he ever became a dentist. "Can it be fixed? Surgery or rehabilitation?"

"Probably—not definitely, but it will require eight to twelve weeks of specialized hand therapy, which can't even start until he's healed."

"Oh, no. What does that mean for dental school and his residency?"

"He's figuring that out. Defer the residency? Figure out if insurance covers therapy? Run away from his overbearing mother and deal with the guilt for going to a gathering that might have cost him everything?"

"Oh, Peter!" She reached for him. "Poor Connor. He can't feel guilty—he was on the wrong road at the wrong time. It could have happened to anyone. And this isn't the end of his career—it's a roadblock. You'll help him."

Peter rubbed a hand over his jaw. "He wants to power through."

"Not a good idea," she said.

"No kidding. You wouldn't know it from a casual conversation but he's a hard worker, an overachiever. Dr. Dunne warned him in no uncertain terms that if he forces use without therapy and healing, he could turn this into something permanent. He's already practicing with his left hand but that won't cut it as a dentist."

He stared out at the water and she waited, sensing he had more to share.

"And then there's Holly," he said.

The overbearing mother, Vivien thought, but stayed silent.

"She's smothering him and I don't know if he loves it or hates it."

"I can't imagine a twenty-eight-year-old young man wanting to be smothered."

Peter looked dubious. "He did say having us all together makes him feel better. Holly was all over that— practically planning our next family vacation."

"And you..." she ventured. "How do you feel having her there?"

He lifted a shoulder. "There's no...acrimony. That's good. I've always wanted that."

"I know."

He turned and looked at her for the longest time. He didn't speak, but she saw something in his eyes—their connection, their history, their relationship.

She reached for his hand on the railing, resting her fingers on top of his.

He looked down at their hands, then sighed. "I better

get home and see how he's doing," he said. "I'm sorry I sent you on a wild goose chase tonight."

The rejection stung.

"It's fine," she said quickly—much too quickly. "I'm going to contact that Natalie person, if that doesn't overstep law enforcement privacy."

"You can contact her. Her complaint is public, just not how he got around it. Can I walk you to your car, Viv?"

The ending of the evening felt abrupt and forced. Did he know what she was thinking and not want to hear it? Did he *not* know? Maybe he thought he'd overstepped the bounds of their undefined and increasingly complicated friendship?

"Yeah, I'm not far. Thanks."

They walked in silence and she realized just how awkward and strained this moment had become. She hated that.

"You don't have to solve it tonight," she said. "He's safe. He's healing. The rest can unfold."

Peter nodded, though doubt still shadowed his eyes.

"Connor could come by the Summer House," she added. "Anytime. No doctors. No schedules. Just beach and noise and Jonah cooking something ridiculous."

He let out a small laugh. "To get him away from Holly?"

"To give him space to think."

Peter's shoulders eased and he smiled, stopping at her SUV. "Thank you, Viv. I'll tell him."

"You could come, too."

His eyes shuttered. "Yeah, thanks. Really busy with the new job."

"I understand." She unlocked the door and opened it, pausing to look up at him and remember a time not so long ago when they would have kissed goodbye.

Why in God's name had she sent him packing? She should just—

"See ya, Viv." With a nod, he walked away, leaving her standing there sad and wishing she could turn back time.

If not, then she needed to...let go.

"Someday, Vivien Lawson. Someday, you will be over that man."

She watched him disappear around the corner and her heart ached.

Someday. But not today.

Chapter Thirteen
Maggie

Maggie stepped into Barbara's kitchen and stopped short, gasping at the table that looked like a low-budget crime lab.

Papers were everywhere. Sticky notes clung to the edge of the table. Jo Ellen's laptop sat open in the center, screen glowing. Three pens, one highlighter, and a half-eaten blueberry muffin added to the chaos.

Jo Ellen looked up, eyes bright. "Good. You're here. We're in Phase Two."

Oh, goodness. "Phase Two of what?"

"Our investigation."

Maggie eyed the laptop screen. "Is that...Oscar?"

Jo Ellen nodded proudly, her love for the ridiculous AI program obvious. "Well, that book didn't help us." She tossed a dirty look to the bright yellow *Private Investigations for Dummies* tome on the table. "Please, with the triangles of infidelity and stakeout snacks. As if I'd spy without sustenance."

"Not to mention the suggestion that we limp when we're on someone's trail."

"Now that idea I don't hate," Jo Ellen said. "Anthony wouldn't suspect it's you or me if we're limping."

Snorting a dry laugh, Maggie walked to the coffeemaker, thanking tea-drinking Jo Ellen for making it as she poured. After adding cream and sugar, she turned and leaned against the counter.

Phase Two was probably absurd, but they had to do *something*.

"All right. What does Oscar say to do after all these nights of nothing but a man who comes home at seven, talks on the phone for five minutes, takes a shower, eats a sandwich, and goes to bed?"

"Nothing," she said. "But what if the woman he's talking to on the phone is not his wife?"

"It's not. Remember, I called Crista once while he was on the phone and she picked up and mentioned she hadn't heard from Anthony all day."

"Then we don't quit until we know," Jo Ellen said.

Maggie walked to the table and muttered a silent apology to her friend Barbara, whose kitchen was normally immaculate. "What was your...what do you call that again? The thing you tell Oscar to do?"

"My prompt," Jo Ellen supplied. "Get with the new age of technology, Mags."

She rolled her eyes and sipped.

"I asked him how to tell if a man is cheating. I told him everything we know. Including that we're two old ladies in a convertible."

Maggie's mouth tightened. "You did not."

"I didn't have to. He remembers us from Miami." She beamed at the screen. "Oscar is wonderful like that. And he totally understands this situation."

Maggie set her coffee on the counter. "Jo Ellen, we are not outsourcing moral judgment and a plan that could impact my daughter and grandchildren to a *robot*."

Jo Ellen swiveled the laptop toward her. "Maggie. Listen to what he says. 'Considering what you've told me,' she read, "'there is one suspicious data point: a man, alone on a deck at night, laughing on the phone. That is not proof of an affair. It is...a question mark.'"

Maggie blinked. "It took artificial intelligence and a legion of teenage tech bros to tell me it's *a question mark?* God save us all from this beast."

"He's just getting started." Jo Ellen scrolled. "'You are wise and loving grandmothers to worry about your precious family, the legacy that you've built, and the permanence of generations ahead.'"

"What is he doing? Giving us information or trying to get a date?"

Jo Ellen snorted. "They call that 'glazing.' It means he, you know, butters you up."

Maggie closed her eyes. "I am not a piece of toast. Read on."

"'You don't investigate the man first. You investigate the *pattern*. Affairs leave footprints. Not emotional ones—practical ones. They require time, privacy, and opportunity. Which means the guilty party will alter routines.'" Jo Ellen looked smug. "Smart, huh?"

"Brilliant, except Anthony's not guilty," Maggie said. At Jo Ellen's raised brow, she sighed. "Well, his routine hasn't changed."

"Exactly," Jo Ellen said, tapping the screen. "The

robot agrees with you. Listen: 'If those answers remain no, then the phone call may simply be...a phone call.'"

"Oh, I get it, Oscar. We just call Anthony and ask him." Maggie scoffed. "Come on, Jo."

"No, Mags, we don't call Anthony. We call..." Jo Ellen looked at the keyboard and adjusted her glasses, typing quickly. Then she plopped her chin on her knuckles and watched as words filled the page like magic. "Meridian Software, Incorporated," she finally said.

"His company?"

"Yup. Here's the number. We'll ask for a Pamela. Why not?" She held out her hand and snapped her fingers. "Phone? No, no." She patted the table. "He'll know your name or number. Mine will come in as Arthur Wylie. Would he recognize that?"

"Not...instantly." Maggie sat back, eyeing Jo Ellen suspiciously. "What are you about to do?"

"What I do best." She tapped a few more keys. "Lie."

Jo Ellen dialed, clearing her throat, readying for battle. All Maggie could do was...watch and listen since she put the phone on speaker.

"Meridian Software. How may I direct your call?"

"Oh, hello," Jo Ellen cooed. "This is bit of a longshot, but does anyone named Pamela work at your company?"

The receptionist hesitated. "Possibly. Can I ask what this is in reference to?"

"Do you have to?"

Maggie frowned, leaning forward. "Jo—"

She answered with a dramatic "shut up" swipe of her hand.

"I'd like to be sure the call is legitimate," the receptionist added.

"So, you do have a Pamela?" Jo Ellen asked.

"Umm...do you have a last name?"

Jo blew out a breath. "Honestly, I do not. But I met her briefly in line at..." She winced and cringed and looked like she might have gas. "Home Goods," she finally said. "She was buying a..." She looked up at Maggie.

"Pillow?" She mouthed the suggestion.

"A pillow," Jo Ellen said, adding a thumbs-up like she approved Maggie's newfound ability to lie. "A beautiful, bright green...actually, it was kind of lime green, you know? The green equivalent of fuchsia? What's that called? Really bright and blinding?"

Maggie gave her a look. Was she serious?

"Chartreuse?" the receptionist suggested.

"Yes! Velvet chartreuse with, um, balls. Like tiny balls hanging off the end. She bought the last one they had, if you can believe it. And you know Home Goods. There might not be another, so I thought I might call the manufacturer...if Pamela knows it."

Maggie dropped her face in her hands, not sure if she should laugh or cry.

The receptionist was dead silent.

"I mean, do you know how hard it is to find the right shade of green?" Jo Ellen continued. "She mentioned that she worked there at, um, Meridian. In Buckhead. That's where you are, right? She was so nice. Lovely woman."

"You probably mean Pamela Wentworth."

Jo Ellen's eyes popped open like saucers. "Wentworth?"

She and Maggie exchanged uncertain shrugs.

"Um, yes, that might be it," Jo Ellen said. "She just said Pamela and I thought, what a pretty name. That's the only way I could remember it, so...is she there?"

"I'll check to see if she's at her desk. Hang on."

Hold music filled the kitchen as Maggie clunked her elbows on the table. "Now what? Are you going to ask Ms. Wentworth if she's having an affair with Anthony or likes chartreuse pillows?"

The phone clicked.

"Anthony Merritt's office, this is Pamela."

They stared at each other in horror. She *was* Anthony's assistant.

Instantly, Maggie leaned forward. "Hello, this is Magnolia Lawson, Anthony's mother-in-law."

Jo Ellen gasped.

"Oh, hello." Pamela sounded surprised. "The front desk told me—never mind. It must have been a mistake. Do you need to speak with him, Mrs. Lawson? He's not in the office right now, but I'll be seeing him soon, so I can give him a message."

"No, that's not necessary, I just wanted to..." Maggie stalled, her mind skidding. "To tell him—"

"Something," Jo Ellen mouthed, wildly gesturing.

"It's not Nolie, is it?" the woman asked quickly. "She's okay, right?"

Nolie? Why would his assistant care about Nolie? And why did that feel…personal?

"Oh—yes. Everything's fine," Maggie said. "I just wanted to tell him we missed him on the Fourth of July. And Crista is…" She searched for a word. "Glowing."

Across the table, Jo Ellen gave her two more enthusiastic thumbs-up.

"I thought he should know how well his *wife* is doing in Destin," Maggie pressed on, emboldened. "She's thriving. Strong. And—well—pregnant. Very pregnant."

Pamela laughed softly. "I know."

The pause that followed was loaded, and both women were weighing it.

"He's out with a customer all day, but I'll be sure to tell him when I see him for dinner," Pamela said lightly.

Maggie's hand tightened around the phone. "Dinner?" she tried not to choke on the word.

"I doubt he'll call in, but I'll get the message to him after his meetings are done."

When they have dinner together.

"Thank you," she said, far too quickly. "Goodbye."

She pulled the phone away as if it might bite her.

"You need to know when to stop, Mags," Jo Ellen said. "The glowing-and-pregnant monologue? Too far."

"She needed to know his wife is pregnant," Maggie said—though her pulse was still racing. "But, oh. That lying is exhausting. I don't know how you do it."

"Practice," Jo Ellen said, standing. "So now we have a plan."

"We do?"

"We're going to follow Pamela to dinner."

"We are?" Maggie shook her head. "We don't even know what she looks like."

"We don't, but..." She clicky-clacked on the keyboard. "Pamela Wentworth...gimme a sec...come on, Oscar. Oh, here we go."

"Is that her?" Maggie asked, leaning forward in shock.

"According to LinkedIn, this is Pamela Wentworth, senior administrative assistant at Meridian Software. Yikes. Look at her. Nothing 'senior' about that babe."

Maggie groaned as she got a good look at a woman who appeared to be about twenty-five with long, honey blond hair, huge eyes, and a smile that would light up Atlanta.

"Holy...cow."

"Please, that picture is Photoshopped to death," Jo Ellen announced. "No one's skin looks like that IRL."

"IRL?"

"In real life," she explained like a teenager exasperated with aging parents. "We have plenty of time, but we should be outside the office building early or we can sit in the lobby. Whatever. We'll case the joint, find our target, and follow her as long as we can. And we'll bring Oscar. He's amazing, isn't he?"

Maggie lifted the yellow book, feeling as dumb as the "Dummies" it was written for. "At least he didn't suggest we limp."

Jo Ellen shot a brow. "If we follow, we limp. That's the rule."

Maggie closed her eyes. "I hate you."

"Inconspicuous? Does the word mean nothing to you?" Maggie waved the scarf that Jo Ellen had produced from her bag, watching in horror as she pulled out giant sunglasses. "It's late afternoon—"

"In the summer, sun's still out." Jo Ellen slid hers on. "Fab, huh?"

"I'm *not* wearing sunglasses or a scarf."

"Maggie, you have short silver hair, high cheekbones, and a very distinctive look," Jo Ellen insisted. "It's entirely possible that Anthony has a picture of you on his desk at work."

"Unlikely."

"Impossible?"

She conceded with a tip of her head, but she doubted it.

"What if he sees us?" Jo Ellen continued, wrapping the scarf around her head. "How do we explain why we're gallivanting around Buckhead? We need to blend in."

"You think he won't notice me in...*this*?" Maggie flicked the silk.

"I gave you the Hermes," Jo said on a sigh. "And I took the one I bought with Artie in Hawaii." She tied her scarf, which covered her hair with a splash of bright pink hibiscus. Maggie's was a much more subtle navy blue with the signature chain design.

It really *was* Hermes, which was sweet, and slightly more acceptable. Maggie took it, and the sunglasses.

"Ridiculous," she muttered, turning to the ten-story building with a bank on the ground floor. "His office is on the fifth floor, as I recall, and the only way to get out of this building is through this lobby and out those doors. Now, once she does that, she could go to one of three parking garages, so what do we do?"

"We follow on foot or by car." Jo Ellen looked up and down Lenox Road. "She could go into either of these giant malls. And there are a bunch of restaurants down that street. I just really don't want to give up this parking spot, since it took us an hour to get it. But who knows? She could drive off to some motel and—"

"Stop." Maggie pulled the scarf on with force. "He's not cheating on her."

"Oh, you're back on Team Anthony?"

"I've never been *off* his team," Maggie insisted. "I was miffed about my roses, but since we sneaked over there the other day and did some pruning, I feel better. He's busy. Crista's pregnant. And Nolie's a kid. Bottom line? They're *my* roses and he's got no one to help with them."

"I love when you have a forgiving heart, Mags."

"Don't count on it." Maggie slid the silly sunglasses on and squinted through them at the bustling shops and offices of Buckhead, half-regretting this fool's errand.

"Maggie!" Jo Ellen grabbed her hand. "Look. Is that her?"

She peered at a young woman in skinny dark trousers, high heels, and a yellow and black top.

"She looks like a bumble bee," Maggie muttered. "But, yes, with that hair? It could be her."

"Are we sure?" Jo Ellen leaned forward, a hand on Maggie's arm. "We have to be ready—to walk or drive. Are you?"

"Just watch her. She's coming closer."

The woman strolled, pulled out her phone, read it, and slowed her step to tap the screen.

"This feels so..." Maggie made a face. "Intrusive."

"Do you want to catch him or not?" Jo pressed.

"Not," Maggie answered.

Jo Ellen stared at her. "You don't?"

"I want him to be innocent, Jo. I don't want him to be having an affair with her."

They both stared at the woman in question, who dropped her phone in her bag, and strolled to the cross-walk, pausing to wait for the light.

"She's walking!" Jo Ellen announced like Maggie was blind. "Bumble Bee is on the move."

"Bumble Bee?"

"Code name," Jo Ellen explained as she gathered her bag and opened the T-Bird's door. "You know, we're like the Secret Service and the CIA."

"Just," Maggie said dryly, slamming her door as she stepped onto the sidewalk. "You've lost your mind."

"Just don't lose Bumble Bee," she said, giving Maggie a nudge toward their target. "She's a fast walker, even in those shoes."

"And we've got a combined age of over one hundred

and fifty, so if you don't want to be taking a detour to the ER, slow down, Jo Ellen Wylie."

"Okay, okay." She slid her arm under Maggie's. "I got you."

"You're as old as I am," Maggie muttered.

"Just move and don't lose sight of her."

"As if I could in that screaming yellow top."

The young woman turned on the next street, making Maggie hope she was headed for the closest restaurant. She passed a sushi place—thank you, Lord. Maggie hated the smell of the stuff—and an eyeglass store, a jewelry store, and a café.

"Where is she going?" Jo Ellen whined.

Finally, she paused, turned on a side street, and disappeared.

"Faster, Mags! We don't want to lose her."

Maggie picked up the pace, considered swearing under her breath, and squeezed Jo's arm.

"Southern ladies do not run in public, Jo Ellen."

"Well, we Yankee girls can make time. Move it, Mama."

They whipped around the corner, catching sight of the Bee disappearing into a store. Reaching it, they both paused as they looked at the sign.

"Second Skin?" Jo Ellen read. "What is...*oh.*"

"Yeah, oh." Maggie bit her lip and peered into the pink-hued display window where three faceless mannequins wore...not much. Something black, something pink, something...that could bring a married man to his knees.

"Buying an outfit for after dinner?" Jo Ellen mused while Maggie grunted. "Come on, Mags, let's go in."

"And do what? Shop?"

"Spy!" She yanked the heavy glass door open and stepped into a surprisingly large boutique. Instantly, the outside world disappeared.

The air seemed hushed inside, as if all the silk, satin, and sin absorbed the noise. Wide-plank pale oak floors felt warm underneath low lighting designed to flatter every skin tone.

They spotted Bumble Bee toward the back, perusing a display of underwear that could also function as shoelaces. They hovered behind a rack of silk camisoles in colors that looked like Easter candy.

Ready to be...nibbled.

"Act casual," Jo Ellen murmured, sliding the hangers as if she fully intended to pick a camisole to wear.

Bumble Bee moved to a bra display, lifting a scrap of white lace with padding, examining it with interest. Maggie squinted.

"A Kleenex would be cheaper," she whispered. "And cover more."

"Hush," Jo Ellen said. "She's talking."

A young sales associate had drifted up to Bumble Bee and smiled. "That one's one of our most popular styles," the woman said warmly. "Very minimal, but incredibly comfortable."

Minimal was one word for it.

"Do you have it in a thirty-two B?" Bumble Bee asked.

Maggie's eyes widened. "Thirty-*two*?" she mouthed.

Jo Ellen slapped her arm.

"We do," the associate said. "And if you're looking for something special, we also have the absolutely most delectable matching thong for a set."

Bumble Bee tilted her head, considering the suggestion. "I do have a...hot date tonight."

Maggie felt the words like a stab in the heart.

"Well, then," the associate said, smiling conspiratorially, "you'll definitely want something that feels good all night."

Jo Ellen leaned closer. "Did you hear that? *All night.*"

"I heard it," Maggie said. "I'm not deaf, I'm just old."

The associate gestured toward the fitting rooms. "If you'd like to try it on, I can set you up in one of our larger rooms."

"Yes, let's do that," Bumble Bee said. "I want to be comfortable. And confident."

Maggie closed her eyes. "Well," she said quietly, "good for her."

"That's it?" Jo Ellen hissed. "That's all you've got?"

"What would you like me to say, Jo Ellen? That I hope she chafes?"

Jo Ellen considered that. "A little."

They shuffled sideways as Bumble Bee disappeared behind a curtain. Jo Ellen craned her neck.

"Can we move closer without looking suspicious?" Jo Ellen asked.

"Pretty sure that ship has sailed, Jo."

They repositioned near a display of robes—blessedly opaque—and pretended to examine the fabric.

"Hot date," Jo Ellen whispered again. "That seals it."

Maggie couldn't argue.

The fitting room curtain rustled. Bumble Bee stepped out, fully dressed again, holding a small stack of items. The associate followed her toward the register.

"I'll take these," Bumble Bee said. "And, oh, use this card." She laughed softly and handed over a silver card. "He's paying."

Jo Ellen gulped noisily. And all Maggie could think about was...the new secret debit card that Crista mentioned.

As the sales associate rang everything up, Bumble Bee stared at her phone, unaware her every move was being tracked.

"Have a wonderful evening," the clerk said when she finished.

"Oh, I plan to," Bumble Bee replied with a laugh. She turned, looking down, and walked straight into Maggie.

"Oh! I'm so sorry," Bumble Bee said, stepping back. "My bad."

Yes, you are bad, Maggie thought as she gave a death stare, looking right into her overly-made-up green eyes and down to her black soul.

The young woman returned a shaky smile, clearly intimidated. "Excuse me," she whispered, sidestepping Maggie. "My car is here."

As she sailed by and out the door, the words registered—her car?

Sharing a quick look, Maggie and Jo Ellen went straight after her, stepping outside just as the woman climbed into the backseat of a dark sedan.

"It's an Uber," Jo Ellen said. "We'll never follow her now."

"But do we have to? She didn't look exactly like that picture. What if it wasn't her?"

On a frustrated sigh, they retraced their steps to the T-bird, neither saying a word about their abject failure to gain concrete evidence that could save Anthony.

"Let's just go home," Maggie said as she fished out her keys

"Okay. We can—" Jo Ellen went silent and froze. "Maggie. Look."

She followed her friend's gaze and landed on...a completely different honey-blonde coming out of the building where her son-in-law worked. She wore a simple cream sundress and carried a tote bag, looking far more professional than the first girl.

"Could *that* be Pamela?" Jo Ellen asked.

Of course it could be.

The woman dashed to a cab, climbed in, and off she went too fast for them to possibly follow.

"We could have been following the wrong girl," Jo Ellen said as they pulled on their seatbelts to drive home. "Sorry."

"It's not your fault," Maggie assured her. "These blonde Gen-whatevers all look alike. I want to get home before it's dark. I'm exhausted."

Six hours later, Maggie was still exhausted. She was

sick of talking about the two girls, sick of worrying about her daughter's marriage, and beyond sick of staying in a stranger's house.

Still, she couldn't sleep because she watched the street constantly and never saw Anthony's car. Did that mean he hadn't come home?

She didn't know but wanted to.

At four in the morning, she lost the battle. She slipped into sneakers and stepped into the dark of night, doing a little of her own sleuthing without the resident expert. No code name, no disguises, no limping.

She had to know if that lingerie was making an appearance in Crista's bedroom or if Anthony was MIA. She had to.

Crista's house was pitch-black inside, but Maggie was determined. She walked up the driveway and peered into the window of the side door, which gave her a perfect view into the garage.

The empty garage.

Anthony hadn't come home.

Chapter Fourteen
Tessa

Tessa sat on the edge of Olive's toddler bed, the small lamp on the dresser casting a circle of light over the bedding and the stuffed animals lined up like an audience. Olive—freshly bathed, already in pajamas—sat near the pillow, calm and watchful, her attention fixed on the open book in Tessa's hands.

Ten days and she'd yet to say one word.

On the floor, Dusty leaned back against the low bed rail, close enough to see the pages. One arm rested loosely across his bent knee, the other reaching up now and then to point at a picture.

Tessa swallowed something tender in her throat, looked down at the cover of *Goodnight Moon,* their final read for the night.

Of course, she had no idea if Olive had ever seen the book before, but she'd bought it at a used bookstore a few days earlier. The spine was worn, the corners soft from years of loving use by children whose names Tessa would never know. She traced her thumb along the edge for a moment before opening it.

Pajamas. Bedtime. A book.

By now, they'd developed a routine—Dusty cleaned

up after dinner while Tessa gave Olive a bath, then they read her a book and said goodnight.

He seemed perfectly comfortable with Olive's silence, certain that at some point she'd speak, always assuring Tessa that she wasn't doing anything wrong.

Tessa so hoped he was right because with each passing day, she doubted herself more. Even silent, Olive was sweet and enchanting. She rarely cried. She slept all night. She wasn't remotely potty-trained but seemed fine with the pull-up diapers. She did everything with precision and care, as if she didn't trust the world around her.

And that just broke Tessa's heart.

"Okay," she said softly, more to herself than to Olive. "Ready?"

Olive didn't respond, but her gaze followed as Tessa opened the book.

"'In the great green room,'" Tessa began, her voice low and gentle, "'there was a telephone...'"

She pointed to the picture as she read, tapping lightly so Olive's eyes could track the movement.

"Which doesn't look like any telephone I've seen lately," Dusty cracked, smiling up at them.

Tessa laughed and continued, "'And a red balloon.'"

Dusty leaned back and looked at Olive. "That balloon looks like it's about to get into trouble," he murmured, barely above a whisper.

Tessa smiled despite herself. "'And a picture of...' What do you think that is, Olive?"

Silence.

"'The cow jumping over the moon,'" Dusty finished quietly, pointing.

Tessa paused again, leaving space the way she'd learned to do, just from gut instinct that developed while caring for a little human who did not, under any circumstances, respond with words. Looks, gestures, nods and headshakes, but no speech.

She glanced at Olive, hopeful, searching.

Olive's eyes stayed on the page and Tessa kept reading.

She noticed the way Olive's gaze followed her finger, and the way her breathing stayed even, the way her body remained relaxed but alert.

Still, she longed for something—any word from her tiny ward. As much as she told herself not to push, the hope lived there anyway, pressing against her ribs.

As she read, she allowed the weight of the moment to sink in. Reading to Olive, especially with Dusty beside her, felt deeply...domestic. Like something she should have been doing for years—even now, when she was nearly old enough to be a grandmother.

The realization hit slowly, then all at once. She'd never done the parenting thing, unless she counted visits with Kate's kids when they were little.

She'd always been off chasing a good time, thinking this was the definition of boring and slow. Yet, here it was, anything but boring or slow. Well, *Goodnight Moon* wasn't exactly riveting, but hanging on to the hope that Olive would whisper something sure was.

Still, she had never experienced these nightly rituals.

These quiet, ordinary moments that stitched a family together over time.

Her brain wandered back to Roman—the child she'd never raised—imagining him as a two-year-old.

She knew she'd made the right choice in giving that little baby to a set of parents who'd longed for one. She had never doubted that. But that didn't erase the ache that came in these quiet moments with Olive.

"'Goodnight kittens,'" she read. "'And goodnight mittens.'"

"Have you ever owned mittens, Olive?" Dusty asked, holding out his hand. "We don't wear them much in Florida."

Olive stared at the page.

Tessa caught Dusty's quiet sigh confirming that even his marvelous patience was wearing thin. Didn't matter— he had top-notch Dad skills, something she added to the growing list of things she really liked about Dusty Mathers.

Tessa pointed to the moon on the page. "Moon," she said slowly, clearly. "Do you see the moon, sweet Olive?"

She nodded, proving she understood so much.

As the story neared its end, Olive's body began to soften. She leaned back slightly against the pillow. Her eyes blinked slowly, lids growing heavy. Her breathing deepened, and Tessa watched her alertness give way to sleep.

She finished the book quietly, her voice barely above a whisper.

"'Goodnight noises everywhere.'" She closed the

book gently and set it on the nightstand. She smoothed the blanket over Olive, tucking it carefully around her small body. Olive's eyes fluttered, then stilled.

Tessa leaned in.

"Sleep tight, little Olive Oyl," she whispered, so softly it felt like a secret.

For just a moment, she let herself hope again. But Olive didn't respond. She drifted off, her face relaxed, her body slack with sleep. Tessa stayed there longer than necessary, watching her breathe.

Dusty's hand came to rest on her back, warm and steady, like he understood exactly what she was feeling without needing her to explain it.

The ache returned, sharp and familiar—the motherhood she'd never experienced layered with this new, fragile affection for the child sleeping inches away.

Dusty nodded gently toward the door, and they moved carefully out of the room, letting him snap the baby gate into place. Tessa leaned against the wall, troubled and wistful all at once.

"You're doing a great job," Dusty said quietly.

"Maybe we should take her to your friend, the expert," she said.

"Not yet. Give it some time. She knows she's in a safe place and that is all that matters now."

Tessa swallowed, emotion welling. "It doesn't feel like enough."

"It is," he said, his tone steady and sure. "I promise you."

"Moments like that are hard for me," she admitted.

"Because I never got to be a mom." She took a breath. "And now I have this chance to be...something. And I keep thinking her silence means I'm failing."

Dusty shook his head. "That's not what it means." He grazed her cheek with his knuckles, his touch sure and loving. "She feels your care. Even if she doesn't say it."

Tessa let out a small, shaky laugh. "No wonder you're such a good therapist."

His mouth curved into a soft smile. "This isn't therapy."

She looked up at him, sensing the moment deepening between them. It had been a long time since they'd had a midnight wine on the roof or shared a meal punctuated with kisses or even walked the beach at sunset, hand in hand.

In the time since Olive arrived, their rhythm had shifted to something very different, something she genuinely enjoyed, despite her concerns for Olive.

"What?" he asked, searching her face.

"I was just thinking how much I like you," she confessed. "Right here, in the hall, on the heels of *Goodnight Moon.*"

"That's funny," he said, lowering his face to brush her lips with his. "I was just thinking how much I..."

He didn't finish and Tessa didn't breathe. Instead, she held his gaze, forgetting everything else in the world but this kind and good and wise man.

"Yes?" she prompted when he didn't finish.

"I like you, too," he finished, then laughed. "Which sounds lame."

"Not to me."

"C'mon, Tess." He cupped her cheek, drawing her close. "I sailed past like a while ago."

"You did?" Her heart tumbled all over the place. "And where'd you land, Dusty?"

Closing his eyes, he leaned in and kissed her lips. "Right here," he murmured against her mouth. "With you, the woman I..." He chuckled and sighed. "I'm as bad as Olive."

She inhaled and pressed against him. "Just say what you're thinking."

"I'm thinking that I'm falling in love with you, Tessa."

She melted, tightening her grip. "Does that terrify or thrill you?" she asked on a whisper.

"It shocks the life out of me," he said. "I didn't...think I'd..."

He didn't expect to love again after his wife died two years ago.

"I didn't, either," she finished for him. "To be perfectly real, I can't remember the last time I felt like this."

Smiling, he kissed her forehead and she leaned into him, frustration fading into contentment.

Tessa was dead asleep when a completely unfamiliar

sound cut through the silence of her home. Was that...an animal outside? A kid in the street? A—

She snapped awake so abruptly her heart slammed against her ribs before her mind caught up. For a second, she lay there, disoriented, her body tense, listening.

The sound came again.

A cry.

Sharp. High. Frightened.

Olive.

Tessa was out of bed instantly, not thinking as she shot toward the other bedroom, the cry pulling her forward like a physical force. The hallway blurred as she rushed down it, bare feet silent against the floor, her focus narrowing to one thing and one thing only—to help Olive.

The crying grew louder, more desperate, and Tessa's chest tightened as she reached the doorway and fumbled with the gate, the movement turning on the nightlight.

Olive sat upright in the toddler bed, hunched over, bawling. She looked up and her face was flushed, her breathing uneven and shaky little gasps breaking through the sobs. She looked lost in it, overwhelmed, her small body rigid with fear.

"Oh, Olive, honey!" Tessa breathed.

She crossed the room in two steps and dropped to her knees beside the bed. She said Olive's name softly, again and again, reaching for her hands, her arms, trying to ground her.

"What's wrong, sweetheart?" she murmured. "I'm here. I've got you."

Olive didn't answer but cried on, shoulders trembling, her distress filling the small room.

Standing, Tessa scooped up the child, grateful Olive didn't resist. If anything, she clung—small hands fisting in Tessa's T-shirt, her body pressing close as if she'd been waiting to be held.

The crying didn't stop, but it lost some of its sharpness as Tessa snuggled her close, swaying in a way that seemed freakishly natural, stroking her back with calming words.

"It's okay," Tessa whispered as she rocked. "It's okay. Did you have a bad dream? Does something hurt?"

No response. No words. Just crying.

After a few minutes, certain she wasn't sick or hurt, Tessa lowered them both to the tiny bed, checking instinctively for signs of pain.

"Nothing hurts? Your tummy? Your head? Your teeny-tiny toes?" She playfully squeezed one of Olive's bare feet, but she didn't smile. She just snuggled closer, which was remarkable.

"I bet you had a bad dream, huh?" Cooing about it, Tessa maneuvered carefully and curled herself on the undersized mattress with Olive. The space was small, barely enough room, but she tucked herself around the little girl, drawing the blanket up over them both, creating a cocoon.

On a shuddering sigh, Olive settled more fully against her chest.

The crying softened and the panic seemed to ebb. It was replaced by hitching sobs and a few hiccups that gradually slowed as Tessa rubbed small circles on her back, steady and rhythmic.

"I've got you," Tessa murmured. "You're safe. You're not alone."

She kept talking, proceeding on an instinct she didn't know she had, keeping her voice low and even, filling the quiet.

"I'm right here," she continued softly. "Nothing bad is happening. You're safe in your room. I'm with you."

Olive's breathing began to even out, the sharp edges dulling into quiet sniffles. Her body stayed tense, but the terror loosened its grip.

At that thought, somewhere, deep in the recesses of her memory, Tessa flashed back to childhood. Kate used to wake up in the middle of the night with something her father called "night terrors."

Tessa remembered that the expression scared her, but sweet old Artie—well, Dad was probably pretty young then—always came into their room and whispered a story to Kate to calm her down.

She could hear his voice, remembered the sound of it from the other bed—they had twin beds in a pink room upstairs in the old house in Ithaca—when she'd been awakened by Kate's unhinged crying.

Dad had always shown up instantly, sat on Kate's bed, gentle, calm, unhurried. He never got mad, he never reprimanded her for waking the house, he just started with...

Once upon a time.

Maybe not the most original opening, but just hearing his voice in her head made her smile.

"Once upon a time," Tessa started, realizing—like Artie Wylie probably had—she had no earthly idea where she was going with this story. "There was a little princess named...Olive."

The shivering eased.

"She lived in a castle," Tessa continued. "A big, beautiful...sandcastle." She added the slightest squeeze, hoping to remind Olive of the ones she herself had made. "It had jewels on the walls and a big drawbridge and... handsome knights and one really...big..."

Big *what?* She winced and dug.

"Mirror! A magic mirror!" Yes, that would work. "In Princess Olive's room, there was a magic mirror and whenever she looked in the mirror, she..."

Olive looked up, as if she were following every word and waiting with bated breath to see what the magic mirror could do.

"She sang," Tessa finished, pretty proud of that option. "Her voice was like an angel in heaven, soft and sweet, and when she sang..."

Now what? She looked at the bed, making out the shape of her stuffies.

"All of her stuffed animals came to life." She spoke slowly, soothingly, letting the words roll out as they came. "Princess Olive was brave," she continued. "And kind. And very, very smart."

She felt Olive's breathing slow further, her small body pressing warm and solid against her.

"The castle had towers and walls and secret rooms. And the sand was always just the right kind—never too dry, never too wet." She described it in detail, letting herself improvise freely.

Olive shifted slightly, then stilled again.

Tessa kept going, not stopping, letting the story flow. No wicked witch, no Prince Charming. In this story, the heroine had a perfect life, she was always safe, and her animals adored her.

Olive's eyes widened, giving Tessa the confidence she needed to continue with a story. Stuffed animals came to life, they danced, they surrounded Princess Olive, and made sure her life was perfect. And they went with her to the beach and collected shells and made her jewelry, and when she was sad, they made her laugh...

Olive sighed into what had to be sleep about ten minutes into the rambling tale.

Tessa let her voice trail off and shifted slightly, adjusting the blanket, careful not to disturb Olive more than necessary. She felt the little girl's grip loosen just a bit, her body relaxing incrementally.

Earlier, reading in the lamplight, the domestic quiet had opened old wounds. It had brought regret. Loss. The ache of motherhood she'd never lived.

This—this didn't hurt at all. In fact, she wasn't thinking about Roman. She wasn't thinking about what she'd missed or what she'd never had.

She was here, holding this child who desperately needed her, feeling wonderfully maternal.

Tessa kept stroking Olive's hair, her back, and when Olive stirred, she continued the story.

Princess Olive exploring her castle. Princess Olive knowing she was loved. Princess Olive safe and warm and protected through the night.

Gradually, Olive's grip loosened completely. Her breathing became slow and even, the tension draining from her small body.

Tessa whispered until Olive's eyes fluttered, nearly asleep, her face pressed against Tessa's chest.

After what must have been another twenty minutes, she eased away, ready to let her sleep. As she did, Olive's tiny hand reached up and grabbed her T-shirt, pulling her closer.

"Are you still awake, baby?"

Two blue eyes opened and looked right at Tessa, the connection palpable and real.

"Do you want me to stay longer?"

She just stared at Tessa, sleep weighing down her lids.

"I'll let you go night-night," Tessa said, leaning over to kiss her head. "Sweet dreams, Princess Olive."

She snuggled into the blankets, then blinked. "Love you, Tess."

Tessa's entire body went still, her breath catching hard in her chest. For a split second, she didn't dare move, afraid any reaction would break the moment.

Emotion surged up her throat, hot and overwhelming, but she swallowed it down, forcing herself to stay calm.

"I love you, too," she whispered back, steady despite the way her heart was pounding.

Olive didn't respond but slipped fully into sleep, her face relaxed, peaceful.

Tessa stayed curled there, holding her, the moment completely and utterly wonderful.

It was only later, when Tessa climbed back into bed and let her head hit the pillow, that she realized two people had professed love for her in the same day.

Now *that* was a good day.

Chapter Fifteen
Lacey

Lacey woke to her phone buzzing on the nightstand, the sound sharp and intrusive against the soft hush of early morning. For one disoriented second, she thought it might be Roman—some sweet, sleepy message about the drive, about coffee, about Jacksonville and the day they had planned.

Then she saw the name on the screen.

Tessa.

Her stomach dropped before she even answered. She was supposed to have today off.

She slid quietly out of bed, careful not to wake her mother—she really did need to change her living situation one way or the other—and padded across the room toward the balcony doors.

The sky beyond the glass was just beginning to lighten, that pale, silvery-blue moment before sunrise fully commits. Lacey stepped outside, pulling the door shut behind her and wrapping her arms around herself as she answered.

"Hey," she said softly.

"Oh, thank God you're awake." Tessa's voice sounded

rushed, breathless, already wound tight. "I thought you might have left for your trip to Jacksonville."

"Not for a while. Why?"

"Look, I know I gave you the day off, but..."

Lacey closed her eyes. "Tess—"

"I just can't do the Tidewater Estate walkthrough. And the couple is only in town today."

A wedding walkthrough? She and Roman were leaving at eleven for Jacksonville and a walkthrough of their own. He'd scheduled a meeting to see a gorgeous downtown penthouse apartment close to the stadium and the airport with a move-in date of August 1st. It wouldn't last if they didn't decide today.

"But I—"

"I know, I know, I promised you two days, and I will totally make it up to you, Lace. But I cannot leave this... child."

Lacey blinked. "The one you're babysitting for Dusty's client?"

"Yes, and she's..." Tessa let out a sigh unlike any Lacey had ever heard from her. "It's a long and private story, as you know. But we—I, actually—had a break-through last night and I think it would be...no, no, I *know* it would be a bad time for me to leave her."

Lacey leaned against the railing, the morning Gulf view forgotten as disappointment and frustration clawed all over her. The irony was she'd wanted desperately to do the Tidewater Estate walkthrough with Tessa for the experience.

If they got that job, it could open up a whole motherlode of wedding planning projects, a business they knew could be their bread and butter. But Roman had worked this schedule out to the minute.

"I was going to get your signed football while I was there," Lacey said, knowing it sounded lame, but longing for Tessa to change her mind.

"I know, but Seamus would be happy with a football at Walmart that Roman autographed. This wedding walk-through is important, too, and a great opportunity for you."

Lacey squeezed her eyes as worlds collided, sensing this wouldn't be the first or last time if she tried to "do both" the way she'd hoped to. She knew it would be difficult to navigate working for Tessa from Jacksonville, even if it meant a lot of travel, but she didn't want to give up either dream.

Okay, Lace, think.

"What time is the walkthrough?" she asked.

"At nine, so just over two hours."

Oof. She'd need to get there, be back, and at Roman's house by eleven. Maybe eleven-thirty.

"Lacey, I wouldn't ask if this weren't important," she said in a hushed whisper. "I was up all night with her and she..." After a long pause, she whispered, "I can't explain it all, but believe me, if I could go, I would."

Lacey believed her. Tessa had been acting very differently—when Lacey even saw her—since the child came to stay with her. Out of love and respect, Lacey hadn't asked any questions or breathed a word to anyone else to maintain Dusty's patient's privacy.

Thinking, she glanced back through the glass at the bedroom she shared with her mother, then out again at the water.

"I can do it, Tess," she said quietly. "I'll...juggle my schedule."

"You are a dream employee," Tessa said on a relieved laugh. "Remember, Rachel Fairchild comes from old money—with the emphasis on *money*. They will spend a fortune on this wedding, and our commission and fee will be the biggest Tessa Wylie Events has had to date. Trust me, I'd love to handle this, but you're totally up for the task."

Lacey nodded to herself, still trying to wrestle the timing. "No chance we can get them there earlier?"

"Tidewater won't open the door before nine," she said.

"That's fine," Lacey assured her. "I'll do it. I don't want to let you down."

"You'll slay this," Tessa promised. "You just go out there and be the face of Tessa Wylie Events. You're ready for this, Lacey. I know you are."

She wanted this challenge—had longed for the chance to really take ownership of one major event without Tessa making the final call on every decision. And she had a raise, a promotion, and endless possibilities.

She also had love, an NFL-playing boyfriend, and the opportunity for a life with him in Jacksonville.

"I can do it," she said, the words tumbling out with

force and certainty. "I'll see if I can push the trip with Roman back a few hours."

There was a brief pause on the other end of the line.

"You're sure?" Tessa asked.

"Yes," Lacey said, forcing confidence into her voice. "I won't let you down. You can count on me."

"Oh, thank you," Tessa breathed. "You're a lifesaver. Just—wow them. Please. The bride knows every rich girl in the South, and this could lead to a ton of business."

The call ended, and Lacey stayed there for a moment longer, phone pressed to her palm, the morning air cool against her skin.

She could do this. She'd call Roman and explain it to him, certain they could adjust the schedule a bit.

Her mother stirred when Lacey slipped back into the bedroom.

"Everything okay?" her mother murmured sleepily.

"I've got a venue walkthrough this morning," Lacey said quietly as she dressed. "Tessa needs me to handle it. *Alone.*"

"Is this the big wedding at Tidewater? Tessa is so excited about that."

At the ensuite door, Lacey nodded. "Huge wedding, huge budget, huge opportunity—for me, now."

"Wonderful, honey." Vivien sat up, more awake now. "Weren't you going to Jacksonville with Roman today?"

"I am," she said, longing to get inside the bathroom. Her mother knew about the trip—but not about the apartment. Lacey wanted to make a decision before announcing the news to her. "I'll handle it. It's all good."

"Then I'll make you coffee and let you get ready in peace." Her mother climbed out of bed and for a moment, Lacey considered sharing her dilemma.

But she was twenty-five. Regardless of the fact that she was bunking with her mother, at some point, she had to make life decisions alone, right? Especially one of this magnitude.

She smiled. "Thanks, Mom. I do want to look sensational for this one."

Almost two hours later, Lacey was certain she'd pulled off sensational—in cream silk pants and a pale blue shell and matching sweater—as she spotted the entrance of one of the most beautiful venues in the whole 30A and Panhandle area.

The Tidewater Estate was set far back from the road, the long drive winding beneath live oaks draped in Spanish moss, the world growing quieter with every curve. The main house rose ahead like something out of a Southern novel—white brick, wide wraparound porches, tall columns standing proud against the morning sky.

Beyond it, the Gulf shimmered.

The place was big, but a walkthrough wouldn't take more than an hour...right? She'd have some time to answer questions for the bride and groom, and zip back to Roman's house by...she cringed.

Eleven-thirty. He said they had to leave by then to make the appointment, and they would.

She let out a breath, then checked her phone again anyway, as if time might suddenly jump forward without telling her. It hadn't. She still had room. She just needed everything to move efficiently.

Kendra Sharpe, the venue event coordinator, met her near the front steps right on time, polished and composed in a navy sheath dress, hair swept back in a low, professional knot. She had the cool, competent air of someone who had walked this property hundreds of times and never once worried about how long it took.

"Morning," Kendra said warmly. "They should be here any minute."

"Perfect," Lacey replied, giving her best calm smile as they exchanged niceties about the property, the weather, the wedding...and time ticked.

Right before nine, a sleek black sedan pulled up the drive. Punctual—thank goodness.

Rachel Fairchild stepped out first, tall and graceful, her dress understated but unmistakably expensive—linen, maybe silk, something that moved beautifully when she walked.

Sebastian Crawford followed, equally composed, tailored slacks, pressed button-down, shoes that probably were handmade in Italy. They looked like people who belonged in places like this. People who were used to being impressed—and unimpressed.

People who didn't rush *anything*.

Lacey straightened her shoulders as introductions were made, more *endless* pleasantries were exchanged, and finally they began walking, letting Kendra do her spiel.

From the start, the questions came quickly—and thoroughly.

Sebastian wanted to know about operations. Valet parking options. Guest arrival timing. Vendor access points. How many shuttle buses could fit on the drive at once?

Rachel, meanwhile, slowed at every turn, taking in the space. She asked about how guests would *feel* moving from ceremony to cocktail hour. Where the light would be at sunset. How the sound of the Gulf carried on still evenings.

All legitimate concerns for any six-figure event, Lacey reminded herself.

Kendra fielded most of the questions, with Lacey chiming in on wedding planning logistics, stressing their capability to keep things moving, anticipate problems, and know how to solve them.

Every few minutes, she surreptitiously checked her open tablet screen to see the time flying by.

They reached the gardens, and, whoa, things got slow.

Rachel drifted from one plant to the next, phone out, taking photo after photo—close-ups of blooms, wide shots of the lawn sloping toward the Gulf, finding angles no professional photographer had probably considered.

She crouched. She stood. She circled back and took the same picture again from a slightly different perspective. And, goodness, she *drawled* on and on with her sweet Carolina accent and her careful, deliberate moves.

"Oh, this would be stunning," Rachel murmured. "Just stunning."

Sebastian powered on about logistics.

"What about noise restrictions after ten?" he asked. "County ordinance?"

Kendra answered smoothly, outlining the cutoff times, the decibel limits.

"And transportation?" he continued. "Guests will imbibe, so we want shuttles. Can they idle here?"

"Yes," Kendra said. "Within reason."

Lacey added, "We can coordinate silent dancing with rented headsets."

"We've been to a wedding at a winery with that," he said. "Great fun."

"And no violating ordinances for our neighbors," Kendra added, launching into a story about a wedding last week that just...took too long to tell.

The garden tour stretched on, and Rachel focused on florals—what was native, what could be brought in, and could they move the sea oats for better water views?

Move the sea oats?

Kendra just smiled at that one while Lacey stole a glance at the time, her heart dropping as she realized they were way past an hour now and pushing two.

Sebastian had a whole new set of practical questions regarding security, timing, and the possibility of arriving or leaving by helicopter.

Seriously?

Meanwhile, Rachel paused at each transition path, testing the walk in heels, asking what happened if the ground was wet. If it rained. If the wind picked up. If the *sky fell.*

Kendra calmly—and slowly—explained everything. Lacey was grateful for her knowledge, but it was thorough enough that she could give the tour next time. And each explanation took forever and generated ten new questions and endless discussions.

She could feel time evaporate—not just intellectually, but physically. At one point, she just gave up the fight. That trip, that apartment, that day in Jacksonville, five hours away, might not happen today.

Lacey's tablet flashed with a new message from Roman.

How's it going? Still going to make 11:30?

She typed back under the pretense of checking notes.

Wrapping up. Almost done.

But it didn't feel almost done, not at all. Rachel wanted secondary spaces, backup ceremony options if it rained, dressing rooms, catering kitchens, the bathroom that guests would use.

Who cared where the guests went to the bathroom?

Rachel did, which meant Lacey should.

Letting go of her own issues, Lacey realized it was the bride who was growing increasingly anxious. She wasn't happy about something and Lacey sure didn't want it to be Tessa Wylie Events.

"What do you think?" Lacey whispered privately when they were leaving the bride's dressing room and Kendra stepped away to take a call.

She winced, which somehow didn't make her any less

attractive. "Compared to the place in Charleston? It would be easier up there, but this has a destination feel. Still, not perfect."

"Nothing's perfect," Lacey replied. "But you cannot feel stressed or disappointed."

Her narrow shoulders sank. "I'm so glad you understand," Rachel said. "That's important to me in a wedding planner."

And if they went back to Charleston and married closer to home, Tessa Wylie Events would lose this job. Lacey did not want that to happen, so she ignored the next text from Roman.

The walkthrough dragged on until Rachel finally took Lacey aside and whispered, "I know it's short notice, but I don't suppose there are other venues nearby we could see today?"

Lacey's chest tightened and her brain whirred. "I... don't know offhand..." She did know, however. "There is one place near Destin—"

"No, Rach," Sebastian said, strong and clearly in charge. "This is a fun idea to come down here for the wedding, but I think we should just stick with Plan A and drop the Florida destination idea."

Rachel looked visibly disappointed as she turned to Lacey. "I want it. His family? Not so much."

"You have the final say," her fiancé assured her. "I promised you that. But another venue would have to be perfect and maybe have more life around it for a party weekend."

Instantly Lacey thought of Seaside Gardens, which

would be perfect. But...*today?* "Is there any chance you could come back? I do have a venue in town with water views and plenty of nightlife around."

"Can we go see it?" Rachel asked, looking up at her husband.

"We're only here through tonight," he explained to Lacey. "So, if you can get us in..."

If she got them in, she was definitely canceling with Roman.

"Uh, let me make a call..." Lacey stepped away, her heart spiraling. *Please be booked. Please be booked.*

"Wait, wait, Lacey." Rachel came closer. "Never mind. Sebastian is right. He's calling the car. We'll let you know what we decide about this estate. If we do Florida, we'll do this, but I don't think he's convinced."

Lacey knew one thing: If Tessa were here, they'd already be on their way to Seaside Gardens.

But before Lacey could whip up her inner salesperson, Sebastian's car arrived. The couple left and Lacey feared she'd never see them again.

No one would know that she'd failed in her job...no one but Lacey.

She rushed her goodbye to Kendra, tried to stay positive, and got back in her car, calling Roman immediately.

"I'm done," she said breathlessly. "I'm on my way."

There was a pause, then, "Okay. See you soon."

Traffic had been as miserable as it could be in Destin, which was pretty darn bad. Lacey hit every light, got stuck behind an accident, sat in blistering delays, and ended up two hours late from her original eleven o'clock arrival time when she pulled into Roman's driveway.

She killed the engine, sat for one breath, then two, staring straight ahead to calm down.

They could still go. It wasn't impossible. Jacksonville was a long drive, but not *space travel*. If they left now, they could make it by early evening. Maybe miss the appointment, but surely they could see the place tomorrow.

She snatched her tote, smoothed her top with a hand that didn't feel steady, and got out. The humid air wrapped around her like a damp towel as she walked to the front door and rang the bell, even though she knew he was home. She'd seen his car.

The door opened quickly.

Roman stood there barefoot in athletic shorts and a faded T-shirt, a baseball cap turned backward. He looked like the version of him she loved most—not a pro-ball player or a face that could be famous. Just a good guy who she really loved.

He didn't look mad—not that she'd know what "mad" looked like on him. She'd never seen him angry, certainly not at her.

Which was a reminder that she didn't really know this man she was considering living with. Well, wasn't that the point of living together?

His expression was gentle, but the corners of his

mouth were set like he'd been bracing himself for disappointment and had finally stopped fighting it.

"Hey," he said.

"Hey," she whispered back.

For a second, she didn't move, and neither did he, and the space between them felt heavy and wide. She wanted him to pull her in—wanted the warmth and the reassurance and the easy laughter that always came so fast with them.

Roman stepped aside. "Come in."

She walked into the cool air-conditioning and the quiet. It smelled like him—clean soap, something citrusy, a faint trace of cologne. The normalness of his living room—the throw blanket folded neatly, the TV off, a bowl on the counter with protein bars like some people had candy—made her throat tighten.

She turned toward him, ready to launch into the apology she'd been writing in her mind for the last hour.

"I'm so sorry," she said. "I didn't plan for it to take that long. They just kept asking questions and I kept thinking it was about to wrap up and then—"

"I know," he said softly. He reached out, touching her elbow to draw her closer. "You look exhausted."

"I am," she admitted, and the truth came out, raw and immediate. "I think we lost the job anyway."

His eyebrows rose slightly. "After all that?"

She nodded and eyed the sofa, which looked inviting. "Are we going now?"

Something shifted in his face and he shook his head.

"No?"

"We're not going to get that apartment," he said.

"How do you know?"

Roman exhaled slowly, then tipped his head toward the couch. "Sit down."

She sat, but it didn't feel like resting. He took the chair across from her instead of sitting beside her, and the choice—small, probably unintentional—hurt a little.

He leaned forward, forearms on his thighs.

"The agent called," he said. "She said someone else requested a showing today. She thinks they'll sign for it today and it's first come, first served. She couldn't hold them off until tomorrow."

Lacey groaned. "I'm so sad."

He gave a quiet, almost-smile. "Yeah. Me, too."

She waited for him to say something sharper. But Roman just looked at her, and the softness in his eyes made her throat burn.

"I kept thinking," he said slowly, "that you were going to walk in the door with your hair all windblown and your smile all bright and say, 'Okay, I'm here, let's go,' like it was nothing. Like work happened, but then you chose us anyway."

Lacey's chest tightened.

"I did choose us," she said, too quickly. "I was trying to. I was trying to do both."

Roman nodded, accepting the words, but not fully soothed by them. "I know you were. And I know what you were doing was important."

"It was," Lacey insisted. "It is. A huge client. A major opportunity. Tessa needed me."

Roman's eyes flickered at the name, not jealous, exactly—but aware that there was another person in this relationship that neither of them had invited, but both of them felt.

Her boss and his birth mother. It would be funny and ironic, except right then? It wasn't either of those things.

"I get that," he said. "I do. I'm not asking you to quit your job."

Lacey let out a shaky breath. "It doesn't feel like that."

He blinked, and for the first time, his disappointment sharpened into something more vulnerable. "I don't want to do that."

"I don't see any other way," she said, and looked down at how her fingers were twisting together.

That was the thing, wasn't it?

He wasn't asking her to choose Jacksonville over Destin. He was asking her to choose him as the center of her orbit. To adjust her life around the gravity of his.

And he was so easy to orbit, she could happily say yes.

Roman was bright, generous, funny and warm and attentive and steady. Roman made her feel wanted in a way she hadn't realized she needed until she had it.

But he was also...Roman Matteo—an NFL player. A man with a schedule that had other people's signatures on it. He had a career that didn't pause for "venue walk-through that ran long." He lived a life where time was money and performance was everything, and there were always other people lined up.

It had been easy to forget that this summer, in this "off-season," as he so casually called it.

But life was about to start up again and it would be "*the* season" and that mattered. A lot.

"Roman," she said carefully, "we haven't known each other that long."

His nodded, as if he'd expected her to say that and had been holding himself back from saying it first.

"And you're asking a lot of me," she continued, voice tight. "Not because you mean to. Not because you're trying to...control anything. But because what you're offering is big. It's like...a whole life. A whole—" She stopped, because the word sitting between them was enormous and ridiculous and terrifying.

Commitment.

"I am asking a lot," he agreed quietly. "And I know that. I know I'm...coming in hot." His gaze held hers. "But that's because when I'm with you, it feels right. I don't want to pretend to be cool about it."

Lacey felt tears prick, sudden and unwanted.

"I'm not cool about it," she whispered.

He smiled faintly at that, but then his expression sobered again.

"I'm not proposing," he said quickly, almost like he had to make sure she knew that. "I'm not saying forever like it's a ring. I'm not trying to scare you."

"You are scaring me," Lacey said, half-laughing through the tightness in her throat.

Roman leaned back, letting out a breath. "Okay. Fair."

He rubbed a hand over his face, then looked at her with honest frustration—not at her, but at the situation.

"I just..." He hesitated. "I think about how fun it could be. You in Jacksonville. Not just visiting. Not just squeezing in between weekends and events and games. Like—living. Doing normal stuff. Grocery shopping. Cooking terrible meals together. You making me watch some reality show and going to Home Depot to buy something mundane and domestic."

Lacey's lips trembled into a smile in spite of herself. "You'd be mobbed in Home Depot."

He choked a laugh. "You severely overestimate my importance to the team. Another reason you should live with me in Jacksonville—to disabuse you of this notion that I'm famous or popular. Second-string all the way, baby. Tradeable, too."

She winced at that.

"Hey, it's a package deal of my reality."

Lacey's heart squeezed because she wanted the whole package with him, but at what price?

Yes, his career was big and rare. Being Tessa's right hand wasn't the same as being a second-string receiver for an NFL team. But, still. It was her life, and she'd just started building it.

"I'm not saying you need to move tomorrow," he said. "Or even this month. I'm asking...can you imagine it?"

"I can," Lacey said quickly. "That's the problem. I can imagine it. And it's...beautiful."

"Then why do you look like you're about to cry?"

"Because I don't know what happens to *me* in that

version," she said, the truth spilling out before she could polish it. "I don't know who I am in Jacksonville. I don't know where my life fits. I don't know if I become...a girlfriend waiting around for your schedule, lost in the background."

Roman's eyebrows lifted, and he looked genuinely pained by the thought.

"No," he said firmly. "No. Lace, I don't want you to be lost."

She stared at him.

"I don't," he repeated, voice steady. "If you ever felt like you had to make yourself smaller to fit into my life, then I don't deserve you in it."

The words hit with a thud in her chest, sounding heroic in the quietest way. Lacey blinked hard.

"So, what do we do?" she asked.

Roman held her gaze. "I'm going to run over to Jax tonight so I can make the team meeting in the morning. I'll come back. We have a few days before I have to check in for training. I'd rather not cram everything into one day like a test."

Lacey let out a shaky laugh. "Yeah, I'm sorry again."

"It's okay," he assured her, and sounded like he really meant it. "I'm willing to wait. Lace, I'm willing to do hard things. I just need to know you're in this with me. Because my feelings for you are only going to get stronger —and your role in your job is only going to get bigger."

The room went quiet again and Lacey's chest felt tight, her emotions tangled—love and guilt and longing and hope braided together.

She stood, restless, walking a few steps toward the kitchen island and then back.

"I am in it," she said, turning to him. "I love you. That's not— Roman, that's not the question."

His eyes softened at the word "love," like it still startled him every time.

"Then what is the question?" he asked.

"I guess it's...can I live two lives at once?"

"Nobody can," he replied without a second of hesitation. "So, no."

They stared at each other for a moment, then Roman stood, too, closing the distance between them, brushing her cheek with the back of his fingers. Tender. Careful.

"You okay?" he asked.

"No," she whispered honestly. "But I will be. I think I need some...space."

He nodded, accepting that.

When she left his house a little later, walking to her car with her heart aching but also strangely full, she knew one thing with sharp clarity—there was only one person who could help her untangle this.

Only one person who could tell her how to be brave without being reckless.

And it wasn't Tessa.

August 1, 1993

I'm writing this in bed with the little reading light clipped onto my book because I don't want to forget tonight, even though it probably doesn't seem like a big deal to anyone else.

After dinner, Tessa and I went out back and sat on the steps, where the wood is still warm from the sun and you can hear the waves. The mosquitoes were bad, but Tessa didn't even notice because I swear they don't bite her.

Tessa had somehow turned an old shirt into something adorable by cutting off the sleeves and tying the bottom into a knot that made her waist look like a pencil. Even when her hair's a mess from a day in the sun she somehow looks perfect.

She was acting weird, though. Not dramatic weird, just quieter than usual. She kept playing with her hair and kicking her flipflops against the step. I thought she was going to tell me she was mad at someone or that someone liked someone else or whatever little gossip we drum up after seeing kids our age at the beach all day.

Instead, she asked me if I thought it was a bad idea to sneak out later.

I honestly thought she was joking at first.

She said this guy she's been hanging out with—Eric Something or Other—wants her to come meet him on the beach after everyone's asleep. At MIDNIGHT. She said it like it was exciting, but I could also tell she was nervous about the whole thing.

I know, I know. Tessa Wylie asking ME for advice about a boy. What are the chances, right?

But she asked me what I would do, which almost made me laugh because when would I ever be in that particular situation? Pretty sure not a single boy noticed my existence today.

Anyway, I had to put myself in her shoes—well, flipflops—and imagine what I would do if I were gorgeous and made an old shirt look like the cover of "Seventeen" magazine.

I would want the kid to really like me, for one thing. So, I asked her if he was her boyfriend, or going to be.

She laughed and said no, not exactly. Eric told her he doesn't want a girlfriend (he's on vacation for a few weeks with his family) and just wants to have fun. He lives in...Texas, I think, so that's a long way from Ithaca.

Anyway, she rolled her eyes like that was normal and said it didn't mean anything, that's just how boys are. Who cares what they call it?

I told her I wouldn't sneak out for a boy who wouldn't be my boyfriend. I said if Eric wants her to risk the wrath of Artie Wylie if she gets caught, then he should at least be willing to come to the door, meet her mom and dad, and take her on a proper date.

She snorted.

And I didn't get that. She's worth a date, right? I told her that and I thought she'd wave it off or get defensive or laugh at me and accuse me of being all "Little House on the Prairie" or something.

But she didn't. She got really, really quiet for a long time. Then—I'm not lying—she put her arm around me and said, "Thanks, Viv. That actually makes sense." She said she didn't want to feel stupid about it later, and that kind of surprised me because Tessa usually acts like nothing bothers her.

After she went inside, I stayed out there by myself for a little while. I kept thinking about how weird it was that she asked me. I'm not the pretty one. I'm not the boy-crazy one. But tonight she wanted my opinion, and she listened to it.

It made me feel older somehow. Or maybe just more real. Like maybe I'm not always the side person in everyone else's story.

I think I like giving advice. It feels good to feel needed. And I'm really, really glad Tessa stayed in the house tonight.

Sweet dreams!

Viv

Chapter Sixteen
Vivien

Vivien had been expecting the board member of the Destin History and Fishing Museum to be an aging docent with silver-streaked hair and reading glasses.

Not this board member. Natalie Cartwright looked to be in her mid-thirties, with dark hair parted down the middle and cascading over her shoulders, and intense brown eyes that sparkled when she walked them through the humble museum that few people in Destin even knew about.

In a modest conference space decorated with framed black-and-white historic photos, she described herself as a "third-generation Destinian" with a love for the town's history that she inherited from her father, and his father, who'd been born and raised right here.

After some small talk, Peter, who had kindly arranged the meeting, took the lead and explained that they were concerned citizens who'd vacationed here as kids and now lived in the area as adults.

And when they mentioned the Left Coast Bridge, Vivien instantly saw a shadow cross the other woman's face, and knew she agreed that the decision to tear it down was wrong.

"That was an, uh, unexpected battle with a disappointing end," she said, adding a smile that didn't reach her eyes. "I wish I had a different story to tell you."

"How did it all come about?" Vivien asked.

"I'm not sure, but there is a salvage company driving the effort," she told them.

Quinn Hargrove. Vivien and Peter shared a quick look and nodded.

"He has a lot of influence then?" Vivien asked.

Natalie gave a soft snort. "If by influence you mean cash, then yes. Pockets are getting lined and, trust me, it's no one in this office."

"Then who?" Peter pressed.

She shrugged. "You said you're with the sheriff's department, right?" When he nodded, she leaned in. "Then you know about..."

"Graft and corruption in small-town government," he finished for her.

"That's what you call it," she countered. "They call it 'public safety infrastructure removal and navigation improvement.' Which sounds like they're doing everyone a favor and also saving baby ducks."

"Navigation improvement?" Vivien scoffed. "That bridge hasn't been used for navigation since—since—"

"Since the dinosaurs," Natalie agreed. "But the phrase hits certain triggers in certain offices."

Peter's jaw tightened. "Whoever is involved in graft and corruption should be investigated," he said.

"Knock yourself out, Detective," Natalie said. "But don't hold your breath. The demo got rubber-stamped and any arguments were ignored. The Left Coast Bridge isn't historically designated at the federal level, it isn't on a protected register, and it's 'functionally obsolete.'"

Vivien winced. *Functionally obsolete.* "Like a flip-phone," she muttered. "What can we do? Mitigation? Documentation? Something?"

Natalie nodded once. "We've tried a lot of those tactics, but we can't even get the paper to do a story or get put back on a city council agenda. The salvage company pushed everything through so fast, we haven't had time to even look for a loophole, let alone find one. I got labeled a squeaky wheel early on, and they're ignoring me."

"Has anyone else taken up the fight?" Vivien asked. "Do we have other allies in this?"

"Not really." She shook her head. "The people with power in this town are those who cater to tourists. That's our life's blood, right? And tourists don't care about the history—they want pretty pictures, busy bars, and white Destin sand."

Natalie leaned back, flipping a lock of silky dark hair over her shoulder. "To be honest? I gave up the fight. When I found out about the plans, I spearheaded a petition, a delay, a second review. All of it. We brought photos. We brought the story. We brought a retired commercial fisherman who cried at the lone city council session when they let us present our side."

Vivien blinked. "That sounds...persuasive."

"It *was* persuasive," Natalie said. "But the approvals

are done. The contracts are signed. The equipment is scheduled. The public hearing already happened."

Vivien's stomach dropped. "When was the public hearing? I swear, if I had seen it announced, I'd have gone."

"You missed it?" she asked with a dry laugh. "I don't know how. It was announced in a 'Notice of Public Hearing' on the bottom of the city website. You don't go there daily to find out what's happening?"

Vivien smiled at her sarcasm.

"Yeah, you missed the meeting on some random Tuesday at eight a.m." She rolled her eyes. "It wasn't well attended, which I'm sure was Quinn Hargrove's plan."

"Do you think he did anything illegal to make this happen?" Vivien asked.

"Define 'illegal.'" She chuckled and looked at Peter. "I guess you do that for a living."

"Generally," he agreed, his expression calm and strong.

"Well, for the record, I'm not saying that's what happened," she continued. "I'm saying I wouldn't be shocked. Quinn has...friends. Friends who like their boats and trips and second homes. And he's been weirdly insistent that everything be fast. Fast is where mistakes happen."

Peter nodded once, the motion minimal. But Vivien saw the way he filed that tidbit.

"If there was an error or a law broken, would it matter now?" Vivien asked, grasping at hope.

Natalie's expression turned apologetic again. "It

could, but I doubt there's anything to find. Even if you discovered some random misfiled paperwork, you'd be fighting momentum. The machine is moving, the demo is scheduled, the salvage company is ready to make a killing."

"I can't believe something couldn't be done," Vivien said on a sigh.

Natalie shrugged. "The fact is, we're outgunned and trying not to get sued into the next century. The museum is a small nonprofit. Hargrove is a man who thinks a lawsuit is like breathing and has legions of lawyers ready to make sure we get suffocated. I'm sorry, I really am."

"I believe you are," Vivien said, looking around at the proof of all that.

"So...different subject?" Natalie asked. "You mentioned that you came to Destin as kids?"

"We did," she said. "My family came for summers and stayed in an old cottage on Gulf Shore from the late eighties to 1995."

"Ah, then Opal hit. The beginning of the end, my dad used to call it."

Vivien nodded, understanding that the storm was truly a turning point in Destin's history.

"But my family was able to buy the property before that," Vivien added, not prepared to get into any of the complicated story surrounding that purchase. "A few years ago, we demo'd the old house and built a new one."

Natalie made a face. "Do you have pictures of the old one?"

"Somewhere," she said. "I have diaries. Why? You need more for this room?"

"Diaries?" Her voice rose with excitement, then she laughed. "I should explain that I'm

working on a passion project. I'm writing a coffee table book about the history of Destin. In my spare time, I run the "Destin from Days Gone By" Facebook page. Any chance I could interview some of your family? Are your parents available?"

"My mother," Vivien said, considering the request. "She and her closest friend, who also vacationed here. They'll talk to you. And we will, if you like."

Her whole face brightened. "I would love that. And the diaries?"

Vivien felt heat rise at the thought of a stranger reading about her teenage crush—especially because he was sitting right here. "I'll have to curate those," she said with a laugh.

"Whatever you can share," Natalie responded. "And I promise I won't give up on the bridge completely. Maybe there's a stone we haven't turned."

They exchanged phone numbers, shook hands, and thanked her again before leaving.

Outside, the day hit them full-force—blue sky, sharp light, the air warm with salt and traffic from the nearby highway. They stepped off the curb and paused near the edge of the parking lot.

Vivien exhaled hard. "Well. That was disappointing," she said. "I guess not for her research but for our bridge."

"Yeah," Peter said. "She wants your diaries."

"Well, she ain't getting them."

"I wouldn't mind reading them myself," Peter said with a sly smile.

She threw him a look. "Over my dead body."

"Really?" He laughed. "'Cause I'm in there?"

In there was one way of putting it. "Because I wrote them as a child and they're silly and I was…"

She turned toward him, and for a second the sunlight caught his face in a way that made him look younger and older at once—stronger around the eyes, more worn at the edges. The Peter from the past, and the future.

"I know what you were," he said.

"Young, annoying, and jealous of Tessa?" she teased, hoping he really didn't know that she was a lovesick teenager who'd obsessed over his every gesture.

Or maybe he *should* know that. Maybe this was the moment to tell him that she'd made a huge and regrettable mistake when she asked for space.

She took a breath and prayed for the right words. "Peter, I—"

"Do not give up hope," he said, interrupting her and bringing her to silence.

"I…haven't." Had she?

"Because I'm not done digging into this bridge paperwork."

Oh, they were on very different wavelengths.

"If someone's palms were greased, it could be indictable," he said. "I can talk to the chief about an investigation, and that would delay the demolition."

She swallowed the confession she was about to make. "Can you do that?"

"It's what you want," he said, as if her wish was his command. "Don't count on it, but I'll poke around some more."

"Thank you," she said on a sigh, knowing this might not be the moment, but she had to tell him soon. "You free for dinner now?" she asked.

Peter's expression shifted, just slightly—something warm passing through it, something almost startled. "Uh, actually, I'm meeting Connor and Holly. You're welcome to join us."

Her heart dropped. "No, no. You do family time."

"You're family, Viv." He winked at her. "All those summers and diary entries? Come on, kid."

Kid. Somehow, she'd ended up right back in 1993. Offering an easy laugh, she shook her head and suddenly wanted nothing more than an excuse. What should she say?

"I'd love—" Her phone vibrated and she seized the opportunity, pulling it out to check the screen. "Oh, dear."

Lacey: *Mom. I need you. Like, now. Please. I'm still in Destin, can we talk?*

Huh. Lacey hadn't gone to Jacksonville with Roman after her walkthrough in the morning? What was wrong?

"What is it?" he asked.

The excuse I needed, she thought. "It's Lacey," she said, reading the next text as it appeared.

Lacey: *I can't do this. I'm going to ruin everything. What do I do?*

"I have to go," she said simply. "She needs me to talk her off a ledge."

"Good luck with that." He gave her a cursory hug and walked off, leaving her feeling...yeah. Disappointed.

There was no other way to describe it.

VIVIEN WRAPPED both hands around a stemless wine glass and exhaled, the tension of the day loosening just a fraction as she leaned back against the cushioned banquette. Lacey had chosen a small neighborhood bar and grill with a forgettable name and an even more forgettable atmosphere.

It wasn't sunny, noisy, or full of tourists, so it did the trick. Instead, the lights were low, there was some quiet jazz playing, and it felt just private and somber enough for both their moods.

Vivien's mood wasn't great—but her daughter looked positively wrecked. She sat across from Vivien, her big blue eyes haunted with a world of hurt and worry, her shoulders slumped. She'd left this morning looking like a sharp and elegant event planner with smooth waves and a slick outfit, but her clothes were a little wrinkled and her hair was downright bedraggled.

They'd hugged when Lacey arrived—longer than usual, a little tighter. Something was definitely bothering her, and Vivien was willing to bet it had everything to do with the fact that she was sitting at a bar with her mother and not hanging out with her boyfriend in Jacksonville.

"So," Vivien said lightly, lifting her glass with a wry smile. "I take it my wishing you good luck didn't help much today."

She made a glum face. "What's the opposite of luck? That's what I got handed today."

"I'm so sorry, honey." Vivien grunted, hating when Lacey was unhappy about anything. "Tell me everything."

She did—a long nightmare at Tidewater, the bride's endless questions, the way time slipped through her fingers no matter how tightly she tried to hold it. All underscored by how much the project mattered to Tessa and how badly Lacey wanted to prove her worth and sign a big and profitable event.

Then came the talk with Roman, and the bombshell.

"Wait. What?" Vivien leaned in. "He asked you to *move* to Jacksonville? To live with him? I thought you two had just planned to spend a day or two there for fun. But the trip was to..."

"Find a place to live," Lacey finished softly.

Vivien leaned back, emotions swirling as she processed this stunning news.

Lacey looked right at her with that mix of challenge and guilt and hope and doubt all in one glance—taking Vivien back two decades to a little girl who'd pulled a doll from a toy store shelf and started a saucy walk toward the cash register as if wanting it made her mother agree to buy it.

"Why are you smiling?" Lacey asked.

"I just had the flash of a memory," she said.

"About what?"

Vivien closed her eyes. "Just you as a little girl."

"Well, I'm not a little girl, Mom, but, yes, Roman has asked me to move in with him. At least for the season."

"Okay," she said, not wanting to react until she knew everything and until she was actually asked for advice. Because this wasn't five-year-old Lacey—this was *twenty-five-year-old* Lacey. Her daughter was a grown woman with free will and a strong sense of right and wrong. And she was in love. "And after the season?"

"I...I don't know," she said softly, probably in the same tone she'd used when Vivien asked how she planned to pay for that doll.

Vivien took a sip and listened as Lacey spelled out her dilemma, which was a classic. Did she choose her relationship or her career? Move or do long-distance? Trust a man she'd known for a few months or wait for a more traditional amount of time to pass?

Lacey shared bits of her conversation with Roman, giving the impression he'd been kind, respectful, but certain in what he wanted to do.

Also, he acknowledged it was a big ask.

A huge ask, Vivien thought, but remained quiet as Lacey laid out the true crossroads she faced and what might or might not be at the end of whatever path she chose.

Finally, Lacey stared at the wine in her glass. "He thinks we lost the apartment. And he's...fine. Disappointed, but fine. He keeps saying it's okay. That we can do long-distance. That he's willing to wait."

"So, the ball's in your court—or end zone, if we're keeping the sports analogy right."

She didn't smile. "He keeps talking about how *fun* it would be if I lived there. Like—*really* lived there. Jacksonville. The season."

"Feels very...finite," Vivien said. "Like it has an ending."

Angling her head, Lacey sighed. "I guess that's good and bad. If it ends, then...it was just a season of football and life. If it doesn't..."

"Then this could be...forever." Vivien leaned in, her breath tight. "Do you think he's the man you want to spend the rest of your life with?"

Because, whoa, it was fast.

Lacey stared at her. "I...think. I don't know. I need your advice, Mom."

Vivien's mind flickered to the diary entry she'd read the night before—remembering the look on Tessa's face that night she was trying to decide whether or not to sneak out with some boy.

That's what Lacey looked like—earnest and scared and wanting to take a risk but rightfully self-protective.

Vivien had counseled her young friend not to break the rules for something half-offered because she was worth more than secrecy, more than crumbs.

Different stakes. Same truth.

She kept her face neutral, her voice calm. This was not the moment to be a Mama Bear. She had to give careful, honest guidance and keep Lacey's eyes wide open. But she certainly didn't want to put a stop to the great love of her daughter's life.

"So," Vivien said slowly, "he's not asking you to marry him."

"No," Lacey said immediately. "He was very clear about that."

Vivien nodded, filing that away. "And you've been dating...what, two months?"

"A little more."

"And he's wonderful," Vivien said, because that was obvious. "And you love him."

Lacey's eyes grew misty. "Yes. I do. Very much. More than anyone, but I know, I know. I'm young. It's fast." Lacey sniffed. "I just don't know how this went from a summer romance with a dream guy to a life choice with major implications."

"Well, you are young enough that decisions like this might feel bigger than they really are." At Lacey's "are you kidding" look, Vivien laughed. "I'm not trivializing this. It's big and important. But it's also...all good."

"Doesn't feel that way."

"You have a fantastic man who loves you and a great job that showcases your natural talent."

She made a face. "He's fantastic and he *says* he loves me. And the job? I wasn't that impressive today."

Vivien leaned in, snagging hold of one word she had said. *Says.* "Do you doubt him?"

"No..." She drew the word out. "But..."

"But what?"

They sat in silence while Lacey searched for words and Vivien fought the need to mother too hard—to protect, to warn, to list every possible outcome.

"There's no question his job is bigger, better, harder to get, harder to keep, and way more 'important' than mine." Lacey used air quotes and Vivien didn't argue. The guy made millions playing professional sports. To equate their jobs would be silly, but she didn't want Lacey to devalue her work.

"This isn't really about work," Lacey whispered, the words sounding very much like a realization she was just having.

"No," Vivien agreed. "It's about your...worth."

Lacey paled. "Yeah, I guess it is."

"And," Vivien continued, "you've yet to say whether *you* want to move in with him. He says it'll be fun and romantic and a memorable season. What do you think and feel when you imagine that life in Jacksonville? Regardless of whether it's for a season or a lifetime, how does the idea of living with him feel in your gut, Lace?"

Vivien had a suspicion she knew the answer but didn't want to back Lacey into a corner. She had to reach the conclusion on her own.

Lacey looked away, staring at the wall. "I don't know."

"But I think you do," Vivien said quietly.

Lacey's shoulders sagged. "I want both. I want him. And I want my career." She let out a soft groan and reached for Vivien's hand. "What should I do, Mom? What's the best and safest choice?"

Vivien threaded her fingers through her daughter's. "Those aren't always the same thing, honey."

"Uh, not helpful," Lacey teased. "I mean, what do *you* think I should do? You have...life. Wisdom. Experience."

Vivien snorted. "And a divorce to prove that none of those things are foolproof and some fools are better ignored."

"Please," Lacey said softly.

Vivien inhaled, then exhaled, steadying herself. She met her daughter's eyes.

"All I can say is to value yourself," she said simply. "Not your job. Not your relationship. *You.* More than a possible future. More than a good time. More than the next adventure."

Lacey's breath caught.

"To me," Vivien continued, voice thickening, "you are the greatest prize ever won. And if someone wants a prize like that...they should earn it."

Lacey nodded slowly, the meaning settling in. "I hear you. You mean, like...with a ring?" She winced. "It's awfully fast."

"I know and I don't necessarily mean with a ring. But with more than...the promise of a season. I mean...what if you don't make the playoffs?"

Lacey rolled her eyes at the sports analogy, then held up her hand. "I hear you, Mom. I know what you're saying. Don't sell myself short."

"Exactly."

They sat back, the moment stretching, then easing. "I

needed to hear that," she whispered. "Not promising I won't sell myself short, but I value your insight. I just don't know if I'm ready for something that long-term and serious. But thank you for the advice."

Vivien withdrew her hand and patted Lacey's. "That's what mothers are for."

"And friends," Lacey said softly, her eyes moist again. "You've been the best one for me."

"Oh, honey, thank you."

She pointed at Vivien. "You're going to be my maid of honor...*someday*."

Chills danced over Vivien at the thought. "I'll probably have to wrestle Tessa for the job, the way she jokes about being your mom." Vivien pointed at her. "Or mom-*in-law*."

Lacey laughed, the moment lighter. "We'll see." She lifted her glass and eyed Vivien over the rim. "Okay. Your turn. Why does this woman look troubled? Bridge problems?"

Vivien laughed weakly. "Not really. Not any more than your decision is a work problem."

"Ahh." Lacey lifted a brow. "It's really about Peter."

"Bingo."

Lacey leaned in. "Do you mean to tell me you haven't told him you're sorry for giving him the old heave-ho?"

"No," she said, giving a dry laugh at the expression. "He's been so busy with Connor. And *Holly*."

"And that bothers you," Lacey said.

Vivien let out a long breath, wanting to be as honest

and self-aware as the young woman sitting across from her.

"Yes. But I know he regretted how that divorce was handled," she said slowly. "But the question for me is about who or what I think I love."

"I don't follow."

"Am I in love with Detective Peter McCarthy, a fifty-three-year-old divorced father of two with a good heart and a solid foundation for a possible future...or young Peter from the beach, the object of my obsession and crush, the unattainable goal of teen Vivien?"

Lacey tilted her head, considering the question with no thought to mocking it. She got what Vivien was going through, which made her basically the greatest daughter ever.

"If you only loved the memory of him, Mom, you wouldn't care."

"I wouldn't care about what?" Vivien asked.

"About everything—his life, his ex-wife, his sons, your future, your relationship. All of it. You'd just laugh it off, try making out with him once, and move on." She cringed. "I'd rather not think about you making out, TBH. But the statement stands. You wouldn't care any more than Uncle Eli cares about Tessa—he crushed on her back in the old Destin days, right?"

"So hard it was embarrassing."

Lacey laughed. "Oh, to go back in time and watch the glory days unfold."

"I met a young woman today who wants to do just

that for a book she's writing." Vivien inched in and stage-whispered, "She wants to read my diaries!"

"And write a book based on them?" Lacey's voice rose in excitement.

"No, a history of Destin. But you're right about the memory," she said. "If it were just that, I'd be like Eli was when Tessa arrived here—"

"The squatter in the empty house." Lacey lifted her glass. "Love that woman."

Vivien laughed at the memory but then grew serious. "When she got here, Eli was affected. Seriously. At first, it was like he couldn't look at her right in the eye."

"Did they talk about it?"

"They might have, but the memory of his crush on her was real. It did not turn into a romance, especially not after Kate showed up and those two were attracted like the magnets she creates in her lab."

Lacey laughed. "My point is made, then. The adult love is different from the teen crush and yours just happens to be on the same person. Peter."

Vivien sighed. "But I did just get divorced. I'm starting a business. I'm finally independent. None of that has changed."

Lacey smiled softly. "Sounds familiar, but here's the thing a wise woman once told me."

"Yeah?"

She leaned very close. "Know your worth, Vivien Lawson. You're not just a job or a divorcee or a single mom. You are a beautiful woman with a lot of life ahead. If you love this man, you *deserve* to be happy with him."

Vivien let the words warm her as much as the last sip of wine. "You're right. But if I tell him, there's no going back. It's the...bridge with no return, if you'll pardon the pun."

Lacey finished her wine, too. "I might forgive it," she said wryly. "If you stop with the sports analogies."

Vivien laughed and agreed to that. After paying, they walked out together into the humid, salty air. The sky was streaked pink and gold, the heat finally releasing its grip.

Without a word, they slipped their arms around each other and stepped onto the sidewalk.

"We're both facing life-changing decisions," Vivien mused.

"And we're sharing a bed tonight." Lacey gave her a squeeze. "You know the best thing about that?"

Vivien slid her a look. "I can wake you in the middle of the night if all the answers come to me?"

"Yep, and you better. You're my best friend, Mom, and I trust you. Thank you for good advice."

Vivien gave her a squeeze, certain of only one thing—this girl was the greatest blessing in her life. Nothing else really mattered.

They had each other.

Chapter Seventeen
Maggie

Maggie woke to a thin gray light just beginning to slip through the edges of the curtains in Barbara's guest room. For a moment, she lay very still, listening—not for anything in particular, just listening. The house was quiet and heavy.

It made her feel...like she didn't belong. Not in this house—she certainly didn't belong here—but not in this *state.*

Which was shocking because Magnolia Fredericks Lawson was a Georgia peach, born and raised, from birth to seventy-eight to...

To something she didn't want to think about yet.

She shoved the thought away and turned over, focusing on the present. But it nagged, that number—seventy-eight. Just a handful of months away from eighty. Then...

Stop it, Maggie. Age never affected her and she wasn't about to start feeling her years now. But the truth was...there weren't unlimited years left.

Was she living them in the right way? In the right place?

She sighed and turned over, forcing herself to think

about more important things, like the whole Crista and Anthony situation.

There would be no spying today. And for that, she was grateful. The time here had been...fine. A lot of laughs with Jo, but nothing concrete. And today, there would be no half-formed plans, no hushed strategy over coffee, no careful timing or driving by buildings and pretending it was coincidence.

It had all gotten them nowhere, to be honest.

Today, Anthony would be working—he always worked—and even if he weren't, they were tired. Bone tired.

The fact was, they'd been on this wild goose chase for too long. They had no proof, only suspicion and unease. Nothing that could be held up to the light and examined.

They'd drawn out the trip, called their kids to say they were alive and well, and went shopping, had lunch, or binged on Barbara's Netflix, watching *Love is Blind* until *they* were blind.

Somewhere along the way, the mission they were on had lost its focus and urgency. She was ready to go back to Destin, but they'd decided to stick around for one more chance to try and follow Anthony, maybe this weekend.

Maggie heard the familiar and oddly comforting ding of a dish and pushed the covers back and sat up, feet touching the floor. Pulling a robe on more out of habit than the need to be warm, she padded out toward the kitchen and the sound of Jo Ellen the Mad Tea Drinker.

"Oh." Maggie drew back when Jo turned, with nary a

flamingo bathrobe in sight. "You're all dressed. Jewelry and everything."

Jo Ellen absently touched an earring as if just remembering she'd put them on. "Because you and I are going... somewhere."

Oh, that sounded vague and Jo Ellen-ish. "Where?"

"It's a surprise," she said in a conspiratorial whisper.

"Which I hate."

"I don't care, Mags. I want to surprise you. Get your coffee, get dressed, and get ready to ride down memory lane."

Maggie narrowed her eyes as realization and a few recent conversations exploded into an explanation. "You want to go back to UGA."

"Oh, Mags!" Her whole body sank in disappointment and frustration. "You ruined the surprise."

"It wouldn't have been a surprise," Maggie countered. "We talked about the Tri-Delt life for an hour last night and I could see you getting all misty and maudlin."

"I don't even know what that means, but didn't you feel it? The call of the past?"

Maggie lifted a shoulder. "It's been sixty years, Jo. Going back will just make us feel old."

"We are old," she said in her most pragmatic voice. "Please, Mags?" Jo Ellen scuttled closer and made praying hands, looking like Nolie when she wanted chocolate ice cream. "Pretty please? I had Oscar make us up an itinerary. It's not a long drive and we could have fun."

"Oh, I don't know."

"You never want to have fun," Jo Ellen said, once again sounding like a seven-year-old.

"We didn't come here for fun."

"Pffft!" She flipped her hand, and turned to the coffee pot, pouring a cup with a flourish. "Take this to your room, get ready, and we can have lunch on campus."

With a dubious look, Maggie took the coffee. "I'll drink it right here, thank you very much, and while I do, I'll talk you and Oscar out of your latest madness."

"It's not madness and we won't be talked out of it."

Maggie took the coffee but didn't sit. She leaned against the counter instead, watching her friend the way one watched weather rolling in—equal parts curiosity and caution.

"We agreed," she said, attempting a different approach, "that today was a down day. No plans. No driving past offices. No...whatever this is."

"This," Jo Ellen said, waving a hand, "is not spying. This is *living*."

Maggie closed her eyes briefly. "That sentence alone makes me nervous."

Jo Ellen laughed. "Relax. We're just taking a little drive."

"Athens is an hour and a half away," Maggie said. "Two, if we take our time or get lost. That is not *a little drive*."

Jo Ellen leaned her elbows on the counter, eyes intent. "Come on. Don't you want to see what's happened to the campus in all these years?"

Maggie rolled her eyes. "I don't have to. The place

will be bigger and shinier and nothing will fit the way it used to. Our sleepy little college town will be gone, replaced by something loud and unrecognizable."

"Don't make me invoke Scarlett O'Hara," Jo Ellen teased in a sing-song voice. "Fiddle de—"

Maggie wiped her hand through the air to halt the bad Southern accent. "Stop."

"I will not. I'll quote Scarlett O'Hara until we're in the car." She cleared her throat. "'Is that...Tara? Oh, Melly! It's still standing! And so are we.'"

Maggie snorted a laugh and shook her head, defeat in the air. "I need an hour to dress for this fiasco."

"Yes!" Jo Ellen practically danced around the kitchen.

THE DRIVE SLIPPED by without ceremony, Atlanta thinning into something greener, quieter. Maggie found herself surprised by how much she recognized as they got closer, the landscape stirring something familiar despite the years layered on top of it. It was bigger, yes. More developed. But it was still the very place that had transformed them from girls to women in the middle of the wildest decade in American history—the sixties.

Downtown Athens was louder than Maggie remembered, and way more crowded. Restaurants pressed shoulder to shoulder. Shops stood where there had once been empty lots. Apartment buildings—most of them ugly as sin—rose to make it all feel polished and urban and important.

They chatted about the differences, finding the occasional place that looked vaguely familiar, but mostly they were quiet as they neared campus.

And that was when the big differences faded and everything looked very much the same.

As if they had the thought at the same precise moment, Jo Ellen and Maggie exchanged a look, the satisfaction in Jo's eyes matching what Maggie felt in her heart.

Thank goodness that so much of it was the same! Stately red brick, comforting arched windows, massive trees, and acres of grass. Yes, there were new buildings scattered around and plenty of students, considering it was July.

"Everyone does summer school now," Jo Ellen mused, proving that her thoughts mirrored Maggie's. "Straight for sorority row, Mags."

"Why not?"

Maggie took a turn, driving from memory, and slowed the car as they meandered down Millidge Avenue. When they reached the cream-colored mansion with three triangles over the front door, both of them gasped softly.

"There it is," Jo Ellen whispered.

Pulling to the curb across the street from the house, Maggie felt a sudden, unexpected rush of gratitude. It was still here! Yep, Jo was right. It was definitely a Scarlett O'Hara "pulls up to Tara after the war" moment.

The bones were the same. Updated, yes. Fresh paint,

new windows, lovely black shutters, beautiful landscaping. But it was unmistakably *their* house.

"It looks...good," Maggie sighed.

"Better than it did back then, even," Jo Ellen said. "But it looks smaller than I remembered."

"Nah. We're just...bigger."

They laughed, memories spilling out easily now as they stared.

Maggie suddenly saw herself sitting on the front steps until they unlocked the door, because she'd stayed out after curfew on a date with Roger...the night he told her he loved her.

She let her gaze move up to a small window on the side, knowing her bed had been in that room. There, she and Jo studied and laughed and shared clothes and experimented with rouge and confessed everything to each other.

"Remember rush weeks?" Jo Ellen mused. "All stress and drama."

"And finals week," Maggie countered. "More stress and drama."

Jo Ellen leaned closer. "And the time we smoked a joint?"

Maggie snorted. "No stress, but plenty of drama."

Sighing together, they sat quietly and looked at the house.

"You know, Jo, I don't really care about getting old."

"Good thing, hon, because that ship has left the port and could sink any day."

"But I don't want to...fritter the last chapter of our

life," Maggie finished in a serious tone that made Jo Ellen turn and look at her.

"No one's frittering," she said. "But I do like that you call it 'our' life."

Maggie smiled, not even realizing she'd said that. "Are we going to look around?" she asked.

"You want to go in the house?" Jo Ellen's eyes flashed. "They love it when legacy alums show up."

"No, I don't need to go in the house, but let's go to campus and see Lyndon Hall."

"Where we met! Ooh, good call."

Maggie pulled out and made her way toward the heart of campus, finding a public lot, anticipation building as they walked in the shadow of the splendid old dorm where they'd met.

They walked toward the dozen stone steps that led to the main door, then up to the window on the second floor.

"That's where it all began," Jo Ellen whispered with nothing but love. "Mags and Jo, inseparable from the day I walked in and announced I was your randomly selected roommate."

The front door popped open and two girls came out, looking...twelve. Maybe fifteen.

They wore shiny, tiny black shorts that could double as decent underwear and what looked like halter tops, but Maggie knew that garment was technically considered a "sports" bra.

One girl had a long blond ponytail, the other had a

fluffy natural afro that looked like an ebony halo around her face.

They jogged down the steps in blinding white sneakers, giving perfunctory smiles to the old ladies as they passed.

Then the dark-haired girl stopped and frowned. "Are you guys lost? Looking for something in particular?"

"Oh, no," Jo Ellen assured them. "We're alum! Class of '69!"

The number cracked up the ponytail girl, but the other's expression grew serious. "Wow, really? That's *so* cool! Welcome back."

"We lived in that hall," Jo Ellen said, gesturing toward Lyndon. "We met our first day of freshman year. I was a Yankee from New York, she's a Georgia girl. We were Tri-Delts."

The blonde's eyes flicked with disinterest and judgment—she probably didn't get a bid on rush week—but the other one came closer.

"I love that!" she exclaimed. "And you stayed friends all these years? Think that'll be us, Courtney?"

"Prolly not," she said, stuffing little white things into her ears. "C'mon, let's run."

But the girl didn't move, studying Jo Ellen and Maggie like they were on display in a museum.

Oh, look, Courtney, dinosaurs from the sixties.

But she said no such thing, instead extended her hand. "I'm Avery," she announced. "I'm the RA on the second floor."

A resident advisor? She looked like a high school senior. Maybe.

"Hello, Avery." Jo pumped the girl's hand. "We lived on the second floor. Room 218."

"That's next to me," she said, glancing up. "It's a room with a good vibe. You must have left your spirits there."

Maggie fought the urge to roll her eyes.

"We had the best year," Jo Ellen gushed, all in with the vibes and spirits.

For a second, no one spoke, then Avery nodded and stepped back, respectful and kind. "I'm not supposed to let you, but if you want to go in..."

"No," Maggie said quickly. "Too many steps."

"Well, we have an elevator now," Avery told her. "But if you do need anything, let me know."

She gave a wave and jogged after her far less friendly pal, who was jumping on two feet, ready to run.

They looked up at the dorm again, then, without talking, walked toward the giant oak tree with an ancient bench under it, stopping to sit in the shade.

"This is making me feel old," Maggie admitted.

"A little," Jo Ellen agreed, looking around like she needed to soak it all in. "But it's also making me appreciate right now. This moment—us."

Maggie's heart, so famously cold for much of her life, melted as she studied her friend.

"How do you do it, Jo? How do you stay so positive?"

Jo Ellen gave a dry laugh. "I wasn't, Maggie. When I was up in Ithaca this past winter, so deep in mourning my Artie that I couldn't see straight, I didn't know the meaning of the word positive. I sat in his recliner for hours on end, with nothing to look forward to, nothing to think about, just...sadness."

"What changed?"

Jo Ellen drew back, looking surprised that Maggie didn't know. "You," she said softly. "You're like Artie."

"I'm nothing like Artie," she said with a humorless laugh.

"To me you are," Jo Ellen replied. "You're...fun."

"Something I'm so rarely accused of."

"With me, you're fun."

"I sure am," Maggie agreed.

"I love you, Mags. Just like I loved Artie."

"Oh." Maggie put her hand to her chest. "That's so sweet."

"It's true."

They sat without speaking, the bench warm beneath them, the shade of the old tree dappling the ground at their feet. Students passed by in twos and threes, backpacks slung low, voices rising and falling in fragments of laughter and complaint. Someone kicked a soccer ball nearby. Somewhere else, music drifted faintly from an open window.

Maggie folded her hands in her lap and breathed, remembering that this had always been a place meant for thinking, for talking things through. A place where decisions had once felt possible.

"This is where I told you I was going to marry Artie,"

Jo Ellen said, as always, her thoughts a mirror of Maggie's.

"You'd been on three dates, and you were so sure."

"You were sure of Roger."

"Never *that* sure," Maggie quipped. "He always... made me work for his affection."

"Oh." Jo Ellen put a hand on Maggie's leg. "I don't remember it that way. He adored you."

"Mostly," Maggie agreed, looking around as a thought formed in her head. A shocking thought, but one that had been niggling for a while. "I'm not entirely happy, Jo."

Her friend turned to her, all humor disappearing. "What's wrong, Maggie?"

"I don't know," she admitted. "I feel like I'm not where I belong and it might be too late in life to do anything about it."

There...it was out. In one simple and ugly sentence. She braced for Jo Ellen's scoffing laugh and assurance that they were not old or far gone and they belonged right where they were.

But Jo just stared at her intently. "Is it being here?"

"Not here on campus," Maggie said. "But here in Atlanta. It doesn't feel like...home."

"Barbara's house is not home," Jo Ellen said. "As if you'd tolerate that paint job."

"I need to do something, Jo, but I don't know what."

"Well, they're expecting plastic surgery. Shall we run over to the med school and sign up for facelifts?"

Maggie shook her head, smiling.

"If it makes you feel better, I have felt the same way recently. Not here, but in Destin."

Maggie slid her a surprised look. "How?"

"Like that place is..." Jo Ellen winced. "Home?"

Maggie nodded slowly. "Destin feels more like home than Atlanta," she said, feeling a strange ripple of relief when the words were out. "And that surprises me."

"I feel the same and it doesn't surprise me at all," Jo Ellen said. "But I don't live on that pretty street with a rose garden and my daughter and granddaughter. I live in a drafty old house in Ithaca where the snow is high, the sun is rare, and Artie's gone, and you're...far away." She added a bittersweet smile. "I can't bear the idea of going back when summer ends."

"I don't want to go back to my old life, either," Maggie said quietly. "Not really."

The words hung between them, honest and unadorned.

Maggie felt something shift in her heart.

"I miss companionship, too," she said slowly, apparently unable to stop a lifetime's worth of true confessions. "Not romance. Not...that. I miss having someone to talk to. To laugh with. To plan with."

Jo Ellen's smile softened. "You mean me."

Maggie met her gaze. "I mean you."

For a few heartbeats, neither of them spoke.

"You know," Jo Ellen finally said lightly, though her eyes shone, "we could become life partners."

Maggie snorted.

"I'm serious!" Jo Ellen insisted. "We're good at this

partnership. We finish each other's sentences and fight over the remote and we never hear what the other one said unless we're in the same room."

"And you bang dishes."

"You don't understand computers," Jo Ellen volleyed back.

"And you snore!" they exclaimed in perfect unison.

"Basically, we're already married," Maggie said. "So, we should just live together in Destin."

Jo Ellen practically jumped off the bench. "You mean it? In the apartment over the garage? On the beach?"

"Assuming my kids don't sell it out from underneath me, which I totally gave them permission to do."

"Maggie!" Jo grabbed her hands. "I do have grand-children in Ithaca, but they'd come down a lot. And honestly, don't you think Kate's going to give up Cornell to marry Eli?"

Maggie choked. "I don't know, but I'm not letting that color my decision."

"*Our* decision," Jo Ellen corrected. "You and me, getting old together, helping each other through, taking road trips and long walks and...oh!" Her eyes filled, proving she was the softest, most tear-prone human alive. "Please say yes! Don't make me get on one knee, Mags!"

They laughed, but beneath it ran something real, something solid. Maggie felt it clearly now—the comfort, the steadiness, the quiet joy of knowing she would not be navigating the rest of her life alone.

"Time goes so fast," Jo Ellen murmured as they rose

and their joints gave a soft protest. "So, let's make the most of what we have left."

Maggie squeezed her hand. "Together."

"I can't wait to get home," Jo Ellen said excitedly as they walked. "To Destin, I mean."

"No more spying?"

"Once more at lunchtime tomorrow. Let's see if he leaves. If not, we'll call him innocent."

Maggie agreed and they headed home, passing the two girls on their jog.

"Hey, Class of '69," the blonde called as they passed.

But the other girl, Avery, waved and blew them a kiss. "You two are gorgeous!" she called.

"Yes," Maggie called. "We certainly are!"

They linked arms and strolled together like a couple of co-eds with their whole lives ahead of them.

Chapter Eighteen
Tessa

The beach was quiet early in the morning, before umbrellas bloomed like loud flowers and music played and kids ran around with footballs and Frisbees. That's when Tessa took Olive for their "jewelry hunt"—also known as looking for shells.

The daily jaunt had become precious to Tessa and, she suspected, to Olive, who thrived on routine. So Tessa had happily arranged to do the same thing at the same time every day.

That kind of structure wasn't Tessa's style—but then, she'd never had a child. Every day with sweet little Olive Oyl, she learned to give up a bit more of herself for this child. And she loved it.

The pain of separation from her mother—who Tessa had made an effort to talk about with love—had completely subsided. Since her breakthrough, Olive talked like any other two-year-old, in single words, with R's sounding like W's, and exuberance for anything that delighted her.

Tessa had even taken her to the Summer House to meet all her friends, who'd been enchanted and politely asked few questions about her mother, all honoring Dusty's professional code of ethics.

Olive hadn't been silent there, either. In fact, she'd squealed at the sight of Jonah's baby, Atlas, begging to "hold, hold" and Jonah let her, with great supervision.

But most days, after breakfast and "clean-up" time—there was a song for that, Tessa discovered from watching Olive's favorite show—they put on beach clothes, sunhats, and flipflops, then slathered on sunscreen with much giggling.

Then Tessa threw a few sand toys, towels, and water in a small backpack, took Olive's little hand, and crossed the street to the beach.

Sometimes on very sunny days, she'd bring an umbrella, but today there were some clouds, so they dropped their things, kicked off their shoes, and walked hand in hand, looking for shells.

The sand under her feet was warm and smooth. Too smooth for great shelling.

"No jewel-wy," Olive muttered as they looked around.

"The tide is rising, though," Tessa told her. "It'll leave a treasure trove, but probably not until later. We can come back after naptime, okay?"

"'kay." Then she gasped and let go of Tessa's hand, running ahead and collapsing on the sand dramatically.

"What did you find, Olive Oyl?"

"Jewels!" She flattened her hand to the sand, then started digging. A moment later, she held up a shell, pale pink with a chipped edge. She turned it over in her small palm, considering it the way grown women examined diamonds.

"That is *excellent* jewelry," Tessa said. "Very rare."

Olive dropped the shell into the little crab-covered canvas bag she wore like a cross-body purse, then reached for Tessa's hand again.

Her fingers were warm and a little damp, her grip confident and tight, a constant reminder of a connection that grew stronger every day.

Maybe too strong, considering she had only eight days, counting today, left with Olive.

Tessa grunted at the thought, but they walked on, the surf frothing around their ankles when they got close to the water. Along the way, Olive pointed at birds and Tessa made up names for them—Isabella the Ibis and Samuel the seagull—making Olive giggle and say their names, waving as they flew away.

Olive set the pace—exceedingly slow—pausing frequently to study the bubbles in the surf or some rocks. Today, a dried palm frond was apparently important enough to warrant a full stop and inspection.

Every now and then, Olive let go of her hand to get a few steps ahead, then turned back, checking to make sure Tessa was there.

"I got you, girl," Tessa called, getting a slow and genuine smile in response.

How was she going to let this darling child go? Tessa swallowed the thought and concentrated on the precious time she had left. She bent down when Olive stopped again and crouched beside her, both of them studying a cluster of shells half-buried in the sand.

"More jewelwy!" Olive exclaimed.

"So much jewelry," Tessa agreed. "You're going to need a vault."

Olive looked up, a question in her eyes at the word.

Tessa smiled. "It's a secret place where you keep all your most precious things," she explained, having decided long ago that every question would be answered, no matter how big or small or if she'd even asked it out loud. Tessa knew—she spoke fluent Olive now.

At the thought, Tessa's chest felt full, as if something inside her was expanding faster than it could be contained.

They passed an older couple, who grinned at Olive and gave a friendly nod to Tessa. Their gazes lingered and she presumed they were trying to figure out if Tessa was an older fifty-year-old mother or a young fifty-year-old grandmother.

But she was neither. Just a happy babysitter who already loved her little charge. But, oh, she wished she could claim mother or grandmother status. She wished in a way that made her ache.

"Tess!"

She straightened, squinting toward the house at the distant sound.

"Tessa!" Dusty jogged across the street in long strides, lifting a hand when he saw she was looking. His expression was unreadable from here, but he sure looked anxious to join them.

She slowed, letting Olive dawdle so he could reach them. While they waited, she crouched again, leaning close, her voice dropping into that conspiratorial tone she used only with Olive.

"Look who it is," she said, nodding toward him.

"Dusting."

She cracked up at the name that had stuck. "Yes, that's our Dusting. He's very handsome, don't you think?"

Olive looked at him, silent, probably not knowing what handsome was anyway.

"And kind," Tessa added, because it was important and they'd read a book last night about a kind kangaroo, so she knew Olive knew what it meant. "And he makes good sandwiches. Also, he laughs at jokes that aren't very funny, which is a fine quality in a man. I say, find a man with a sense of humor, a good heart, and a decent toolbox and you're golden, Double O."

Olive picked up another shell.

Tessa kept going anyway, because she needed to say it out loud, even if Olive had no idea what she was hearing. She had to give voice to her feelings and who better than this tiny bestie?

"You know, I think I'm falling in love with him," she said softly. "Girl to girl, I'm here to tell you, I think that's what's happening. And I hope—when you're big—you meet someone just like him. Someone who is there when you need him, and even when you don't. Someone who looks that good when he runs."

She stood as Dusty reached them, breathless, hands braced on his knees for a second before he straightened.

"Hey," he said, smiling automatically—then something in his face shifted.

"What's wrong?" Tessa asked immediately.

Dusty blew out a breath, inching back away from Olive. "Morgan's out," he whispered.

Tessa blinked. "Out?"

"She checked herself out. Which she can do at any time. I got a call from a doctor who said she'd made some progress, but not enough. Still, they can't keep her, so…"

Tessa's stomach dropped. "When did she leave?"

"Break of dawn this morning. I called her and she said she took an Uber home and now she's…on her way."

"Here?" Tessa's world tilted when he nodded. "I thought—we thought—I had another week."

"I know," Dusty said quickly. "I know. I'm sorry. I didn't imagine she'd—"

"Tess?" Olive ambled over. "Jewel?" She held up a slimy black pouch that had probably once held a sea oats pod.

"Oh, I think a mermaid must have dropped her wallet," she said, getting wide eyes from the little girl and a soft snort from Dusty. "Better leave it for her. And I have very exciting news about your—"

"Not yet," Dusty muttered. "In case she changes her mind."

Tessa nodded. "Dusting is making the sandwiches for lunch!" she said instead, her voice rising brightly. "Are you hungry?"

She shook her head, looking from one to the other. "More jewelwy."

"We'll come back later," Tessa replied, hating herself for lying but not as much as she hated Morgan for shaving a week from this bliss.

No, no, she mentally corrected herself. She didn't hate anyone. Especially not Olive's mother. But she wasn't happy.

"Come on, princess. Let's go get you lunch and I'll..." She swallowed. She'd pack up her clothes and toys and... and cry.

She took Olive's hand again, careful and cheerful while Dusty helped them gather their things. They walked toward the house talking about lunch and naps and how they'd put all the jewelry in one place so it wouldn't get lost.

"A vault," Olive murmured, proving that she listened and was smart as a whip and Tessa could try but she couldn't love the child more.

Inside her chest, something cracked cleanly in two, the pain too deep to even make a fuss over Olive's brilliance, which she usually praised.

Back in the house, Tessa moved with calm efficiency. She laid Olive's clothes out on the bed, all of them neatly folded and rolled. From the kitchen, she could hear Dusty's voice.

"Peanut butter *and* jelly, or just peanut butter?" he asked.

"Boff," Olive said decisively.

"Good choice," he said. "That's also my choice. More is better. Or more is just...whoa. Not that much more."

There was a pause, then laughter—Olive's giggle, breathy and delighted. Tessa didn't know what Dusty had done to earn that, but she could see his face, animated and playful, and Olive's, beautiful and innocent.

Tessa pressed a folded T-shirt to her chest and closed her eyes, a loud voice echoing one question in her head: *How did she miss this part of life?*

The question came unexpected, sharp as a blade that sliced her heart in two.

But how could she *not* ask herself the obvious question? Why hadn't she gotten *this*—the mess, the noise, the weight of loving someone who needed you completely? Why had she not chosen differently when she'd had the chance?

Not just Roman, though that decision was very deliberately safe and selfish at the time. She'd told herself she was choosing freedom. Possibility. A full life—and giving one to her newborn.

Frankly, considering Roman Matteo's personality and upbringing and outcome, she'd done the right thing giving him up for adoption.

But other times in life—when a man got too serious, when a job wasn't the be-all and end-all, when she could have made a commitment—she ran. There'd been so many times she could have taken the marriage and motherhood path, and she so vehemently and desperately took off in the other direction.

Why?

She'd always said no man could hold a candle to her father, but was that just an excuse for a girl who had been too wild, too impulsive, and too addicted to a good time?

She hadn't been stupid or careless. She'd made the best decisions she could with what she knew at the time. And she chose pleasure over responsibility.

But standing here now, listening to Dusty laugh softly and talk about the evils of crusts on bread, she felt like she'd missed the *real* pleasure in life.

Was there anything worse than regret?

Letting out a groan, she leaned against the dresser, breathing through the sadness, reminding herself—again —that those emotions wouldn't change history.

Normally, she didn't give a second thought to her decision to remain childless. She had a niece and nephew, and now she had Lacey, who was like a daughter. She had Jonah's little baby to scratch that infant itch and she had—

A car pulled into the driveway.

She had run out of time.

She walked to the window and looked down to see a small blue compact car and, a moment later, the driver's door opened and a young woman stepped out.

Morgan looked much better than she had when she'd dropped Olive off—straighter, stronger, cleaner. Ready to take her daughter away.

Not away. *Home.*

And Tessa had to face the fact that this brush with faux and temporary motherhood was officially over.

She pressed her hands together, blinked away tears, and walked toward the hall at the sound of footsteps coming up the outside stairs.

Loving Olive had been worth every second. Even this one.

TESSA WALKED into the living area just as Morgan knocked. Dusty was at the sink rinsing a cup, sleeves pushed up, sunlight catching in his hair. He turned at the knock, and the look that passed between him and Tessa was brief, but it said everything: *This is going to hurt.*

Olive looked up, eyes bright with surprise. They didn't get a lot of visitors here.

"It's a happy surprise, Double O." Tessa's voice came out practiced and strained.

Olive beamed at her beloved nickname, then returned to her crustless sandwich and blueberries.

Dusty dried his hands on a dishtowel and crossed to the side door, with Tessa a few steps behind. She didn't know why, but her whole being wanted to stay close enough to feel his steadiness and let him lead. Her heart hammered.

When Dusty opened the door, Morgan stood there with her car keys in her hand and a tote bag slung over her shoulder, hair brushed and down. She wore a simple T-shirt dress and sneakers, looking more like Olive's older sister than her mother.

She did not look awful. She looked like a young woman who had been told, very firmly, to drink water, sleep, and try to present as stable.

But her eyes gave her away.

They were too shiny, too wide, like she had rehearsed herself into a version of calm and could feel the seams splitting.

"Hi," Morgan said in a quiet, controlled voice.

"Hello, Morgan," Dusty replied, gentle but solid. "Come in."

Morgan stepped inside, and the moment she crossed the threshold, her composure wobbled. Her gaze flicked past Dusty, scanning the large, open floor plan, then landed on Olive at the kitchen table.

Olive paused mid-chew, blueberry-stained fingers hovering. She stared with a stunned stillness that made Tessa's stomach drop. Instantly, Tessa remembered the moment Olive had collapsed when her mother left and how she'd cried when the ocean "stole" one of her flipflops.

Olive hated sudden change. How could they forget that? She should have been warned but—

"Oh, my...baby." Morgan covered her mouth with one hand. "Hello, sweet girl. Hi, my Olive."

Olive did not answer, staring at her mother as if Morgan were a stranger wearing a familiar face.

Morgan took one shaky step forward and then stopped.

"I...I don't know," she whispered. She glanced at

Dusty, then at Tessa, her cheeks flushed. "I don't know what to do. I don't know how to just...take her. I don't want to scare her. She looks like I'm—she looks like I'm—"

Dusty took a step closer and she recoiled. Her shoulders folded inward, breath catching, tears spilling out.

"I'm sorry," she choked. "I'm sorry, I'm sorry, I'm sorry. I did this so wrong. I did this so wrong."

Tessa stood frozen, a dozen competing instincts fighting for control—protect Olive, comfort Morgan, disappear into the back bedroom and scream into a pillow, rewind time, bargain with God, beg for one more week.

"Morgan," Dusty said gently, "look at me for a second."

Morgan tried. She blinked hard and lifted her face, tears tracking down her cheeks.

"You are here," he said, firm and reassuring. "That matters. Your brain is telling you that you are failing because everything feels intense. That does not mean you *are* failing. It means you are feeling it."

Morgan let out a sound that was half-laugh, half-sob. "I feel like a child. I feel like I need an adult."

Tessa watched in awe. Dusty could steady people the way that her dad used to steady a boat—hands sure on the rope, eyes on the horizon, no drama, no flinching.

He put a light arm around Morgan. "Let's go up on the roof and talk for a moment."

By "talk," Tessa assumed he meant "do therapy."

Morgan wiped her face with the back of her hand, then looked at Tessa with a desperate sincerity.

"I'm not good at hard things," Morgan said on a hushed note. "I just found that out. I guess I run. I shut down. I disappear. I am trying not to do that now."

"You're doing great," Tessa said, her chest aching at the rawness of it. She had to remember that this young mother had done nothing wrong. She'd been in a hospital bed holding a newborn when her parents and husband were killed on their way to get her.

Who could judge her for anything?

Morgan kept her gaze anchored on Olive, who had gone unnaturally still in her booster seat, eyes wide and fixed on Morgan.

Morgan swallowed. "Hi, Olive," she tried again, softer. "I've missed you, angel girl."

Olive's mouth opened slightly, like she might speak— then her jaw closed again. She looked at Tessa, and in that look was something so sharp it nearly cut Tessa in half.

Are you letting her take me?

Tessa forced herself into motion.

"Okay," she said, brighter than she felt. "I'm going to go get her things. I already started packing, but I need to grab her favorites."

With an approving nod from Dusty, she crossed into the kitchen and easily lifted Olive from her booster seat with hands that were steadier than her heart. Olive didn't resist. She just let her body go limp in Tessa's arms.

"Come on, Olive Oyl," Tessa murmured, pressing her lips to silky blond curls. "Let's go get your treasures while Dusty and Mommy talk."

As Olive dropped her chin on Tessa's shoulder and they passed him, she whispered, "Dusting."

Tessa didn't dare look at Dusty to see how that hit. Instead, she walked Olive back to the bedroom in a warm and solid grip. There, she lowered her to the floor, but Olive's small fingers tightened in Tessa's shirt. "Stay, Tess."

The words were like a two-by-four to the heart.

She turned so Olive didn't see her tears, looking at the sunlight spilled across the pink comforter and three rows of stuffed animals. Olive's suitcase was open on the bed, half-filled with neatly folded clothes and pajamas and tiny socks rolled into perfect little donuts.

Tessa sat on the edge of the bed and Olive scrambled onto her lap, glassy-eyed as she gazed up.

"It's okay," Tessa said softly. "We're just getting your things."

Olive's lips trembled. "Mommy...mad?"

"No," Tessa said immediately, even though she had no idea what Morgan felt. "You know Mommy loves you. She's not mad. She's just been...away, like I told you. But she's back now."

"She sad."

Oh, this child was bright.

"Yes," Tessa said, smoothing Olive's wavy locks. "Sad like when your sandcastle falls down. But you build again."

Olive stared at her, absorbing, trying to understand with a two-year-old brain what grown-ups could barely understand.

"Scared," Olive whispered.

Who was? Morgan or Olive? At this point, what difference did it make? They were all scared.

Tessa reached for the stuffed bunny with the floppy ear Olive had gotten attached to the past few nights.

"Okay, first things first," she said, in that cheery, practical tone she used on the rare occasions Olive was upset. "Bun-bun goes in. Very important."

Olive sniffed, watching as Tessa tucked the bunny carefully into the suitcase.

"Dino Star," Olive said, voice wavering.

"Yes," Tessa said quickly. She grabbed the green dinosaur and set it beside the bunny. "Dino Star is absolutely coming. Dino Star is not staying behind."

Olive let out a tiny, shaky breath that sounded like relief.

"And *Goodnight Moon*," Tessa continued, reaching for the book on the nightstand, their absolute favorite. "This is coming, too. Mommy will read it with you."

Olive's face crumpled. "Tess read."

Oh, please, child, don't make this harder. "I know," Tessa whispered, kissing her temple. "I know you like when I read."

Suddenly, Olive's arms tightened around Tessa's neck and a sob escaped.

Tessa held her, rocking slightly, letting her cry

without trying to stop it too fast. She *hated* change. Tessa could feel the fear in her bones.

"Olive, listen to me," Tessa whispered, voice low and sure. "You are going to be okay. You are loved so much. You are loved by Mommy. You are loved by...a lot of people. You are loved by me."

Olive sobbed quietly. "Stay."

Tessa's eyes burned. "You do have to go," she said, choosing honesty because Olive deserved it. "But you can take all your things. You can take your jewelry bag. You can take your sand toys. You can take your books. You can take every single animal friend, and you can take my love with you."

Olive hiccupped, her breath catching.

"And you keep all our special memories right here..." She pressed her hand over Olive's heart. "In your vault."

Her blue eyes flashed, as if she actually understood that.

After a moment, Tessa let go and finished the job of packing, snagging a sturdy shopping bag for the animals.

Olive watched every motion with silent intensity, her eyes tracking the disappearance of her world.

Tessa zipped the suitcase slowly, the sound loud in the quiet room. Then she pressed her forehead gently to Olive's.

"Thank you," she whispered. "Thank you for being my little pal for three weeks."

Olive's voice was barely audible. "Tess...mine."

"Yes, dear one, I'll always be yours."

A soft knock came at the bedroom door. Dusty stood

there, his gaze taking in Olive's tear-streaked face and Tessa's trembling hands.

"Hey," he said softly. "How are we doing in here?"

Tessa tried to breathe. "We're...getting there."

Dusty nodded, stepping in slowly. "Okay. Time to transition."

She smiled at the therapist word that implied movement instead of...catastrophe.

Dusty knelt near the bed, not reaching for Olive but holding her gaze.

"Olive," he said, "Mommy is in the kitchen. She's ready to take you home. Tess is going to walk with you."

Olive's eyes snapped to his. For a heartbeat, she looked like she might protest. Then her face closed down and she went quiet. The kind of quiet that Olive could hold for...days.

Dusty rose and lifted the Hello Kitty suitcase in one hand and the shopping bag in the other.

Tessa scooped up Olive's little body and held her close, following Dusty.

Morgan stood near the kitchen table, hands clutching her car keys like she might snap them in half. When she saw Olive, she stepped forward, then stopped again.

Dusty turned and gave a look to Tessa, silently telling her to hand over the child to her mother.

"Olive, your Mommy is going to hold you now," Tessa told her.

Olive did not move, speak, or stop staring at Tessa, who felt like a traitor. She kissed the sweet cheek and whispered, "It's okay, Olive Oyl. It's okay. You're going to be okay."

Morgan stepped forward and took Olive from Tessa's arms, gently and with no fight.

In Morgan's arms, her eyes wide and shining, Olive stared over Morgan's shoulder at Tessa with sheer agony in her sky-blue eyes.

Tessa's lungs forgot how to work.

Morgan's voice shook. "Say bye-bye to Miss Tessa."

Olive did not speak.

Morgan's face crumpled again. "Oh, God," she whispered, then caught herself, wiping her cheeks fast like she was embarrassed by her own emotions. "I'm sorry. I'm sorry. I'm not trying to make this harder."

"You're fine," Dusty assured her under his breath.

Morgan nodded, swallowing. "Okay. Okay. Mommy's got you."

Olive's eyes stayed on Tessa like she didn't believe that promise for one second.

Tessa forced herself to smile. It felt like lifting a weight with broken arms.

"Bye, Double O," Tessa whispered. She raised her hand in a small wave, hoping Olive would mirror it, but she didn't.

Dusty picked up another bag with more toys and extra shoes because Olive's world had expanded in this house and it was hard to compress it back down. "I'll take these down if you've got her."

Morgan shifted the child on her shoulder and turned

to look at Tessa, "Thank you. I...I know it must be weird, but thank you for...being her person."

Tessa's smile trembled. "She made it easy," she said quietly. "She's magic."

Morgan nodded, tears slipping again. "I know. That's what scares me. I don't want to mess it up."

They trudged down the stairs in silence and Tessa followed because she couldn't help herself.

In the driveway, Dusty placed the suitcases in the trunk, then got the car seat from his truck. In a few minutes, Olive was strapped in her seat, and the three of them stood in the blazing sun, silent.

Dusty finally leaned slightly closer, lowering his voice. "Call me, keep meeting me, and follow through with your doctor at the clinic. You don't have to do this alone."

Morgan swallowed hard. "I will," she whispered. "I promise."

Tessa stepped to the back window to see Olive strapped in her seat, cheeks blotchy, eyes still shining. She stared out the window at Tessa with a longing so clear it felt like a physical force.

Tessa's heart clenched so hard she thought she might actually collapse. More for support than anything else, she lifted her hand and pressed it to the glass.

Olive did not lift her hand in return.

Tessa gave a tight smile, then a nod to Morgan with a murmured wish for luck. Then she tore up the stairs before anyone heard her sob.

She cried for a while, letting out tears that had been

kept in lockdown for years, down to just shudders by the time Dusty came back.

He sat next to her on the sofa, wrapping his arms around her.

"I love her," Tessa cried, the admission ripping out of her with no filter. "I love her like she was mine. I loved her like I—like I should have loved—"

She broke on that thought, the old ache surging up with new violence.

Dusty's hands moved slowly on her back, grounding and rhythmic. "Let it out," he murmured.

Tessa's sobs intensified. "I made choices," she gasped. "I made so many choices. I acted like I wanted freedom, like I wanted the big life and the fun and the...the control, and I do, I do, but God, Dusty, I missed something. I missed something so huge."

He listened, holding her.

"I missed it," she continued, voice shaking. "I missed the sticky hands and the songs and the routines and the way she checks to make sure I'm still there. I missed the feeling of being someone's home."

Dusty's arms tightened. "Yes," he said gently. "Olive woke something primal in you. That does not mean your past was wrong. It means your heart has more room than you thought."

Tessa shook her head, tears soaking his shirt.

"I wish I could do it over," she moaned. "I wish I could go back and be different. I wish I could take every moment I ran from something serious and shake myself by the shoulders and say, 'Stop. Stop running.'"

Dusty lifted her face slightly, not forcing her to look at him, but making sure she could hear him.

"You did what you could with what you had," he said firmly. "Your younger self was making decisions with the information and the fear and the pressure she had at the time. You cannot punish her forever for not being the woman you are now."

Tessa's breath hitched. "But it hurts."

"I know," he said simply. "It hurts because it mattered."

Tessa pressed her face back into his chest, shaking. "I am alone," she whispered, the fear underneath the grief finally surfacing. "I always end up alone."

"No," he said, his voice sharp with conviction "Not anymore."

Tessa pulled back slightly, eyes swollen. "Dusty—"

"I love you," he said, steady and clear. "I love you, Tessa Wylie. I am not saying it because you are sad. I am saying it because it is true. I want a life with you. A real one."

Her tears spilled again, slower now, heavier.

Dusty cupped the back of her head gently, anchoring her. "Listen to me," he said. "We can build a life that honors what you just discovered about yourself. This does not have to be the end of something. This can be the beginning of something."

Tessa's voice shook. "How?"

Dusty exhaled slowly, thinking for a minute. "We can foster," he said. "If you want to. We can take in kids who need routine and safety and parents. You are good at that. You did it without even realizing you were doing it."

Tessa swallowed hard, imagining it, and the image hurt and soothed at the same time.

"We can get dogs," Dusty continued, a faint smile in his voice. "We can get a ridiculous number of dogs if that makes you happy. We can have a house that is loud and messy and full of life. We can do that together."

Tessa's throat tightened as she caught the image he was describing. "We can babysit Atlas. And maybe Lacey and Roman will have kids. I'll be Grandma Tess."

"In short shorts," he teased. "We can do that, Tess. We'll have that generation to grandparent whether they want us or not."

Tessa clung to him, letting his vision settle into the empty space Olive had left behind.

"But I still wish..." Tessa whispered, voice cracking. "I still wish I could undo it. I still wish I could have had... more time. I still wish Olive could have stayed one more week. I still wish..." She huffed out a breath. "Well, I don't wish for a better man in my life. There isn't one."

He smiled at the compliment, and held her while she cried a little more, but the sobs were quieter now, less frantic, like the storm had moved from hurricane to steady rain.

She pressed her forehead against his chest, breathing him in.

"I hate this," she whispered.

"I know," he said.

"I love her," Tessa whispered.

"I know," he said again.

"And I love you," she admitted, the words quiet but clear.

Dusty's arms tightened. "Good," he murmured. "Because I am not going anywhere."

For now, that was enough.

She let herself lean into the future he had painted—not as a replacement for the past she wished she could change, but as a promise that her life still had chapters left to write.

Chapter Nineteen
Lacey

The *Good Time Girl* had a way of making everything feel as close to perfect as it could, so Lacey was happy she and Roman had decided to take it out on this, their last night before he left for training camp.

Tessa's twenty-nine-foot cabin cruiser had a low, confident profile and a name in a looping script across the stern that Lacey had watched an artist hand paint a while ago.

The boat had been Lacey and Roman's happy place since they'd met, but tonight felt more bittersweet than joyful.

Lacey stood near the bow with her bare feet planted on warm fiberglass, one hand curled around a champagne flute, the other braced on the rail. The sun was dipping into the horizon, dragging gold across the Destin harbor like somebody had spilled a jar of honey on the water.

In the distance, a charter boat was easing back in, tired and slow. Closer by, a pair of teenagers laughed loudly on paddleboards, their voices carrying across the slick surface. Pelicans glided over the water, wings barely flapping, as if they had all the time in the world.

Lacey wished she could borrow that feeling.

Behind her, Roman adjusted something at the helm, turning them away from another boat's wake. He loved this boat, too. Born and raised on the water, a fisherman from both his birth and adopted families, Roman loved the freedom of being out here away from the world.

Lacey loved it because it was familiar. The boat carried the memory of earlier, lighter days—Tessa at the wheel with her hair in a messy knot, a playlist blasting, with Lawsons and Wylies sprawled across the seats like sun-drowsy cats, laughing about nothing, everything.

But there was no lightness tonight, their last date in Destin—at least for a while. Lacey had been telling herself all afternoon that this was simply a sunset cruise. Champagne. Harbor breeze. Salty kisses. A moment of softness before reality slammed back in.

She hadn't given him an answer about moving, but then, they hadn't really discussed it after he came back from Jacksonville. The topic had been tabled, she assumed, and he was waiting for her to bring it up.

That had to happen tonight. Now, even.

Her pulse had been jittery all day, her thoughts skipping and sprinting, as if something inside her already knew this was a threshold.

A line she'd cross and couldn't uncross.

Roman came up beside her and slid his hand into hers, their fingers threading naturally. He kissed her temple, a warm brush of lips that made her want to turn into him and stay there until the sun sank completely.

"How you doin'?" he asked, low and gentle, as if he could feel the tension humming beneath her skin.

She tried to answer lightly. "I'm great. We're on a boat. The only thing I'm responsible for is...not dropping my phone in the water."

He gave a soft laugh, but he didn't let it go. "Lace," he said quietly. "Talk to me."

Lacey stared out at the water, at the marinas and docks and condo balconies all fiery with sunset light. Boats rocked gently on their moorings. Music floated from somewhere—a distant speaker, a bar on HarborWalk.

"Okay," she said, and her voice came out too tight. She cleared her throat and tried again. "I've been rehearsing it, actually, because I didn't want to ruin tonight, and now I'm worried I'm going to ruin tonight anyway, so I'm sorry."

Roman's mouth curved, but his eyes stayed steady. "You can't ruin anything by telling me the truth."

She swallowed and looked down at their hands. His thumb stroked the side of her finger in a small, loving motion.

"I've been thinking about Jacksonville," she began, and felt her chest tighten immediately. "About what it means if...if we do this. If I go."

Roman didn't speak but waited, listening intently.

"It isn't just moving," Lacey said, words tumbling, because once she started, she couldn't stop. "It isn't just changing my address and learning the fastest way to the grocery store. Tessa's offered me a bigger role in her company and it's a huge opportunity. I can't do that job from Jacksonville, not the way I'm doing it now. And it's becoming a huge part of my identity. Like I wake up and know exactly who I am when my feet hit the floor."

Her eyes burned, and she hated that. She hated crying when she wasn't even sure what she was crying *about* yet.

"I love you," she said, and that part came easy, because it was the clearest thing she'd ever felt. "I'm not questioning that. I'm not questioning us."

Roman's grip tightened slightly, but he still didn't interrupt her.

"But I'm scared," she admitted, voice shaking. "And I'm embarrassed that I'm scared, because you do things with such confidence and I keep...spinning."

His gaze softened, but his jaw tensed. "Tell me what you're scared of," he said.

"I'm scared that if I go, I'll lose myself," she said, quietly. "And I'm scared that if I don't go, I'll lose you."

Roman exhaled, slow, as if he'd been holding his breath.

She gestured vaguely at the harbor, at Destin, at everything. "This place has become a home to me. My family is here. My mom, who really is my closest friend. Tessa, who is so much more than a boss. Uncle Eli and my cousins, Jonah and Atlas. Meredith is here at the moment, and Grandma Maggie. Somehow, they all ended up in Destin—"

"For the summer," he interjected.

She made a face. "My mother and Uncle Eli—and I

assume Aunt Crista—aren't giving up that house. It's our new family home and...and..." She huffed out a breath. "I'm not ready to leave them all."

Roman's gaze stayed steady on her face.

"So I guess we need to talk about long-distance," she added. "And how that might work for us."

He gave her a look that said he didn't think it could work, but didn't say anything.

"You see what I mean, don't you?" she continued. "I don't want to resent you because I followed you to Jacksonville and gave up my job and family. And I don't want to miss out on the greatest guy because I was scared."

Roman lifted his free hand and brushed the hair off her cheek, his fingertips grazing her skin.

"I'm sorry this is such a struggle, Lace."

"Well, it is," she confessed, and there it was—the core truth she'd been skirting. "I feel like I'm two versions of myself fighting in my head. One version wants to be brave and say yes to everything and be like Tessa, a world beater who doesn't need a man. Or like Meredith, superstar workaholic. The other version wants to run back to your arms and hide in your incredible shadow forever."

Roman's eyes flicked down to her mouth and back up, as if he wanted to kiss her and anchor her there, but he didn't. He stayed with her words.

"You aren't going to hide in anyone's shadow, Lacey Knight. You aren't Tessa or your mom or your cousin or any other role model. You're you. Beautiful, smart, funny, inquisitive, and perfect."

She let out a sigh. "Eh, you had me at beautiful," she

joked, then looked up at him. "Can we talk about how long-distance could work? I could come for game weekends and when you travel, I—"

He put a finger on her lips, quieting her. Then he glanced past her toward the open water where the sun was sinking fast, the sky turning flushed and bruised. Then he looked back at her, and something in his face shifted—resolve settling in, unmistakable.

"Actually," he said, and his voice had a new steadiness, "the sun is almost where it should be."

She drew back, a frown forming. "For what?"

"Come to the back of the boat. I want to move us to another spot."

Before she could ask why, he guided her to the helm. She sat on the back cushions as the engine changed pitch. The boat angled into a wider arc, leaving the busier channel behind and sliding into a calmer stretch of water where the surface smoothed and reflected the sky like glass.

"Where are we going?" she asked, trying to keep her tone light.

"The perfect spot." He steered the boat with practiced ease, then lowered the throttle until the *Good Time Girl* slowed to a gentle drift. He cut the engine to full silence.

"Look," he said, pointing behind her. "Dolphins."

She turned and squinted into the sun-dappled water but must have missed the millisecond that they jumped. She waited for one to rise in an arc but didn't see anything.

After a beat, she turned, surprised to find him in front of her, holding out a hand to bring her to her feet. Then he took both of her hands and looked right into her eyes, not at dolphins.

Wait, had he just made her turn away for some reason?

"I wanted to be right here," he said, "when the sun hits the water."

She wanted to look to the west and see that, but she couldn't take her gaze off his face. No sunset could be as enticing to her eyes.

"Look, Lace, I know we haven't had much time, but sometimes time isn't the measure. Sometimes clarity is."

Lacey's throat went dry at the serious tone, but Roman's gaze didn't waver.

"I've talked to my parents," he said. "I've talked to my friends. I've talked to my coach, teammates, and anyone else I trust completely."

She blinked at him, aware of her eyes stinging again.

"I've sat alone and asked myself if I'm being impulsive or if I'm being honest."

His hands tightened around hers, which was good, because she felt like she might actually sway with this boat.

"And every time I ask, the answer comes back the same."

He released one of her hands and reached into his pocket.

Oh, God. Oh, God.

The world narrowed to that small movement and a

box appeared in his palm, the sight of it stopping her heart. Then it started again, too fast.

"Roman," she whispered, and didn't even realize she'd spoken.

Very slowly, very gracefully, Roman lowered himself to one knee.

The deck felt impossible beneath her feet. The sunset light hit his face, turning his skin warm, his expression almost unbearably open. A man on his knee on the deck of a boat in a harbor at sunset was supposed to be a fantasy. A scene in a movie. Something you watched and thought, *That would never happen to me.*

And yet—here it was, happening.

"Lacey Rose Knight," Roman said, her full name sounding downright poetic on his lips. "I love you. I've never met anyone like you and I never will. You're solid, you're real, you're smart and funny and, yeah, you overthink everything, but you are going to be the best wife and mother."

Wife and mother? She stared at him, tears threatening to spill.

He opened the box and she couldn't help herself— she looked.

The ring caught the last bright edge of the sun and flashed—elegant, stunning, far more exquisite than anything she'd ever seen in person.

"I refuse to ask you to move to Jacksonville without this on your finger, officially my fiancée and then my wife. You're worthy of that and so much more."

Her mother's words about worth danced in her

head...but her pulse was pounding too hard for her to remember what Mom had said.

"I'm asking you to marry me," he said, as if she hadn't figured that out yet. "I want you to know that when I ask you to do something hard—like changing your life—I'm not doing it casually. I'm doing it because I love you, and I'm choosing you."

Lacey couldn't speak.

Her chest felt like it was caving in, not from sadness, but from the sheer weight of being loved that directly.

Roman's eyes glistened, just slightly, and that tiny crack in his control undid her.

"I know people will say it's fast," he said. "They can say it. Let them. I don't live my life based on what people say from the outside. I live it based on what's true." His thumb brushed her knuckles. "You're true."

A sob rose up her throat, and she swallowed it back hard. She loved him, so much it scared her.

Roman watched her face like he could see every thought rushing through her. He didn't pressure. He didn't plead. He simply stayed there, on one knee, offering her his life.

She tried to breathe. But what rose up first was panic—bright and sharp, a reflex she hated.

"Roman..." Her voice broke.

"Take your time," he said immediately, gentle. "I'm right here."

She shook her head, tears falling. "I don't—I can't think. I can't—"

He stood then, smoothly, putting the ring box back in

his palm as if he didn't want to trap her in a tableau she couldn't escape. He didn't pocket it yet. He just held it, waiting.

Lacey pressed a hand to her chest, trying to steady her heartbeat.

"I love you," she managed, and it came out like a plea. "Please hear that. This isn't me rejecting you. This is me...being terrified of making the wrong decision. I guess I am overthinking again."

Roman's face softened. "Kind of."

Tears blurred her vision. "We haven't even known each other three months."

"I know," he said.

"That's not enough time," she whispered, even though some part of her hated the logic of it. "Not for something this big."

Roman's jaw tightened slightly, not in anger—more like pain. "What would enough time be?"

"I don't know," she said, and it sounded lame. Because it wasn't the time stopping her—was it? It was fear.

Fear of making a mistake, of losing everything, of... ending up like her parents—divorced.

Because the truth was that no amount of time could guarantee safety. No amount of time could promise she wouldn't lose herself. No amount of time could keep her from getting hurt.

On a sigh, Roman looked out at the water for a long moment, the sun now half-gone, the sky deepening into a richer, darker gold.

Then he looked back at her.

"Tell me what you *can* say," he said quietly, "right now."

Lacey squeezed her eyes shut. Her lungs burned.

"I can't say yes tonight," she whispered. "Not yet."

Roman nodded once, slowly.

"Not yet," he repeated. "Okay."

She opened her eyes and a tear fell. "I need time. I need to go home and think without the sunset and the champagne and—" She gave a broken laugh. "—without you looking like the best man in the world on one knee."

A faint smile touched his mouth, but his eyes stayed teary.

"I don't want you to say yes because the moment is pretty," he said. "I want you to say yes because you mean it."

"I do mean it," she insisted, desperate. "I mean...I mean the love part. I mean the us part. I just— Roman, I'm scared."

He stepped closer and pulled her into him, wrapping his arms around her in a firm, steady hold. Lacey clung to him instantly, burying her face against his shoulder, breathing him in—salt, clean cologne, warmth.

"I know," he murmured into her hair. "I know you are."

She shook, a silent sob, because being held like this felt like everything she wanted...and everything she feared losing.

After a long moment, Roman eased back just enough to look at her.

"Here's what we'll do," he said softly. "We'll go back. I'll get you to your car at my house. You go home. You take tonight. You take tomorrow morning. I leave tomorrow afternoon."

Lacey's chest tightened again. "Not yet might not mean by tomorrow," she whispered.

"I know." His gaze locked on hers. "I'm not going to drag you there. You get to choose this."

She nodded, miserable. "Okay."

"I love you," he said again, simply. "And I trust you."

The last statement echoed over the engine as he restarted it and played in her head as they motored back through the harbor with the sunset fading behind them.

When they reached the marina, Roman tied off with calm efficiency. He helped her step down to the dock, his hand steady at her elbow. For a second, she thought he might kiss her, might try to pull her back into the warmth.

But he didn't.

He drove back to his house in a quiet that felt right, given the circumstances, and pulled in next to her car.

When they both got out, he walked her to the driver's side and stopped. He looked at her like he was memorizing her face, as if he needed to carry it with him into the hard, lonely hours ahead.

"What time do you leave?" she asked on a whisper.

"I figured I'd take off before noon. But wait—I need to get something for you. Don't leave."

The fact that he thought she might take off made her realize how tenuous this all was. Of course, she waited and two minutes later, he jogged back holding a football.

A signed football—with what looked like forty Sharpie autographs.

"It took a little longer to get it for Seamus's fundraiser. But I managed to snag the whole team, which is worth a lot more than just me."

The humility—and the gesture—touched her as she took it.

"And you need this." He added a long white envelope. "It's the certification that it's real from the NFL. That adds value, too. Tell Seamus I hope the right little guy in his ministry gets to take this home."

She swallowed hard, taking the ball, not sure what to say. "Thank you. Tessa will be overjoyed."

"But not if I take you away to Jacksonville." He brushed his thumb under her eye, wiping away a tear with a smile. "But that won't stop me from trying."

She leaned into him and he kissed her on top of the head.

With one last hug, Lacey slid into the driver's seat before she fell apart in front of him.

She pulled out of the driveway slowly, hands shaking on the steering wheel. The road blurred, lights streaking, and by the time she reached the first stoplight, she was crying in earnest—ugly, shaking sobs that made her chest hurt.

Because somewhere deep inside her, beneath the fear and logic and panic, a quiet, steady voice whispered the question that would not leave her alone as she drove home in tears:

What if she'd just made the biggest mistake of her life?

THE NEXT MORNING, after a sleepless night, Lacey was at the dining room table at the Summer House, laptop open, coffee cooling untouched at her elbow. She hoped diving into work would clear the fog in her head and lift the pain in her heart.

The house was unusually quiet for a weekday morning. No baby crying or Meredith on the phone with a client. No music drifting from someone's room. No Jonah in the kitchen, whipping up some unimaginably delicious breakfast.

She told herself that quiet was good. Quiet meant she could work.

She clicked through the file on her screen, forcing herself to focus on the Gilsons' anniversary party. Seventy-five people, three generations, a Gulf-front dinner, a sunset vow renewal, kids' activities that would keep the youngest entertained without exhausting the grandparents. It was the kind of project she loved and normally, she would have been energized by it.

This morning, she felt like she was pushing herself through mud.

She hadn't told anyone about last night, not even her mother. The words Roman had said, the sight of him on one knee on the *Good Time Girl*, the weight of the ring between them—those felt too fragile to speak aloud.

Like if she talked about the proposal, it would become real in a way she wasn't ready to manage. And they'd all have a conflicting opinion.

So she adjusted seating charts. She made notes about catering timelines. She drafted an email she didn't send.

Her phone buzzed on the table and she grabbed it, convinced it would be Roman. It wasn't. A florist she had a meeting with tomorrow—they could wait.

She was just getting into the rhythm of pretending she was fine when the front door popped open without a knock.

"Hey."

Lacey looked up, hand flying to her chest. "Tessa?"

Tessa stood in the doorway, sunglasses pushed up on her head, hair pulled back in a low ponytail that looked hastily done. She was wearing linen pants and a loose white tank that had seen better days. She looked...off. Not her usual bright, capable self.

"What are you doing here?" Lacey asked automatically. "Did you—" She glanced past her into the entryway. "Did you bring Olive to work?"

Tessa's mouth twitched, and for a second Lacey thought she might actually laugh.

"No," she said. "She's...gone."

She didn't say it dramatically, just flat and factual.

"Gone...where?"

Tessa crossed the room and folded into the chair across from Lacey, dropping her bag at her feet like she didn't care where it landed. She braced her elbows on the table and leaned forward, scrubbing her face with both hands.

"With her mother," she said.

"Oh, okay. I think. You don't look great, Tess."

"I am a wreck," she murmured, her face in her hands. "Just so you know. Absolute, full-blown mess."

Lacey stared at her, the Gilson anniversary event disappearing entirely from her brain.

"I mean—I knew you liked her, but..." Lacey proceeded carefully. "I thought it was just a babysitting thing."

Tessa dropped her hands and looked up, eyes tired and unguarded. "So did I." She let out a breath that sounded like it had been stuck in her chest for days. "It was supposed to be that. Temporary. It was my brilliant idea to help Dusty's struggling patient."

"And..."

"And then somehow, without me noticing when it happened, she became...mine."

Lacey felt something in her chest tilt. "Yours? How?"

"I have no clue." Tessa laughed, short and humorless. "But I knew her routines—no, no. I *created* her routines. I read to her, bathed her, shell-hunted with her. I knew her tastes, her cares, her fears, her little...soul." She let out a grunt. "And it hurt to let her go."

Lacey didn't know what to say to that. She'd never seen Tessa this stripped of polish or humor.

"How did that happen?" Lacey asked quietly.

Tessa stared at the table, fingers tracing an invisible line in the wood.

"I don't know," she said. "That's the thing. I don't know when it crossed from a favor to...love. It just did."

She looked up then, gaze locking onto Lacey's face with an intensity that made her sit back slightly.

"Listen to me," Tessa said. "And I know you didn't ask for this advice, but I'm giving it to you anyway."

Lacey blinked. "Okay..."

"Do not make the mistakes I've made," Tessa said, her voice sharp and urgent. "Do not convince yourself that freedom is the same thing as fulfillment. Or that fun matters more than meaning. Or that work will hold you when everything else falls apart."

Lacey opened her mouth, then closed it again.

Tessa barreled on. "I built a great life. I did. I traveled. I had a very successful and fun career. I had control. And it all felt impressive and shiny and safe until suddenly it didn't."

Lacey didn't speak, but stared at her friend and mentor, who pressed her hand to her chest as if it hurt.

"And then a two-year-old with a weakness for blueberries and kind kangaroos looked at me like I was her everything, and my whole life suddenly rearranged itself."

Footsteps on the stairs made Lacey look to her right and she spotted her mother coming down. Vivien paused on the threshold, taking in the scene. "Am I interrupting?"

"No," Tessa said, waving her over. "Sit down."

Vivien hesitated, then came closer and took a chair at the table, concern etching her brow.

"Everything okay? You got up early, Lace."

"Tessa is, um, talking about something," she said, not answering her mother's question. "Go on, Tess."

"Life is short," she said, obviously needing no more

encouragement than that. "I know that sounds like a bumper sticker, but it's true. Family matters. Fun doesn't matter. Work doesn't matter—not the way we pretend it does when we're using it to avoid something else."

Lacey felt her pulse start to climb, her body reacting before her mind caught up.

"Fall in love," Tessa said. "I know it sounds simple, but it's not. But I'm telling you, Lacey Knight—fall in *love.*"

She already had.

"And then—honestly, I don't care if this flies in the face of feminism—have *babies* if you want them. A few! A lot! Raise them yourself. Be there. Do not wait for perfect timing or the perfect version of yourself or for the stars to line up. Create a family!"

Lacey didn't know whether to laugh or cry, so she turned to her mother.

Vivien cleared her throat softly.

"I mean—" She gave a small, wry smile. "I'm divorced, so I'm not exactly a poster child for perfect decisions. But I will say this—having a family, even one as small and broken as ours, was a highlight of my life."

The stairs creaked again, and Eli appeared in a T-shirt and shorts, a coffee cup in one hand, his Bible in the other.

"What's happening?" he asked.

"Group intervention," Tessa said. "You're welcome to join."

"I was going to sit outside and read, but..." He came

to the table, placed his book and cup down, then took a seat. "This sounds just as holy."

"If you mean, holy moly, Tessa's on a roll, yeah," Lacey joked.

"About?"

"About the importance of getting married and having kids," she said.

"Well, that's biblical." Eli put his hand on the leather cover. "It's on most every page, starting with Genesis. 'Be fruitful and multiply,'" he said, then glanced around at the three women. "Has one of you...multiplied?"

They laughed. Well, Vivien and Lacey laughed. Tessa looked like he'd kicked her.

"No!" she exclaimed. "And that's the problem."

Before anyone could respond, footsteps thundered on the stairs that came up from the first level, followed by Jonah's voice singing, "You are my sunshine, who slept all night long..."

Atlas cooed as if on cue.

Jonah appeared at the top of the stairs with Atlas strapped to his chest, facing out, wide-eyed and smiling, cheeks impossibly round in the morning light.

Lacey's heart did something painful and sudden.

Jonah grinned at the room, shaking back his long hair. "If anyone needs proof that life is chaos and magic at the same time, I give you Atlas Lawson—sleeper and superstar!"

Eli laughed, standing up. "Give me my grandson!" he demanded, extracting Atlas from the carrier with ease. "Hello, handsome!"

"What's the powwow about?" Jonah asked, loping to the table and looking at them. "Would a nice onion and cheese frittata help save the world? 'Cause my kid slept all night and I'm in the mood to cook."

Suddenly, the room felt full and alive and vibrating with love. Even Tessa perked up and they were all talking, all meaning well, all completely unaware of the weight pressing down on Lacey's chest.

Because they didn't know Roman had been on one knee in the sunset. They didn't know she had said *not yet*. They didn't know he was leaving today.

They didn't know that she might have tossed the chance for the very thing they were so wildly singing about this morning.

But she did and she—

A hard knock on the front door stole all their attention.

Roman! Lacey practically leaped from her chair, knowing deep in her heart that he'd had the same sleepless night and he was back to ask again and this time—

"Anyone home?" a gruff voice from outside demanded.

With a punch of disappointment, she opened the door to see Seamus Donahue, the weathered old fisherman, holding the football she'd dropped off last night at the marina on her way home.

"Seamus? Is something—"

He powered by her. "Tessa! Are you here?" he called. "Oh, you're all here. Well, good, 'cause I have something to say."

"Join the crowd," Eli replied, coming closer with Atlas. "Look at my handsome grandson."

"I can't look at anything but this." He lifted the football the way Jonah had lifted Atlas.

"Oh, the whole team signed it!" Tessa smiled for the first time since she'd walked in. "I love that boy."

"You better!" Seamus said, letting Jonah take the football to examine it. "I know you didn't raise him, Tessa—I learned that the hard way when I walked into a pile of... not my business."

They all laughed at the memory of how Seamus took one look at Roman and saw Artie Wylie, and they'd all missed it. Not Lacey, but she knew that Roman was the baby Tessa had given up for adoption.

"It's a great donation," Tessa said. "You didn't have to come all the way—"

"Oh, yes, I did! This is going up for auction tonight and I...I just had to..." He looked around, his voice cracking. "Is he here?"

"Roman?" Lacey asked. "No, he's home or..." On his way to Jacksonville, she added glumly in her head.

"Then I'll tell you, since he's your boyfriend and"—he turned to Tessa—"your son."

"What?" they asked in unison.

"Did you look in this envelope?" He pulled out the white paper from his jacket.

"That's the official certification," Lacey said. "To prove the autographs are real."

"Yeah, yeah, yeah, but it's also..." He pulled out a sheet of paper from the envelope, snapped it open and cleared his throat. "'The Arthur Wylie Memorial Youth Fishing Scholarship to cover gear, rods, tackle, payment for charter fishing days, and one annual Artie Day Fishing Tournament for underprivileged children.' Fully funded for five years by an *anonymous* NFL player who also agreed to give the scholarship winner private fishing lessons for the next five summers."

For a moment, no one spoke. Then Atlas let out a squawk, but it wasn't loud enough to erase the echo of the last few words. They hung in the air like...like the answer Lacey had been so desperately seeking.

With one quiet and meaningful gesture, Roman showed exactly who he was. Not just a great guy with talent and good looks, not just the dreamboat she'd fallen in love with this summer, and not just someone temporary looking for companionship for the season.

He understood the concept of family, of legacy, of permanence and personal commitment. Could it be any more obvious?

As she stood there and they started to react, Lacey searched the room, her gaze landing on her mother first, then Tessa. The two of them were looking hard at her, with matching expressions that stated the obvious: *You know what to do, Lace.*

She nodded as if they'd spoken out loud.

What in the heck was she thinking? *Not yet? Was she out of her mind?*

"I have to go," she said.

Tessa blinked. "Go where?"

"To answer a very important question Roman asked me yesterday."

That silenced everyone—including Atlas.

Lacey grabbed her purse from the entryway and yanked open the front door the very moment a sleek and familiar Porsche rolled into the driveway, stopping her in her tracks.

Roman.

She bolted out, running into the driveway as he stopped. He climbed out of the sports car, confusion flickering across his face as Lacey dropped her bag and every doubt she ever had and ran to him, arms outstretched.

"Roman! Roman!"

He blinked in surprise but scooped her up when she crossed the driveway and launched herself at him, arms wrapped around his neck, legs around his waist.

"Yes," she said, breathless and laughing and crying all at once. "Yes, yes, *yes!*"

Roman laughed, stunned, arms catching her automatically as he spun them once before setting her down. "Lace—"

"Yes," she repeated, pressing her forehead to his. "I'm terrified and I'm sure and I love you and I'm done pretending I don't know what matters. I will marry you, Roman Matteo. I will happily and joyfully marry you!"

Lowering her to the ground, he inched back, and for one horrifying second she thought he was going to say he'd changed his mind.

Instead, he reached into his pocket, pulled out the

ring box, and dropped to one knee again right there in the driveway.

"Yes," she said, tears streaming before he got a word out. "A thousand times, yes."

He slid the ring onto her finger, stood, kissed her deeply. Her heart thumped, her lungs squeezed, and somewhere behind her, she heard the noisiest cheer from her family on the porch.

Seamus hooted like a fan in the stands and Tessa screamed at the top of her lungs.

When Roman lifted her and twirled her in the air, Lacey just dropped her head back and soaked up the best moment of her life.

Chapter Twenty
Maggie

"Another escapade?" Maggie whined with the same high pitch she'd heard her little granddaughter give when she simply did not want to do something.

She sure as heck did not want to go back to Buckhead and spy. All Maggie wanted was to go home—and by home, she meant Destin. She was equal parts exhausted, discouraged, and sorry she and Jo Ellen had ever embarked on this adventure.

"We've seen nothing," she said as she backed out of Barbara's driveway, confident that she and Jo Ellen had left the house in the same perfect condition they'd found it.

"We have one more shot," Jo Ellen said. "Let's do a drive-by at lunchtime and see if he leaves the office with her. If not, we can chalk it up to suspicions but no lipstick on collars, no hotel rendezvous, no canoodling."

Maggie adjusted the rearview mirror and mentally planned her route to Lenox Road. "Canoodling? That's the gold standard now?"

"It has always been the gold standard," Jo Ellen replied primly. "You cannot cheat without canoodling and the only canoodling Anthony did was spend a whole lot of time on that ride-around mower last Saturday."

"And never even noticed I'd tended my own rose garden." Maggie narrowed her eyes. "He's not forgiven for that sin."

"But he's not a cheater."

"We *think* he's not," Maggie corrected.

As they drove into Buckhead, the mid-morning sun slanted across the glass buildings, and Maggie felt the weight of uncertainty press on her chest.

"I hate this," she said quietly. "I hate doubting him."

"You're not doubting him," Jo Ellen corrected gently. "You're doubting Crista's doubt."

Maggie blew out a breath. That was uncomfortably accurate.

Crista's voice had been so steady when she'd said it. *I feel it, Mama. Something is wrong.*

Maggie had dismissed it. Hormones. Anxiety. Pregnancy. She'd defended Anthony fiercely.

And yet...the debit card. The deleted texts. The password. Who was he talking to on the phone so often? Staying out all night, once, she reminded herself.

"All right," Maggie said, peering at the street sign and cursing Atlanta traffic. "One more time."

"One more lunchtime observation," Jo Ellen agreed. "If he walks out alone and eats a sad sandwich by himself, we go home victorious. If he leaves with a woman..." She lifted a shoulder. "Then we won't clear his name to Crista."

And, really, that was all Maggie had ever wanted.

They parked two blocks from Anthony's office building just before noon, the T-bird well hidden, their stupid scarves tied on, sunglasses firmly in place.

The Lenox Road area hummed with weekday energy all around as Maggie adjusted her scarf. "I look ridiculous."

"You look incognito," Jo Ellen corrected.

"I look like I'm about to rob a bank in Palm Beach."

Jo Ellen patted her hand. "Focus."

They sat on a bench in front of the building, pretending to scroll through their phones while actually staring at the entrance like two extremely obvious spies.

At twelve fifteen, the doors swung open, shocking them both when Anthony stepped out. And right beside him, a brunette. Not either of the women they thought might be Pamela, but a whole different one.

Who was this?

Maggie's stomach dropped so abruptly she felt it in her knees.

"Well," Jo Ellen breathed. "There's your canoodling candidate."

Not exactly. They were walking briskly, side by side, talking, laughing, nodding to each other. A business meeting? A paramour?

"Wherever they're going, it's on foot," Jo Ellen said, sitting up. "Let's follow but stay back."

"And if he sees us?" Maggie slid a look to Jo. "We limp."

Snorting a laugh, they fell into step half a block behind Anthony and the woman, doing their very best to appear casual, but probably sticking out like seventy-eight-year-old sore thumbs in the middle of this upscale, urban, youthful environment.

Suddenly, Anthony fooled them by turning and jaywalking across the street.

"Oh, dear. We're not doing that," Maggie said.

"Just keep him in your sights, Mags, and hustle to the light. It's green."

"Hustle?" Maggie rolled her eyes. "The last time I *hustled* was in college dancing—and I was three vodka tonics to the wind and still had my original hips."

Somehow, they caught up across the street, watching as Anthony paused at another massive office building. He looked down at the woman next to him, who gazed right back up at him, and for one horrifying second, she thought they were going to kiss.

But they shook hands, burst out laughing, then hugged.

"Canoodling?" Jo Ellen asked.

"Not quite," Maggie declared.

Together, they walked through the building's large glass doors. Maggie and Jo Ellen exchanged a look, a nod, and followed.

"It's not a hotel," Jo Ellen whispered as they stepped inside the sleek marble lobby. "That's a blessing."

"Look," Maggie said, watching them march to large glass doors of a law firm on the lobby level.

"They're visiting an attorney?" Maggie rasped the question. "Oh, that's not good."

"It could be for work," Jo Ellen said, squinting at the

many partner names on what looked like a large and prestigious firm.

"Or for a divorce," Maggie whispered.

"No!"

Maggie launched a brow and eyed a leather bench next to a tall Ficus tree in the lobby. The plant would hide them, but they were close enough to see when the couple—no, not a *couple*!—left the offices.

"Let's wait and watch," she said.

Jo Ellen agreed with a sigh, the two of them taking the bench and leaning back so they were hidden.

"Is this what my life has come to?" Maggie muttered.

"No, your life has come to moving to Destin and having the best decade of all." Jo elbowed her. "Don't forget that."

"I can't think about it now. Not with Anthony in there getting a divorce."

"Will you *stop?*"

Maggie's heart began pounding in her ears. *Law office.* Why would Anthony need a law office? There really was only one possibility—he was filing for "dissolution of marriage."

"We don't know what he's doing in there," Jo Ellen said quickly.

"Why else would he—"

"Estate planning? Business contracts? Wills? His work?"

"He's a software engineer...manager...thing. They have attorneys at that company—a whole department full of them. And it's lunchtime. This is personal." Maggie chewed on her lip. "This is serious."

Time slowed while they waited, but Maggie's mind did the opposite. It raced ahead in awful, vivid detail—Crista's face crumpling, Nolie asking why Daddy didn't live with them anymore, the baby born into fracture.

She pressed her palm against her chest. "I should have taken Crista more seriously."

"You took her plenty seriously," Jo Ellen countered. "We're here, aren't we?"

True enough.

Finally, after what had to be an hour, they spotted Anthony in the law firm's lobby with the nameless brunette and a man, all of them shaking hands. The man clamped his hand on Anthony's shoulder and beamed at him.

A moment later, Anthony and the woman walked out, too busy talking to notice the old women in scarves hiding behind a tree. They were only fifteen feet away and Maggie could see her son-in-law's face clearly.

She knew that face and the happiness etched on it. She'd seen that expression when he hoisted Nolie on his shoulders or clapped for her from the auditorium during a Christmas play. She'd—

"It's done!" the woman said, reaching a hand up to high-five Anthony.

He grinned at her and held up the fat file folder. "Signed and sealed, baby."

Baby?

"Are you happy?" she asked.

"Over the moon." He made a face like he couldn't contain his joy and reached for her, hugging her hard.

Hugging? Embracing, more like. A triumphant, exuberant squeeze of affection.

Maggie felt something inside her splinter.

Anthony pulled back, still smiling. "I can't wait another minute, Evelyn."

Evelyn? Who was this woman?

"I have to tell Crista and pray she doesn't murder me for doing something so life changing. She *has* to know the truth. I can't go on lying to her any longer."

The words detonated, each like a little bomb in Maggie's head. She shot to her feet so abruptly she nearly toppled the Ficus.

Jo Ellen grabbed her arm. "Maggie—"

Too late.

Maggie marched forward, ripping off her head scarf like a battle flag.

"*Anthony.*"

She kept her voice low, but the tone of it cracked through the lobby like a whip, and Anthony jerked around, blinking. Then every drop of blood drained from his face.

Of course—guilty.

"Maggie? What...what are you doing here?"

"What am *I* doing here?" Maggie demanded, advancing, working to control her tenor. "What are *you* doing here, Anthony John Merritt?"

Evelyn's eyes widened. "Is this your mother?"

Anthony glanced between them. "No...I—this is—"

"You," Maggie cut in, stabbing a finger toward his chest, staying close so she could make her point without causing a scene. "You are about to destroy the best thing that ever happened to you."

"Maggie—"

"Crista is the greatest woman on this planet. She is carrying your child. She has given you a beautiful daughter. She has stood by you through promotions and pressure and stress. She made you a gorgeous home and you're willing to destroy it with the same cavalier attitude you used when you totally forgot about my roses?"

"Maggie—"

"And this—" she gestured toward the law office "—this is how you repay her?"

Anthony stared at her as if she'd been speaking in Greek. Stunned, he looked around, his gaze landing on Jo Ellen, who gave a weak and pathetic wave as she shuffled closer.

"What are you doing here?" he asked, still sounding stunned.

"We've been following you," Jo said, making Maggie groan. Did that matter now? He was ruining his life and needed to know that.

Anthony's jaw dropped. "You've been—what? *Why?*"

"Because I believed in you." Maggie ground out the words. "When Crista came to me scared and suspicious, I defended you. I told her there was no universe in which you would cheat. And this—this secret debit card, these deleted texts, these clandestine meetings with your *young, attractive assistant—*"

The woman made a small choking sound.

"—and now *divorce* papers? And you're worried she might murder you? She should move fast because I am very close to doing it myself!"

Anthony started to speak, then he laughed. A short, startled, incredulous laugh, and added insult to injury by looking at his lover, who also giggled like a schoolgirl.

Maggie's mouth fell open.

"You think this is *funny*?"

Evelyn, to her credit, tried to contain herself, but failed. Another chortle escaped.

Anthony scrubbed a hand over his face. "Maggie," he said carefully, fighting a smile. "You think I'm *divorcing* Crista?"

"You just said you can't go on lying to her."

"Yes, but—"

"And you're in a law office. With...*her*."

"True," he conceded.

"And you hugged and got all gooey and said Crista might kill you, but I guess you and your little hottie don't care."

"Hottie?" He drew back and looked at the other woman as if...well, as if he'd never considered her that way. Which was probably an act.

Jo Ellen leaned closer to Maggie. "We may have miscalculated, Mags."

"The only person who miscalculated is my son-in-law. He underestimated me."

"Uh, never, Maggie," he said, inhaling deeply. "Sadly, you *underestimated* me."

She stared at him, her heart rate too high to continue her tirade.

"I am not divorcing your daughter." He opened the thick folder in his hands and pulled out a piece of paper with a picture at the top and grids of numbers and lines. "I am surprising her."

She leaned in, squinting at the picture of a sweet house with white siding, soft gray shutters, and a small front porch with two rocking chairs. Palm trees dotted the background and there was water in the distance.

"With...that?" Her voice cracked.

Anthony's smile softened. "I know, it's small. Not the Summer House and not meant to be. But it's five minutes away from that beach and perfect for us to spend long weekends and summers. In Destin."

Maggie stared at him. "You...bought a house."

"I knew if I breathed a word of it to her, she'd talk me out of it. She'd say it's crazy and too much money, but since Eli and Vivien have been down there, and now you, I know she feels lonely. And with another baby..."

"You bought a second home." Maggie breathed the words, then frowned, looking from him to the woman. "Why is she..."

"This is Evelyn Brookstone, my real estate agent."

"Oh." It was all she could manage, plus a look at Jo Ellen, who was biting her lip to keep from laughing.

"Look, Maggie, I know Eli and Vivien aren't selling the Summer House. And I suspect..." His lips curled up. "...you're never leaving it."

Maggie opened her mouth. Closed it.

"And that place is huge, but there are four of us—or will be when the baby is born—and I thought we should have our own space down there," he continued. "I wanted to surprise her."

Evelyn stepped forward, smiling warmly. "I've never seen a man so concerned about making his wife happy. You're Crista's mother? You should know she's in very good hands."

"I...did know that." Maggie winced and looked around, hoping she hadn't made a spectacle, but no one seemed to notice—except Anthony, her beloved son-in-law.

He gave a wry smile. "Sounds like you had some doubts."

"I'm sorry," she said on a sad breath. "Truly. Crista was suspicious because of you taking calls outside and getting a different bank account and erasing texts and..."

"I didn't want her to stumble onto anything." His expression crumbled. "Oh, man, I blew it if she thinks I'm cheating. But how could I blame her? The lying was killing *me*, and I knew why I was doing it."

All Maggie's anger and doubt evaporated like the air from a balloon. "I came to prove you innocent. We followed you and called your assistant and...you didn't come home one night."

"I slipped down to Destin to see the house before I signed on it, and I didn't tell Crista I was there, obviously." He laughed softly. "You are one of a kind, Maggie Lawson."

Jo Ellen stepped in, looking smug. "For the record," she said, "I *suggested* estate planning when you got here."

"Where are you staying?" he asked. "How long have you been here?"

"We were in Barbara Johansen's house," Maggie explained. "And we've been here...a long time."

He dropped his face into his hand and shook his head in sheer disbelief, but Maggie slid the paper from his other hand to get another look at the new house.

"You bought this for her," she whispered, awe in her voice.

"For us," he corrected gently. "I knew she wanted to feel part of the whole Destin experience, which apparently is where the Lawsons live now."

Maggie pressed the photo to her chest.

He gave her a look. "Next time, just ask me."

"There will not be a next time," she said softly.

"You say that now," Jo Ellen muttered.

"Look, Maggie, I really do need to get back to work, but..." He hesitated as he led all of them outside. "Can you keep the secret? Until I can get down there and surprise Crista and Nolie and baby-to-be?"

Maggie's lips curved slowly. "Can *I* keep a secret?"

They all laughed and started walking down the street, but as they fell in step, Maggie leaned closer to her son-in-law.

"Anthony. Just one more thing."

"What's that, Maggie?"

"Can we talk about the roses?"

Chapter Twenty-one
Tessa

"Two years?" Tessa gasped as Dusty scrolled to the next page on the rabbit hole known as the Florida Department of Children and Families, the gateway site for the foster process.

They'd been digging through online information and Reddit threads and privatized foster services for—

Tessa glanced at the time. "Oh, dear. We're supposed to go to the Summer House for Vivien's bridge-jumping thing." She grunted and dropped her head. "Please, can I be sick and get out of it? Because this quagmire of acronyms and processes and home studies and a...what is that again? A *social-emotional audit of my life*—whoa. This is definitely giving me a headache."

Dusty pulled off his glasses, squeezing the bridge of his nose. "Same, Tess. But if we want to foster, it's a full-time job just to get considered."

"And then, after two years of training and classes and interviews and references up the wazoo..." She pointed to the screen. "They prioritize one thing—*reunification with the family.*"

"Can you blame them?" Dusty asked. "Most times you support the child only to..."

"Pack them up and send them back to their parents," she finished, her voice taut with a pain that was still fresh. "I don't know if I can go through that again, Dusty."

"We have to if we want to foster."

"If we foster *kids*. Can't I just get a nice little puppy and call her Olive?" Her voice cracked on the last word. "Who I miss so—"

"Yes, but...hang on." He picked up his phone and put it to his ear, too quickly for her to see who'd just called.

"Is everything okay?" he asked, walking out of the room and lowering his voice. "Where are you now?"

She knew a patient emergency when she heard one, having been with him long enough to know his many clients called on the weekends more often than mid-week. She supposed that must be when grief hit the hardest.

Pushing back from Dusty's desk, she blew out a breath. This wasn't about loving a child and giving him or her a beautiful home. This was about navigating a system, and honestly, at fifty, was that what Tessa wanted to do?

What Tessa wanted was...

She picked up her phone and tapped the photos, scrolling through the eight billion she'd taken of Olive.

She wanted her little Olive Oyl. Not...bureaucracy. Yes, she understood the need for it and respected the process and the people who put it in place to protect children.

But this was too much.

"Hey." Dusty came back in, tucking his phone in his

pocket, his expression serious. "I'm sorry, Tess, I have to go."

"Oh, who is it? Everything okay?"

He just shook his head, which she now knew was code for "don't ask, 'cause I can't tell" and she held up a hand.

"It's fine. I'm going to make the briefest of appearances at Vivien's shindig and come home." She pushed up from her chair. "I wanted to surprise her with that boom box I found in a thrift shop."

"With the '90s cassette?" His brows lifted. "I really don't want to miss that playing when we all jump off the bridge. Look, I already have a bathing suit on. I'm ready to let go."

"Of?"

"A future without a perfect woman by my side." He kissed her lightly. "'Cause you are not going anywhere, Tessa Wylie."

She smiled at that. How could she not?

"Well, I know what I'm letting go of." She waved a hand at the computer.

"Being a foster parent?" he guessed, wrapping her in a hug. "Don't worry, honey. We can navigate this mess together. We'll figure out our family, no matter how it looks."

She gave a whimper and dropped her head on his shoulder, loving the sheer strength of it. "What I'm letting go of is Olive. She's gone forever and I have to let go of my not-so-secret hope that she'll come back."

He kissed her on the head and stepped back,

searching her face. In his expression, she saw the deepest and most profound understanding.

No surprise—he was a grief counselor and she was grieving.

"I'll be there tonight, I promise. I'll try to get to Vivien's before you all leave to jump. If not, I'll meet you at the bridge."

She kissed him again and stood very still, listening to the sound of him getting keys and his wallet and heading out to his truck.

When the door closed, she dropped back into the seat and stared at the screen, reading the words.

PRIDE training is Parent Resources for Information, Development and Education. Eight to ten classes, three hours each.

"Three hours?" she whined.

Dusty was right. She was letting this go—tonight. With Vivien and her stupid idea that they all make one more jump before the bridge was taken down.

"God help me," she murmured as she walked out carrying the boom box. "Because I'm gonna need it."

THE SUMMER HOUSE was alive with a warm chaos that almost made Tessa forget her blues. She forced herself to greet friends and family, acknowledging that she was only just emerging from a cocoon she'd spun to protect herself since Olive left.

She started with her mother, who'd returned from an

extended stay with Maggie. Neither one looked like they'd had much "work" done, but something had brightened their faces. Looking at Jo Ellen, Tessa suspected that her mother and her bestie maybe had a few treatments and abandoned the idea of anything that caused pain and just drove around and had fun.

There was an aura of joy around the two older women that everyone seemed to chalk up to their lifelong friendship, but Tessa sensed it might be more than that.

"So where did you stay the whole time?" Tessa asked her mother.

Jo Ellen lifted a shoulder. "Here and there. You know Mags. She loves a good, unplanned adventure."

Tessa slid a side-eye to Maggie, who was standing with Crista and Anthony, cooing over pictures of the second home here in Destin they'd purchased.

"Maggie doesn't love adventure," Tessa corrected. "But she is kind of glowy. You two get in trouble with some bikers again?"

"Not this time," her mother said. "But we did make kind of a monumental decision."

"Do tell."

"Only if you promise not to share with Kate—yet."

Tessa drew back and raised her brows. "I don't usually keep secrets from my twin, Mom. Maybe you shouldn't tell me."

"Well, I will. And I'll tell Kate myself if she ever comes back here." She inched closer and lowered her voice. "We're not leaving."

For a moment, Tessa wasn't sure what she meant.

Not leaving for the bridge? Not leaving on another adventure? Not leaving—

"Ever," Jo Ellen clarified. "We're moving into the garage apartment permanently and I'm selling the house in Ithaca and—don't get mad—everything in it but the memories."

Tessa stared at her, then blinked. *Mom not in Ithaca? It was...*

"Perfect," she breathed.

"You think so?" her mother asked.

"Yes, I do," Tessa assured her. "And not just because I'm here and I selfishly want you nearby. Because it's cold and far and life is here—in the sunshine. Anyway, you and Maggie are as much sisters as Kate and I are. You deserve this, Mom."

"Oh, honey!" She threw her arms around Tessa and they hugged, the action getting the attention of Maggie and those around her.

"What's all this?" Maggie asked, coming closer.

Tessa didn't answer but put the rare arm around Maggie Lawson and—even more rare—the usually chilly woman didn't bristle. Instead, she just shook her head.

"Jo Ellen never met a secret she could keep," Maggie said.

"Why keep it secret, Mags? I'm so happy."

"Well, so am I. And look who's going to live five minutes away." Maggie beckoned Crista and Anthony closer, and they moved as one, arm in arm.

"Let me see your real estate," Tessa said, taking

Anthony's phone while Crista yammered on excitedly about having a place down here.

"Guess no one is selling this behemoth," Tessa said, eyeing Crista. "You were the wild card."

"I say we keep the Summer House as a family compound," Crista replied, glancing up at her husband. "I love that he wants that for all of us."

He smiled, clearly basking in his Husband of the Year Award.

"Hey, boss." From behind, Lacey wrapped her arms around Tessa's waist and squeezed her, getting a gasp in response.

"Lacey! You're here!" Tessa spun and hugged her, then looked around for Roman. "And where's my boy?"

"He's getting me a drink, since we just walked in. Surprised?"

"Yes! I didn't think I'd see you for...ever."

Lacey made a face. "Stop. We're there for the season, then back here for the off-season, and you know you'll see me plenty. Guess what?"

"You found an apartment?"

"We did—on the water in town. Gorgeous. But I also..." She bit her lip with a sly look. "Got our first client for the satellite office of Tessa Wylie Events. I wanted to tell you in person."

Before Lacey left engaged and joyous, she and Tessa decided that *they* would be the ones trying to make long-distance work. If Lacey could scare up business in Jacksonville, Tessa would provide all the support and resources and take a cut of the profit. Lacey could run a satellite office and build her own event planning business.

But honestly, she'd made the decision in a fog of missing Olive, so Tessa wasn't quite sure how it would work out. She only knew she couldn't be the one holding Lacey back from happiness.

"It's actually for the Jags," Lacey told her. "I met a woman in the PR department and she's always looking for help setting up fan events and player appearances. She asked if I wanted a job, and I said no. But she could be our client."

Tessa's jaw loosened. "Are you serious?"

"We have three events in August."

"Lacey!" She threw her arms around her young friend, squeezing before drawing back. "You sure you don't want a job with her? Or just take this as your own business?"

"I'm positive! I can't do this without you, Tess. We'll Zoom every morning, you give me pointers and assistance, and I'll help you hire someone here if you need it."

"I don't need anyone," Tessa said softly. "Without Olive..."

Lacey made a face. "I know that was hard."

She swiped her hand as if to say it was too much to talk about. "Another time," she murmured. "No sadness today. Let me look at that rock again."

As she admired Lacey's engagement ring, Roman came over and hugged her, the three of them clustered together like the strange little mix of a family that they had become.

How could she not be happy when she realized that?

"What are you smiling about?" Roman asked, eyeing Tessa.

She lifted a shoulder. "Just the fact that after not having any kids, I now have a son *and* a daughter and that is what our darling Eli would call a blessing. I'm just... overwhelmed by that."

They hugged her just as Vivien clapped her hands and got everyone's attention.

"Hey, all!" she called. "Sun's going down, so we should start walking to the bridge."

"Where's Peter?" Eli asked, coming next to his sister.

Vivien shrugged. "He said he had a work issue," she replied. "But I don't want to be out there too late. We have young ones with us and..."

"Not-so-young ones," Maggie said dryly, making everyone laugh. "And this oldster is not jumping off any bridge, so if you want to leave Atlas with me, Jonah, that's fine."

"You are jumping!" at least three, maybe four different voices chimed in unison.

"I am not," Maggie replied.

"Mom, it's not high," Eli assured her. "Honestly, the bridge isn't that far off the water, and it is very warm and safe. It'll be fun."

She lifted a brow as if she were *allergic* to fun.

"Ignore her," Jo Ellen said. "She's going and if all she does is cheer me on, then that's a win."

Maggie rolled her eyes to the comments and laughter,

and everyone started gathering towels, drinks, flipflops, whatever they would need.

Tessa peered out to the driveway from the front window but didn't see any sign of Dusty. She considered texting him, but he'd find her. She wasn't in a celebratory mood anyway.

In fact, she considered not going at all, but Lacey slid an arm around her and Roman picked up the ridiculous boom box she'd brought, and somehow, they were all traipsing outside in a massive group of Lawsons and Wylies.

"Like old times, huh?" Vivien said, tugging at Tessa's sleeve.

"We're missing Kate," Tessa said. "You know she'd jump in with her glasses on."

Vivien laughed and agreed. "Where's Dusty?"

"He's—"

"Pulling up," Lacey said, pointing to the truck turning into the driveway.

"Oh, good, he made it." Tessa was only a little surprised at how much his arrival lifted her spirits. "Let me go get him."

She broke away from the pack as they moved along the driveway, jogging over to the side where he was parking.

She was squinting into the tinted windows, trying to see his face, when the back window slowly lowered, offering her a view into the cab. Was he—

She nearly tripped over herself coming to a shocked dead stop.

Her jaw opened. Her heart stopped. Her hands flew to her mouth to keep from screaming, but she couldn't help it.

"Olive!"

Dusty was out and around the front so fast, he left his driver's door open. His face was on fire with a smile that lit his whole being.

"What is happening?" she muttered as she charged to the truck. She reached the door and pulled it open, squealing at the sight of her angel.

"Tess," Olive whispered.

"Double O!" She scrambled into the seat. "I missed you, baby girl!"

She smothered her with giggly kisses, getting her out of the car seat with trembling hands. Scooping her up, she turned to Dusty, who stood in the open door, grinning like an absolute fool.

She was vaguely aware that the pack of family and friends had detoured from the trip to the bridge to move closer to this new arrival, all of them trying to figure out what was going on, as was she.

"What? How? Dusty!" She simply couldn't form a sentence as Olive climbed onto her, squeezing hard.

"Come on down, I'll explain." He took Olive and set her on the ground.

"Baby?" Olive asked, looking past him. "Baby Attas?"

"She wants to see Atlas," he translated as he took Tessa's hand.

"He's here!" Jonah called, coming to them with Atlas in his baby pouch. "Hello, Olive!"

As the family gathered around and gently greeted her without overwhelming the tiny creature, Tessa landed on her two feet and looked up at Dusty.

"Did Morgan go back? How long can we have her? That last week? You know I'll take it, so—"

"Forever."

She opened her mouth to speak, then closed it, unable to process what he'd just said.

"Morgan did go back—I checked her in. On the way, she told me she has accepted the fact that she is not in any way capable of raising Olive. She realized it after she got her back. She just can't manage the responsibility, not emotionally or psychologically. Her doctor agrees."

"What does that mean?" The question came out strangled.

"She's going to put Olive up for adoption and—"

"No! I mean, yes. Let's adopt her. Now. Tomorrow. As soon as possible. Morgan can see her when she wants, but we'll raise her. We'll take care of her and teach her and love her and everything!" The words spilled at the same time as her happy tears. "I'll go through a bazillion hours of training, I'll do anything!"

"Anything? Because there's a catch, Tess."

"I don't care what it is. I don't care where I have to go, what I have to do, who I have to pay or how much. I love her and I want her."

Dusty's smile grew wide and slow. "The catch is that Morgan will only adopt her to a married couple."

She blinked at him. *That* was the catch? That wasn't a *catch*. It was...a dream come true.

"So," he continued, drawing the two-letter word out. "If you and I got married in the next couple of days—"

She screamed and threw her arms around him, laughing as he lifted her off the ground.

The others came closer, questions flying.

Still in Dusty's arms, feet floating in the air, she looked at them over his shoulder.

"Guess what, everyone?" she called out. "We're getting married!"

August 6, 1993

I swear Destin weather is actually insane. Almost as insane as what happened to me when the sky decided to have a crazy mood swing and unleash a monsoon on us.

Tonight started out simple and fun. We all walked down to the Ice House, that place by the boardwalk, to get ice cream after dinner. Of course, some of Eli's friends were there, so that turned into a whole thing. But, still, I was happy with my mint chip cone even though Tessa says that flavor tastes like toothpaste (she's so wrong it hurts).

We all sat with our treats at the picnic tables out front where you always feel like you're sitting in the middle of a parking lot but somehow it's still fun. The whole group was there. Mom, of course, trying to keep everyone from getting sticky. Eli being with the annoying college boys (except Peter, he's so much more mature than them) and acting like he's twelve even though he's definitely not. Crista complaining about who knows what, the usual.

Kate and Tessa and I were laughing about it, and I remember thinking, this is what it's supposed to feel like. Just summer. Just best friends. Just ice cream melting too fast.

And then Peter walked over to our table, and

I tried too hard to be cool. I probably failed. I don't even remember what he said, but I remember the way my stomach did that stupid drop thing anyway. Yes, I still love Peter McCarthy.

Everything was loud and busy. There were so many people. Kids running around. Cars pulling in and out. Music blasting from somewhere. It felt chaotic in a normal way.

And then it wasn't normal.

It happened so fast. One second the sky was still kind of pink from sunset, and the next second it was like someone poured black ink across it. The wind came out of nowhere. Not a breeze, but a real, serious storm kind of wind. Someone uttered the word "tornado" when napkins and wrappers were flying everywhere.

Tessa literally squealed and grabbed my arm. Then the first raindrop hit my shoulder, and it was huge! Like a warning shot. And then the sky totally opened up, I mean full-on Florida apocalypse rain. Sideways, like a sheet, enough to make you feel like you're being drowned just standing there.

Everyone started yelling and scrambling at the same time.

Mom was shouting Crista's name. Eli got serious, fast. Parents were grabbing kids and sprinting to cars. Someone knocked over a chair.

The ice cream shop door kept slamming open and closed.

It was chaos. Total chaos.

And somehow, in the middle of all of it, the group splintered.

Tessa and Kate ran toward one car with some of the other teens, screaming and laughing like it was a fun adventure. Eli took off in the other direction and got into someone's van with some friends. Mom and Aunt Jo Ellen were trying to herd people and calling out names.

I was right there, and then I wasn't. I don't even know how it happened. I turned for one second—one second—because I thought I saw Kate's glasses go flying, and when I turned back, it was like everyone had vanished.

The parking lot was a blur of headlights and water. Windshield wipers going crazy. Doors slamming. Engines starting.

I stood there soaked, my hair plastered to my face, my shirt sticking to my back, and my heart exploding.

They LEFT. Not on purpose. I know that. But still. I was left behind. Truly, I'm not sure I've ever felt more invisible in my life.

I started running between cars, calling out, but the rain swallowed my voice. I couldn't even see where I was going. And then I had this horrible thought: What if they think I'm with someone else? What if everyone assumes someone else has me?

The cars were all gone and I was freaking out. I could be here all night! I could be struck by lightning!

I was blinking rain and tears out of my eyes when I heard an engine slow down and saw a truck pull into the lot, headlights cutting through the sheets of rain. It stopped right in front of me.

Do I even need to say who my heroic rescuer was? Peter McCarthy always saves the day.

Peter leaned across the seat and yelled, "Vivien! Get in!"

For a second I just stood there, frozen, because it didn't feel real. He came back. He actually came back for me.

I ran to the truck and climbed in, soaking the seat, not even caring.

Peter looked at me, his hair damp, his jaw tight in this way that made him look older, and he said, "You okay?"

"I got...turned around," I managed.

He shook his head like he couldn't believe it but said something that made me laugh and relax and get butterflies all at the same time.

He drove out of the lot carefully, wipers going full speed, and I sat there trembling, not from cold exactly, but from adrenaline and embarrassment and a bit of a thrill to be in a car alone with him. I had assumed he went with Eli and the other boys, but I'd been wrong.

After a minute he said, "You're good. I've got you."

Yes, I melted faster than my mint chip cone.

By the time we got back to the house, everyone was inside, towels everywhere, Mom was frantic and relieved all at once, Eli swearing they didn't mean to leave me, Kate and Tessa wide-eyed and apologetic.

But all I could really think about was that in the middle of all that chaos, Peter was the one who came back.

Peter McCarthy, my hero.

Love,

Viv

Chapter Twenty-two
Vivien

No doubt they attracted some attention, this posse of more than a dozen people ranging in age from a few months to nearly eighty meandering down Gulf Shore toward the construction site and jetties.

They didn't move fast but stayed in clusters of two or three along the sidewalk, spirits high.

Well, most spirits were high. Tessa was obviously on a cloud, her ecstasy palpable as she and Dusty took turns holding little Olive on their hips, kissing her and each other, and accepting congratulations and answering a slew of questions.

Lacey and Roman had the newly engaged glow, too. Even Jo Ellen and Maggie were a little giddy, talking endlessly about their "new life" together.

Crista and Anthony swung a very excited Nolie between them, and siblings Jonah and Meredith were deep in conversation, taking it slow because Atlas had fallen asleep against his daddy's chest.

That left Vivien and Eli walking side by side, somehow at the back of the pack, even though they'd been the ones to initiate caring about the bridge demolition in the first place.

"Are you down because the bridge will be?" Eli asked.

She smiled up at him. "I'm not down," she said, fluttering the white sundress she wore over her bathing suit as if the playful move would support the statement.

Eli wasn't buying it.

"I'm just not...on their level," she admitted, gesturing toward the crowd in front of them, a few currently dancing to an old Wilson Phillips song thumping from an equally archaic boom box that Dusty carried.

"What do you know," Eli leaned in to remark. "The youngins figured out how to work a cassette tape."

She smiled but knew it looked as sad as it felt.

"Missing Peter?" he asked, confirming that.

"Missing Kate?" she fired back.

"Always. I talked to her a little while ago. She's...not great."

Vivien slowed her step. "Why? She wants to be down here?"

"Yeah, but we're the last thing on her mind," he said. "She thinks her project might lose the government grant, and that could have catastrophic effects on her lab, her staff, even her job. She was distant, and preoccupied."

Vivien sighed, hurting for her friend. "I'll call her tomorrow. I've been terrible about staying in touch while she's gone. I keep expecting to come down the stairs and find her in the kitchen cooking something with Jonah, and life as it was."

He just sighed. "Same."

"Summer's ticking away," she said. "And Kate was supposed to be here the whole time. I'm sure that's a huge disappointment for you."

"It is. And I probably need to get back to Atlanta, but I want to close that Pippin Lake deal and then set Meredith up to stay here and run it." He squinted at his kids, who were a few feet ahead, laughing. "It's the closest she and Jonah have been since Melissa died. And Meredith is so helpful to him with the baby."

"Or you could just close Acacia in Atlanta. Or let your top dog up there run it for you, and open Acacia Destin."

"Don't think I haven't imagined that," he said. "But you never answered my question, Viv. Is it Peter or just the end of the Let Go Bridge that has your smile in hiding?"

She gave him the best one she had. "I am sad about the bridge, but I don't know why. Well, maybe I do."

"Tell me."

Taking a deep breath, she looked up into his blue eyes, a familiar warm affection spreading through her. She adored her big brother and trusted him. And if anyone would understand this, it might be him.

"The two are tied together—the bridge and Peter."

"How so?"

"Well, somehow they are tangled up in my heart," she started, trying to put her thoughts in a way that made sense. "The bridge was always there—and not just the summer we let go. Every summer. There for parties and shade, a symbol of connection, a landmark that lasted. And Peter was the same to me. Always there, always had my back—even the time you bolted from the ice cream place in a storm and left me behind."

He laughed and shook his head. "Blame—"

"I'll blame Tessa," she said dryly. "You *never* left her behind."

"Didn't help my pathetic cause," he joked. "But explain Peter and the bridge to me."

She let out a noisy sigh. "The bridge reminds me that I've had a crush on Peter since time began. And it's going to be gone."

"And...?"

"And maybe I'm more in love with the memory, the crush, the heady, crazy high I got when he looked at sixteen-year-old Vivien than I am with Detective Peter McCarthy of today."

He considered that, nodding.

"I mean, I 'let go' of my crush back in the day, but..."

"You didn't let go of him."

"Well, I did, two months ago. And I just can't seem to find a way to tell him that was a mistake, which makes me wonder if it was or not. And if the bridge comes down, maybe my past—and present—with Peter does, too."

Eli was quiet, carefully watching Jo Ellen and Maggie navigate a tricky turn around some fencing and the narrow path to the jetty. When they made it, he put a hand on Vivien's shoulder.

"There's a verse that says, 'For here we have no continuing city, but we seek the one to come.'"

She glanced at him, mixed feelings about his use of the Bible for any problem. It helped, but she didn't understand it. No wonder Kate was confused. "That sounds...like something you'd say."

He smiled faintly. "It's in Hebrews, a book which doesn't actually have an author attached to it. But as an architect, that verse has always resonated with me."

"What does it mean, exactly?" she asked as they rounded the last corner and started marching on sand up toward the bridge in the distance.

"That nothing built in this world—nothing built by men—is meant to last forever. Not homes or monuments or bridges. And that's good, because God doesn't anchor us to steel structures. He anchors us to Himself. And He was anchored to wood and nails on our behalf. That's grace and it's a gift."

She smiled, but as always, Eli's deep biblical knowledge left her lost. "And Peter?" she pressed.

"He isn't tied to a bridge or even a memory. He's tied to *you*. And if you want my opinion..." He squinted into the fading light, seeming to lose his train of thought.

"Your opinion?" she urged.

"What is he *doing*?"

"Who? What?"

"That guy with the impact driver on the side of the bridge."

Vivien shifted to the side to see past the people in front of her, many of whom were stopping at the sight.

Finally, she could see that a man had climbed up the side railing of the bridge and was using a noisy tool, pulling off sections of the bridge and tossing them into a flatbed truck parked on the sand. The metal and wood had been marked with bright orange spray paint, and whole pieces of the side had been stripped off.

Even from here, she made out the stocky form she recognized.

As people called out questions and exclamations, Vivien broke through the crowd and took off, yelling the man's name.

"Quinn! Mr. Hargrove! Hey, you can't do that until tomorrow!"

He stopped and turned, pushing a ballcap up to get a better look at her. "I sure can."

"No, no. The demolition is scheduled for tomorrow." She caught her breath and slowed as she reached him, looking up at the damage he'd already done. Not too much, but it wouldn't be long until no one could climb it.

The steps to get up the side weren't that far off the sand, but he did seem to loom over her and looked big and dangerous with the power tool in his hand.

"I don't have to wait." He yanked a crowbar out of a bag resting near him, slamming it into wood. "I can get the old-growth lumber now."

"Because it's the most valuable," Eli said, rushing up next to Vivien. "Who are you and what are you doing?"

"I could ask the same thing, pal. Back off." He looked past them at the small crowd, his gaze flickering. "You brought your posse, Vivien? No broody boyfriend this time?"

Her jaw dropped as she rooted for an answer, but

before she gave one, an engine roared from a small workers' access road.

A small truck rumbled closer and Vivien's heart dropped. Another worker? They were starting tonight?

The driver's door opened and a woman leaped out, long dark hair whipping around as she turned, waved to someone behind her, then pivoted and ran toward the bridge.

"Oh, no you don't, buddy!" she yelled.

It was Natalie Cartwright from the fishing museum! Vivien hustled closer, just as a green and white sheriff's SUV showed up and both doors flung open, the sight nearly knocking Vivien off her feet completely.

"Peter!" she gasped. "And Connor!"

Peter shot closer, arm out, badge extended. "Touch one more board, Hargrove, and I'll arrest you."

"You cannot demo this bridge," Natalie called, practically jumping on her sneakers as she waved a piece of paper. "These are archival affidavits proving that the bridge qualifies for a heritage protection review."

He flicked his hand. "Back off, girl. We've been through that and it doesn't qualify for squat." He punctuated that by yanking a board and tossing it toward the truck, but Peter punched the wood as it fell, flipping it to the sand.

"Step off from the structure," Peter demanded.

Quinn laughed. "Got a contract and a schedule."

Pocketing his ID, Peter stepped right under him. "Then you better find your permit," he said. "Because I don't see one posted, and under the Florida Building

Code, you don't touch a public structure without it displayed on-site."

Quinn didn't move.

"And as of this afternoon, this bridge is under cultural resource review," Peter added.

Natalie lifted the papers higher. "Filed and logged."

Quinn's jaw flexed as he yanked the crowbar over wood again.

"That triggers an automatic hold on alteration," Peter continued, hands resting on his hips like he had all the time in the world. "You start tearing it apart now, that's willful violation."

"And what are you going to do about it?" Quinn shot back, tossing the crowbar and picking up the other power tool, squeezing the trigger and aiming the tool at Peter with a vile look. "You and the old ladies and babies are going to stop me?"

Peter moved so fast, Vivien didn't actually think she saw it happen. One second he was at the base of the steps and the next he launched up them—three long strides, no hesitation. He clamped a hand over Quinn's wrist, the other caught the back of his shoulder to turn him with precise force.

The impact driver died mid-snarl as Peter twisted it cleanly out of Quinn's grip and it dropped to the planks with a hollow clang.

"You've already removed material from county property without authorization," Peter said, low and controlled, right at Quinn's ear—but every word carried. "So here's what you're going to do, Mr. Hargrove: Pack up, unload the lumber you salvaged, put your tools in the truck, and get out."

Quinn jerked free just enough to sneer a curse at Peter. "You can't do a thing to stop me."

"Watch me."

Peter's weight shifted as his hand slid behind Quinn's arm, guiding—not shoving—using Quinn's own resistance against him. The motion was so fast it barely registered as force.

Quinn's balance disappeared.

Peter muscled him down the short embankment beside the bridge and drove him into the sand in one controlled sweep. He planted a knee square between Quinn's shoulder blades.

One hand locked his wrist, the other already reaching for cuffs Vivien didn't even know he had.

It was over before anyone processed it. Before anyone *breathed.*

"You are being detained for performing construction and demolition without a valid permit, violating a stop-work order, and interfering with a government order," Peter said, his voice like iron. "And you are going downtown."

Quinn swore into the sand.

Vivien *might* have swooned.

Leaning in just enough to be heard, Peter got right in the guy's ear. "You don't get to dismantle historic public property because you're greedy and in a hurry."

He pulled Quinn's arms back, secured the cuffs, then

finally looked up at the stunned circle Eli had managed to hold back. His gaze traveled over all of them, but landed directly on Vivien, as warm and heroic as that day in the rain.

"Aren't you going to read me my rights?" Quinn asked.

"Sure." He stood them both straight up, moving Quinn like a helpless puppet. "You have no right to talk to women who are out of your league," he said in a perfectly dry voice as he walked right past her and winked. "Don't jump without me, Viv. Don't let go of a thing until I get this menace booked."

He pushed Quinn forward and guided him into the back seat of a sheriff's SUV, slamming the door as a final punctuation.

Everyone stood stone still as Peter drove off, except for Tessa, who sidled up to Vivien and whispered, "And *that's* why you've spent thirty years mooning over the man."

Vivien smiled. She had a feeling she was about to spend thirty more.

THEY ALL DECIDED to wait for the hero of the day before they jumped. The result was an impromptu party, a massive bonfire, and endless songs from the early '90s on cassettes that Jonah pronounced "epic."

As Tessa, Olive, and Nolie danced on the sand to "Walking on Broken Glass," Meredith sat with Connor, talking over a sleeping Atlas, while Eli and Jonah stoked the fire.

Dusty and Anthony had run back to the house and returned with a truckload of chairs, blankets, drinks, and snacks.

Before she left, Natalie explained how her meeting with Vivien had gotten her fired up for one last effort to save the bridge. She'd been the one to go to the sheriff's office when a certain piece of documentation was missing, and Peter had glommed onto the case to help her.

Vivien hugged her and promised to stay in touch.

It was dark by the time Peter returned to a rousing round of applause that he waved off.

"You all look too dry to have jumped off that bridge," he said, laughing. "Or are you worried it isn't safe?"

"It's structurally sound," Eli assured him, placing an arm on Peter's shoulder. "And you, my friend, made us proud."

Peter grinned at him and said something under his breath and the two of them laughed at one of their inside jokes.

Peter's gaze flicked over the crowd, and he spotted Vivien and held her gaze just long enough for her to know...they may not need that talk after all. Some things didn't need to be said out loud.

After accepting a few more accolades for the arrest, he came over to Vivien and lowered himself onto the blanket next to her, the firelight catching his warm expression.

"Hey," he said. "Hope that didn't upset you."

She chuckled. "Did a number on my hormones."

Laughing, he put an arm around her and pulled her a little closer. "We got the goods on that guy, and he won't be sniffing around the bridge for a while. Kudos to you, Natalie," he added to the other woman a few feet away. "You *do* love the history of this place."

"It fascinates me," Natalie said with a smile, looking up at the shadow of the bridge in the darkness. "Although I've never jumped and let go."

"Then start us off," Peter said. "Surely you have something to let go of."

She gave a wistful smile and stood, walking toward the bridge just as Roman and Lacey leaped to follow.

"We're giving up the single life!" she called.

Peter snuggled closer, giving Vivien a delicious whiff of soap and his cologne.

"You showered before the jump into the water?" she asked, leaning into him.

"I smelled...and not like teen spirit."

She laughed. "That was the song Dusty played when we were sixteen and jumped."

"I know."

Inching back, she frowned. "You weren't here. You were watching the four hundredth sequel to *Lethal Weapon*."

"Don't knock it. Where do you think I learned the slick cop moves? And, yes, we were here."

"No," she insisted. "You and Eli were watching the movie and we came alone. Do *not* question the veracity of my diaries."

"I don't question the diaries, but I do question your ability to know when you're being trailed. You think Eli and I were going to sit on our butts watching a movie when our girls were out in the dark with the likes of Dustin Mathers?"

She didn't know whether to laugh or be aghast. "You *followed* us?"

"Of course. I saw you jump. Made sure you got out and home okay." He closed the tiny bit of space between them, ignoring the cheer that went up when Roman and Lacey splashed in the water. "We beat you home, had a beer on the beach, and you lied and said you didn't let go of anything."

Now she *was* aghast. "How do you know I lied?"

"Because I can read your eyes, Vivien Lawson. I know what you gave up then, and I know what you gave up two months ago."

She stared at him. "You."

He angled his head, his dark eyes glittering. "And now I think you need to let go of letting go of me."

Oh. He was so right. She dropped her head back and looked toward the first few twinkling stars, not bothering to argue.

"Ready?" he asked, rising and reaching for her hand.

"Our turn!" Dusty and Tessa scooped up Olive and carried her to the very lowest rung of the ladder up the bridge. The two of them stood in knee-deep waves, holding her to help her jump.

"Let go, Olive Oyl!" Tessa cried. "Life is about to change!"

The little girl had no idea what it meant, but she jumped into Dusty's arms and called out, "Again! Again!" While the happy couple let her jump over and over, Meredith and Connor stayed deep in conversation.

"Are you going to jump, Mer?" Peter asked they made their way to the bridge.

"Connor can't, so I'll stay in solidarity."

Connor lifted his cast and gave her an apologetic look. "You sure? Go jump."

"Nah. Tell me more about the workload at dental school. It sounds wonderfully daunting."

Vivien and Peter shared a knowing look. "Over-achievers, both of them," she said.

"Well, he hasn't stopped talking about her since they met on the Fourth of July, so..."

She lifted a brow and filed that little piece of juicy gossip. "Where's Holly tonight?"

"Back in Pensacola for good," he said.

She kind of hated the relief that washed through her. "Oh, are you..."

"Still divorced," he said with a wry smile. "But not at odds anymore, which is all I ever wanted. Why? Were you worried?"

She slowed her step as they reached the bridge, looking up at him, vowing to never play another game with him again.

She took a breath and exhaled. "I missed you," she said simply. "I wanted to be with you and felt I couldn't."

He draped an arm around her and eased her onto the

step in front of him. "I missed you, too, Viv. Come on, let's get up there."

She climbed the few steps, feeling the strong warmth of him behind her, basking in the joy that not only had she not lost him, they felt closer than ever.

Looking down, she had to laugh.

"Why did we think it was such a big risk?" she asked.

"Because letting go of anything is a risk," he said, guiding her over the rusted metal and wide wood planks to the center point, helping her to the edge. "And sometimes, so is holding on."

Just then, the boom box crackled with more volume and the opening strains of "I Will Always Love You" floated up.

"Oh, Tessa." Vivien shook her head. "Predictable is her middle name."

"What's yours?" he asked.

"Leigh," she replied. "Yes, I'm Vivien Leigh. Have you met my *Gone With The Wind*-loving mother?"

He glanced at Maggie, deep in conversation with Jo Ellen by the fire.

"Why do you want to know?" she asked.

"So that when I propose, I can do it with full authority and sound exactly like the movies."

Her jaw dropped and she leaned way back, so far, he caught her from falling. "Peter!"

"What? We both know where this is going. I'll wait for the right moment. Unless...now feels good."

"Everything with you feels good," she whispered, wrapping her arms around his neck. "I'm in no rush but that doesn't mean I'm letting you go, Peter McCarthy. The only thing I'm letting go of is doubt, fear, and whatever has ever held me back from telling you and the world that...I love you."

He closed his eyes on a sigh. "Finally."

He lowered his head and kissed her just as the music hit its iconic crescendo and Whitney wailed her famous chorus.

"What are you letting go of?" she asked into the kiss.

"A future without you." He pressed his lips to hers. "I love you, Viv."

Still in a warm lip-lock, they pushed off, falling the short distance in an instant, still clinging to each other as they went under the dark water.

Coming up for air, they paddled to the side, and climbed out, arm in arm, knowing the one thing they'd never let go of—each other.

Chapter Twenty-three
Maggie

"No." Maggie sliced her new "life partner" with a look that she hoped conveyed how serious she was. "Absolutely, unequivocally no. Do not ask again or I shall throttle you."

Jo Ellen just giggled in response to that, which only made Maggie scared enough to take a deep drink of the gin and tonic that Jonah had promised he'd made "light." But, goodness, it tasted more like gin than tonic.

"Mags. You know you want to."

"You know I don't," she volleyed back, watching Anthony climb the stairs carefully with a giddy little Nolie. "Thank goodness Crista has a brain and is watching from the sidelines."

"She'd go if she weren't pregnant," Jo Ellen said.

"And I'd go if I weren't seventy-eight. You? Knock yourself out, Jo. You probably will."

"I'm not doing it without you," she said sternly. "And I *am* jumping." She leaned closer from her lawn chair, lifting her drink, her bright eyes proving the gin-versus-tonic theory. "So that means you are, too. We're in this together and we're letting go of lonely widowhood and embracing our new, fun, adventurous, hilarious, perfect life."

Maggie waved her off and let her gaze drift over the party around her, deeply content. In this chair—where she intended to stay.

"It's not even as dangerous as a motorcycle," Jo Ellen said, "which you have ridden multiple times."

"Don't remind me."

"Have you talked to Brick?" Jo Ellen asked.

"No. Why would I?"

"To tell him you're staying local. He's not far from here, you know. You two could ride his hog all the time."

Maggie's eyes shuttered. "Don't make me regret my decision to stay here with you, Jo."

Her friend just laughed and leaned back with a smug smile. "No regrets, Maggie. No regrets."

They turned to the bridge at the sound of Nolie squealing in delight with her father, followed by a splash.

Maggie sat up, waiting for that little head to pop up, which it did, joyfully laughing. *Thank goodness she was safe.*

They heard movement behind them and turned to look up at Vivien, who gestured at the bridge.

"Your turn, Mom and Aunt Jo."

"We're not—"

Jo Ellen rose quickly, like she'd been waiting for the invitation. Reaching her hand to Maggie, she angled her head toward the water. "Buckle up, buttercup. We're jumping."

"We are *not*."

A few others called out encouragement, and those who were standing came closer.

"Come on, Mom!" Eli said on a laugh. "I wouldn't let you jump if it were dangerous."

"Really, Grandma," Jonah chimed in. "We're not leaving until you two go."

"Stop it," she said, shifting in her seat.

"Don't you have something to let go of?" Vivien asked. "Something that's weighed you down for a long time? This is freedom, Mom."

"This is insane, Vivien."

"Jump, Grandma!" Nolie yelled, rushing over to dance on the sand, still dripping and clinging to a towel. "It's not scary at all!"

"Jump! Jump! Jump!" They started clapping and acting like a bunch of fools at a sporting event. Soon, every single person who was there was in on the nonsense.

When it died down, Jo Ellen braced her hands on her thighs, bending over to get right into Maggie's face.

"Listen to me, Magnolia Fredericks Lawson. You do have things to let go of, and this is a rite of passage."

"I'm too old and too ladylike and—"

"Too stubborn," Jo Ellen finished, literally pulling Maggie to her feet.

She came to a stand, doing her level best to stay steady on the sand. "Would you please—"

"Would *you* please just come with me and cheer me on?"

She narrowed her eyes. "I know what you're doing, Jo. I know you so well. You'll get me up there and—"

Laughing, Jo dramatically unzipped Maggie's coverup to the delight of the crowd and tossed it to the sand. "You wore a bathing suit."

"Because I came to the beach."

"Off we go, Mags." Jo threw her arm around her and started walking them both toward the bridge. And Maggie, God help her, went along with it.

She let Jo guide her to the wobbly stairs.

"This is crazy," she muttered, but didn't stop.

She held on to the railing and climbed to the top of the bridge, looking down. It really wasn't far. She'd been on diving boards that were higher. Fifty years ago.

"To the middle," Jo urged, never letting go of Maggie's back.

When they got there, Maggie turned to her. "Are you happy now?"

"You know what? I *am* happy," she said. "Because this is symbolic, Mags. This is us letting go of loneliness, cold, boredom, and waiting to die."

A soft breeze ruffled Maggie's short hair and blew over her nearly naked body. It felt...liberating. Alive. Terrifying and wonderful and so, so light.

"That's not what I'm letting go of," she whispered, accepting the fact that she *was* going to jump.

"Then what?"

She let out a long, slow sigh and put her arm around Jo Ellen. "Roger."

"Roger?"

"I've never really forgiven him for what he did."

"Yes, you did," Jo Ellen countered. "When that FBI agent came here and told us what he and Artie did and you found out that he tried so hard to make up for his petty crimes, you forgave him."

"I didn't, not really," she replied, closing her eyes to enjoy the next whisper of wind and the message it held. "I have always resented what he did to our family, what he did to me, and what he did to us—you and me. Keeping us apart for thirty years!"

"That's over now."

She nodded, aware of the small group below them still calling out encouraging words and their names.

"It's over but I have to let go of that last little bit of anger and resentment," she said. "Even though, in the end—and with Artie's help—he probably managed to slip into heaven by the back door, I have carried the weight of my feelings for so many years. I've awakened with that dark pit in my stomach so frequently, thinking..." She huffed out a breath. "Never mind. I'm jumping and letting go of any last vestiges of bitterness. It's time to let go, Jo."

Jo Ellen threw her head back with a hoot and gave Maggie a soft push, jumping with her.

For one split second, the world blurred, the air rushed, then the water covered her like she was falling into black space—the brackish liquid washing away all the things that had plagued her heart for so many years.

She didn't, couldn't, and wouldn't hate Roger Lawson ever again.

They pushed to the surface at the same second, the sound of a noisy cheer from the sand filling her ears. Immediately, Eli and Jonah waded in, arms out to help them from the water.

Overwhelmed, she hugged her son when they landed on solid ground and he lifted her an inch into the air.

They were wrapped in towels and love and cheers in no time, and someone who needed to die actually flashed a picture.

"Delete that immediately," she ordered, still smiling.

"No chance," Jonah called from several feet away. "That one's going in the Lawson archives."

"Proof that Magnolia Lawson is officially living her best life." Jo Ellen declared proudly, wrapping an arm around Maggie and steering her toward their chairs again.

Jo Ellen plopped down beside her and lifted her drink in a triumphant toast.

"Look around, Mags," she said, gesturing toward the sand where everyone was still laughing and talking and reliving their jumps. "Your kids are happy. Your grandkids are happy. My Tessa has a *wedding* coming up! Crista and Anthony have a place here and a healthy little one on the way. Meredith's a huge success, Jonah's a wonderful father, there are babies and new romances and parties and sunshine and all kinds of adventures ahead of us."

Maggie watched the group for a moment—Vivien laughing with Peter near the waterline, Eli helping Jonah with Atlas, little Nolie still dancing around in the sand with Olive.

Jo Ellen leaned closer, her eyes sparkling with that familiar reckless optimism. "I'm telling you, Maggie. The future looks amazing."

She couldn't deny, it was amazing.

Maggie lifted her glass and clinked it gently against Jo Ellen's. "You never really know what's around the corner, Jo," she said, her voice softer, more thoughtful.

Jo Ellen gave her a sideways look. "Always the cautious one."

"Someone has to be," Maggie replied.

But as she leaned back in her chair and let the evening breeze dry the last drops of water from her skin, she felt comfort settle warmly in her chest.

Whatever came next—storms, surprises, troubles she couldn't yet imagine—she wouldn't face anything alone.

Don't miss the next book in the Destin Diaries series, *The Summer We Celebrated,* carrying the families of the Summer House into a month marked by unexpected new beginnings and life changes. Kate and Eli face the tender, complicated work of aligning not just their lives, but their hearts and their beliefs—and their new love faces the most difficult challenge yet. Meredith makes a surprising connection at her dream job that stirs emotions—and possibilities—she never saw coming.

And Jonah discovers that chasing the career of a lifetime while raising a baby alone may be the hardest recipe he's ever attempted—until an unlikely encounter changes everything.

As the families gather to celebrate Tessa's breathtaking beach wedding, they'll discover that the biggest risks aren't the ones behind them—they're the ones that require trust, friendship, and a leap of faith.

Can't wait for the next book? We've got lots more to read...

Other family saga beach reads by
Hope Holloway and Cecelia Scott

Hope Holloway

Coconut Key
Shellseeker Beach
Seven Sisters

Cecelia Scott

Sweeney House
Young at Heart

Collaborations by Hope and Cecelia

Carolina Christmas
Christmas in the Canyons
The Destin Diaries

To find out when we have new releases, sign up for our
mailing list!
https://www.hopeholloway.com/newsletter-signup
https://www.ceceliascott.com/newsletter-signup

About The Authors

Hope Holloway is the author of charming, heartwarming women's fiction featuring unforgettable families and friends, and the emotional challenges they conquer. After more than twenty years in marketing, she launched a new career as an author of beach reads and feel-good fiction. A mother of two adult children, Hope and her husband of thirty years live in Florida. When not writing, she can be found walking the beach with her two rescue dogs, who beg her to include animals in every book. Visit her site at www.hopeholloway.com.

Cecelia Scott is an author of light, bright women's fiction that explores family dynamics, heartfelt romance, and the emotional challenges that women face at all ages and stages of life. Her debut series, Sweeney House, is set on the shores of Cocoa Beach, where she lived for more than twenty years. Her books capture the salt, sand, and spectacular skies of the area and reflect her firm belief that life deserves a happy ending, with enough drama and surprises to keep it interesting. Cece currently resides in north Florida with her husband and beloved kitty. Visit her site at www.ceceliascott.com